MAGIC

WHITE HAVEN WITCHES (BOOK 3)

UNLEASHED

TJ GREEN

Magic Unleashed
Mountolive Publishing
Copyright © 2019 TJ Green
All rights reserved
ISBN 978-0-9951163-5-1

Cover design by Fiona Jayde Media
Editing by Missed Period Editing

Other Titles by TJ Green

Tom's Arthurian Legacy Series
Excalibur Rises - Short Story Prequel
Tom's Inheritance
Twice Born
Galatine's Curse
Tom's Arthurian Legacy Box Set

White Haven Witches Series
Buried Magic
Magic Unbound

Invite from the author -

You can get two free short stories, *Excalibur Rises* and *Jack's Encounter*, by subscribing to my newsletter. You will also receive free character sheets of all the main Whitehaven Witches.

By staying on my mailing list you'll receive free excerpts of my new books, as well as short stories, news of giveaways, and a chance to join my launch team. I'll also be sharing information about other books in this genre you might enjoy.

Details can be found at the end of *Magic Unleashed.*

Cast of Characters

Avery Hamilton - owns Happenstance Books
Alex Bonneville - owns The Wayward Son pub
Reuben Jackson - owns Greenlane Nursery
Elspeth Robinson - owns The Silver Bough
Briar Ashworth - owns Charming Balms Apothecary
Mathias Newton - DI with Cornwall Police
Caspian Faversham - CEO Kernow Shipping

1

Avery stood on the cliff top looking out over White Haven harbour and the sea beyond. It was after ten at night and the moon peeked out behind ragged clouds, casting a milky white path over the water.

Alex stood next to her and sighed. "This is crazy. I told you it was a waste of time."

"We have to check. The old guy was insistent he'd seen something. He looked panic-stricken."

"He'd probably had a few too many rums."

"You didn't see him," Avery persisted. "He looked white, and he said he'd only seen something like it once before in his lifetime, and that was just before a couple of young men disappeared and were never seen again." Alex snorted, and Avery punched his arm. "I can't believe you're scoffing after all we've seen recently."

It had been just over a week since the five witches had broken the binding spell beneath the Church of All Souls, marking the end of a fight that had been going for centuries with the Favershams, a family of witches who lived in Harecombe, the town next to White Haven. The binding spell had been cast centuries earlier by Helena Marchmont, Avery's ancestor, and the other four witch families in White Haven. It had trapped a demon and the Faversham's ancestor beneath the church using a huge amount of magic. Breaking the spell had been difficult, but with the help of Helena's ghost they had succeeded, releasing magical energy that increased their own power. They had then defeated Sebastian Faversham, rescued Sally, and regained Reuben's missing grimoire. But Sebastian's final warning had proved correct. Strange things were indeed happening in White Haven.

In the last few days a dozen reports of strange noises and ghostly apparitions had been the centre of town gossip. Lights had appeared up at the ruined castle on the hill in the dead of night, and one fishing boat had reported seeing green lights in the depths of the sea, before they had hurriedly left the area and sailed for home.

On top of all that, Helena had reappeared, if only briefly, in Avery's flat. The scent of violets had manifested first, and then the smell of smoke and charred flesh, and Avery had yelled out, *"Helena! Stop it!"* Fortunately—or not, Avery couldn't work out which she preferred—she couldn't see Helena very often now, but it was unnerving to detect her unique presence in the flat. She hadn't resorted to warding the flat against her, but was seriously considering it.

Although Avery hoped these manifestations would settle down, she suspected they were only the beginning. And then that morning, an old man had appeared in the shop. He looked around nervously, and then approached Sally, who in turn escorted him over to Avery as she sorted some new stock in a quiet corner.

"This is Avery," Sally said cheerfully. "I'm sure she can help you, Caleb." She gave Avery a knowing look and left them to it, Caleb wringing his cap as if it was soaking wet.

"Hi Caleb, nice to meet you. How can I help?" Avery adopted her friendliest smile. Caleb looked as if she would bite. "I've, er, got something to tell you that you might find interestin'."

"Go on," she nodded encouragingly.

"I hear you may have abilities others may not," he said, almost stumbling over his words.

Oh, this was going to be one of those conversations.

She hesitated for a second, wondering what to say. "I may have, yes."

"I was on that fishing boat the other night."

Avery was confused for a second, and then realisation flashed across her brain. "The boat that saw the lights?" She looked at Caleb with renewed interest.

His hair was snowy white, but thick and brushed back from his face, falling to his collar. He had a full white beard, and wore a heavy blue jacket despite the heat, thick cotton trousers, and wellington boots. His face was covered in wrinkles, but his pale blue eyes were alert and watchful. He reminded her of the old sea captain from the fish fingers adverts.

"Yes, the boat that saw the lights. I wasn't going to say anything, but I remember only too well what happened the last time I saw them."

"You've seen them before?" Avery said, surprised. "Are you sure it wasn't just phosphorescence?"

"I know what that looks like, and this was different."

"Different how?" Avery asked, narrowing her eyes and feeling a shiver run through her.

"The lights circled below the boat, even and slow, three of them in all, and then started to weave a pattern below us. The young ones were transfixed. A wave crashed over the side and broke my concentration, but I could hear something." He stopped and looked away.

"What?" Avery insisted.

"Singing."

"Singing?"

"Strange, unearthly, hypnotic. I started the throttle and headed out of there, almost breaking our nets in the process."

Avery knew she should laugh at his outlandish suggestion, but she couldn't. He was so serious, and so absolutely believable. "And then what happened?"

"They disappeared. And I didn't look back."

"And the others?"

"Couldn't remember a thing."

"What happened the last time you saw them?"

"That was a very long time ago—I was only young myself." Caleb looked away again, shuffling uncomfortably, and then lowered his voice. "Young men disappeared. Vanished—*without a trace.*"

"But, how do you know that was related to the lights?" Avery felt bad for asking so many questions, but she half-wondered if he was winding her up.

"They'd been spotted with some young girls, and … Well, things weren't *normal.*"

Avery blinked and sighed. "I know I'm asking a lot of questions, Caleb, but why weren't they normal?"

"They were last seen at the beach, and their clothes were found there, but nothing else. And no, it wasn't suicide." He rushed on, clearly not wanting to be interrupted again. "I think they want something, I don't know why I think that, but I do. I *know* it. And it's only a matter of time before they arrive, so you need to stop them."

"How can I stop something I don't even know exists?" she asked, perplexed.

"I have no idea. I'm just offering you a warning." And with that he left the shop, leaving Avery looking after him, bewildered.

She sighed as she remembered her earlier conversation, and rubbed her head. "It sounds like it's out of a story book.

Mysterious lights in the sea, weird singing, loss of memory. Sebastian warned us that creatures would come. What if our magic sent a wave of power out into the sea? I guess it's possible."

Alex nodded, his features hard to see in the darkness on the cliff top. "The old myths talk of Sirens who sing sailors to their doom, but the old guy's story also reminds me a little of the Selkie myths."

"The seals that take human form?"

"Pretty much." He turned to her. "The myths haunt all coastal communities. They were popular in Ireland, particularly where I was on the west coast. And of course here in Cornwall there are Mermaid myths—they come looking for a man to take back to the sea with them to become their husbands and make lots of mer-babies."

"Great, so green lights and mysterious singing under the sea could be a rum-soaked hallucination, or maybe one of three weird myths."

He grinned. "Or a few others we haven't thought of, but I'll keep watch for women shrouded in seaweed or seal coats shed on the beach."

"You're so funny, Alex," she said, thinking the complete opposite.

He turned to her and pulled her into his arms. "I don't care how alluring they're supposed to be, they wouldn't be half as alluring as you."

She put her hands against his chest, feeling the strong beat of his heart and the warmth of his skin through his t-shirt, and looked up into his brown eyes. She could feel her own pulse starting to flutter wildly and wondered if he realised quite what he did to her. "You're very alluring yourself."

"How alluring?" he asked, his lips a feather-light touch on her neck.

"Too alluring." She could feel a tingle of desire running through her from their contact.

"No such thing," he said softly. His hand caressed the back of her neck and pulled her close for a long, deep kiss as his hands tangled in her hair. Pulled so close to him, she felt his desire start to grow, and he stepped away, a wicked gleam in his eyes. "Let's go back to mine. I've got better things in mind than standing on a cliff top."

***

However, when they arrived at Alex's pub, The Wayward Son, Newton was at the bar, sipping a pint of beer.

Mathias Newton was a Detective Inspector with the Cornwall Police, who also knew that they were witches. His history was as complicated as theirs, and although their relationship had started badly, they were now friends. He turned from where he'd been scowling into his pint, half an eye on the football highlights that were on the muted TV screen in the corner, and half an eye on the door. He was in casual clothing, his short dark hair slightly ruffled, and his grey eyes were serious. "Where have you two been?"

"Nice to see you, too," Avery greeted him. She slid onto the seat next to him while Alex leaned on the bar and ordered the drinks.

Alex groaned. "Your timing sucks, Newton. I had better things in mind than a pint."

He just grunted. "Get over it."

"You look as grumpy as hell," Avery said.

"That's because I am. We've had some odd reports at the station."

Avery felt her heart sink. *Not more strange things.* "Like what?"

"Odd disturbances—noises at night, people thinking they're being broken into, electrical shorts, missing items, but no signs of a break-in."

Alex raised an eyebrow and passed Avery a glass of red wine. "People report electrical shorts to you?"

"You'd be surprised what people report to us. But yes. We've had a flood of reports over the last couple of days. I wanted to know if you've seen anything."

"Lots of rumours of weird happenings, but nothing concrete." She related the story the old sailor, Caleb, had told her. "We've been up on the cliff top to see if we could spot anything, but…" She shrugged.

Newton rubbed his hand through his hair, ruffling it even more. "I'd hoped things would go back to normal after the other night, but they're really not. Briar and Elspeth have both had people coming into their shop sharing strange tales, and Elspeth has been selling lots of protection charms."

"Really?" Avery asked. "I must admit, I haven't spoken to them in a couple of days."

"It's my job to, Avery." He finished his pint and ordered another. "Have you heard about the meeting?" Newton was referring to the Witches Council.

She nodded. "Yes. It's tomorrow evening, at eight."

To celebrate defeating the Favershams and breaking the binding spell, they had all met for dinner at Avery's flat, but it had been interrupted by the arrival of Genevieve Byrne, another witch who organised the Witches Council, a group they hadn't even known existed until that night. She had invited them to the next meeting, actually almost insisted that they attend, and after that their celebrations had taken a downward turn as they each debated the merits of whether to go or not. For Avery, it was an easy decision. They'd been invited to something they'd been excluded from for years, and she had no intention of letting the opportunity pass her by.

Reuben had not felt the same. "Screw them all, why the hell should we go to their crappy meeting?"

"Because we'll learn something, Reuben," Avery had answered, exasperated. "Aren't you the slightest bit interested in knowing who they are and what they do?"

"No," he'd answered belligerently.

"Well, I am," Briar said. "But I'm too chicken to go."

"I'm not sure I trust her or any of them," Newton said, "but maybe that's the policeman in me."

Alex had nodded in agreement. "I don't entirely trust them either, but I agree with Avery and Briar. We should go. We need to have a stake in whatever's going on around here."

"Well, unless anyone else really wants to go, I'd love to go first," Avery said. "Someone else can go next time."

Alex rolled his eyes. "Just when I thought things might start to get back to normal around here."

But at least most of them had agreed on attending.

However, now, in the warm comfort of the pub, Avery felt a bit worried about going and the reception she might receive. The other night beneath All Souls now felt like a dream—if it hadn't been for the headlines that proclaimed the death of Sebastian Faversham in an electrical fire at the family home. A fake report. He had actually died after being attacked by Helena's ghost, her spirit made stronger by the extra surge of magical energy that pulsed through her like a bolt of lightning.

"Where?" Newton persisted, drawing her back to the present.

"Some place called Crag's End."

"Where the hell's that?"

"Around Mevagissey, somewhere just off the coast. It seems to be a very large, private residence."

He looked concerned. "I'm not sure you should go alone."

"That's what I said," Alex agreed, gazing at Avery.

Avery twisted to look up at him. "Alex, I'll be fine. They're all witches, I'm sure I'll be quite safe."

"We don't know any of them."

"We were invited. Stop worrying," she said, as much to reassure herself as him.

"Someone should go with you," Newton said.

Avery looked between the two of them. "Something is very wrong with the world when the two of you start agreeing. No. I'm going alone. Trust me. I'm a witch."

2

Avery eyed the house in front of her warily. It looked like a small castle, with three turrets and a stone tower. All it needed was a moat and a portcullis. She hoped boiling oil wasn't about to be poured on her.

It was not the type of house she had expected, and although it looked sturdy and well maintained, the grounds were wildly overgrown and romantic, filled with tumbling roses, honeysuckle, and immense shrubs. Halfway up the drive she wondered if she'd taken a wrong turn, but then the drive opened out and the castle appeared, silent and aggressive in the falling dusk light.

She turned off her van's engine, trying not to panic and get the hell out of there. As she walked up to the front entrance of the castle, she noted only two other cars on the drive. She'd aimed to get there early and find her feet, but now she wondered if she should have arrived late and snuck in quietly.

The castle was slightly inland, set on the edge of the moor. The high walls and hedges protected it from prying eyes, and from the winds that would sweep in off the sea on this elevated position.

She was about to knock on the front door when it swung open in front of her, revealing a large entrance hall softly lit with candlelight. The floor was a chequer board of black and white tiles, and a round table was placed in the centre, on which rested a vase filled with exuberant flowers, the scent filling the room.

As she entered the hall, a deep voice manifested out of the shadows on the stairs, making her jump. "You must be Avery Hamilton. Welcome."

Avery squinted into the darkness and a figure stepped into the light.

The man the voice belonged to was tall and gaunt, and Avery estimated he was in his sixties. His hair was long, slightly unkempt, and streaked with grey, and he wore an old-fashioned velvet jacket and trousers.

He smiled as he came closer and shook her hand, his grip dry, bony and firm. "I'm Oswald Prendergast. Welcome to my home."

Avery looked up at him and smiled back. "Thanks for the invite. I hope I'm not too early."

His sharp eyes appraised her, and Avery hoped she was appearing confident. She wasn't at all sure she knew what she was doing here. "Not at all. A few have already arrived. Come into the drawing room and I'll introduce you."

Drawing Room? Avery felt as if she'd stepped back in time.

He led her up the stairs, the smell of furniture polish surrounding them. "I should warn you that some of our members were unwilling to have you on the Council, but I agreed with Genevieve. In the end we took a vote, and there were more fors than againsts."

"Thank you, we—all of us in White Haven—appreciate it. My grandmother mentioned the Council to me, but I must admit, I thought she was rambling."

"I remember your grandmother. Of course, I didn't really know her, but she's a fine witch. Anyway," he said, gesturing to the door on his left and pushing it open, "we're in here."

Avery entered a room that looked out to the rear of the house. Three large, leaded glass windows filled one wall, revealing the gardens beyond, but it was the interior that really caught her eye. Despite the fact that it was midsummer, a roaring fire filled the large fireplace and the room was stiflingly hot. Someone had thrown open a window to invite a wan breeze in, and in front of it stood three diverse individuals. There was an old man with a huge beaked nose and a shock of white hair and white eyebrows, and he wore a plum silk smoking jacket and black trousers. Next to him was a middle-aged aristocratic woman with auburn hair, a long, straight nose down which she peered at Avery, and she wore a chiffon gown. She reminded Avery of Margot from the sitcom *The Good Life* and she tried to keep a straight face. The next person was the one she least wanted to see—Caspian Faversham. He wore a smart suit and he turned and narrowed his eyes as Avery approached beside Oswald.

Oswald smiled at them warmly. "I'd like to introduce you to Avery, our newest recruit. Avery, I believe you know Caspian, but this is Claudia Everley and Rasmus James."

Avery presumed Oswald must know what had happened with the Faversham, but his tone didn't betray it.

The older two witches looked at Avery with interest, but it was Caspian who spoke first. "Avery. I must admit I hoped never to see you again. I'm sure you're aware that I was against your invitation to this group."

Avery could feel her anger rising already. "I hoped never to see you again either, Caspian, especially after you killed my friend, Gil, and kidnapped Sally, but here we are, having to tolerate each other."

Oswald intervened immediately, his warm, friendly tone disappearing. "Caspian, I warned you. Your family's behaviour in recent days almost meant you lost your place on the Council, so don't push your luck. Your probationary period is not yet over—you haven't got as many supporters as you think you have."

"My father has died too, Oswald…"

"But not by Avery's hand. You know it was Helena's fault."

Caspian shot Avery a look of pure loathing. "You let her in."

As much as Avery didn't want to start a full-blown argument, she was not about to be blamed for everything. "I don't control her, Caspian! She's not a pet."

Oswald laughed bitterly. "You are a victim of your own crimes, Caspian. Stop blaming others."

Rasmus interrupted. "Spirits are wildly unpredictable, you know that, Caspian. I suggest you let it lie." His voice was deep and gravelly, as if it had been dredged from the bottom of the sea. "The Council advised your father against the course of action, and he insisted on doing what he wanted anyway. He brought it on himself."

"Indeed," Claudia said, finally speaking. "I am heartily sick of this vendetta against White Haven."

Avery suppressed the urge to whoop with delight, and instead turned to Claudia and Rasmus, thinking she detected a twinkle of delight in Claudia's eye that was swiftly hidden. "I'm sorry, it was not my intent to argue. It's a pleasure to meet you both."

They both shook Avery's hand, and Claudia pulled her to the drinks cabinet. "Welcome, Avery, let me pour you a drink. Wine, whiskey, brandy, gin and tonic?"

"Gin and tonic please," she said, relieved to be away from Caspian.

"I meant what I said," Claudia continued, dropping her voice. "But others agree with Caspian. You may find you're in for a tricky evening."

"That's okay, I'm a big girl," Avery said, grinning. "But thanks for your support anyway. I'm very curious about tonight, and looking forward to meeting everyone, friendly or not."

Claudia passed her the drink. "This meeting doesn't encompass everyone, just families or coven representatives, much as you are representing your own coven."

"I don't know if we're anything as formal as a coven," Avery said.

"Whether you have declared it or not, you really are. And powerful, too. We all felt that wave of magic you unleashed from beneath the town. It nearly knocked me over. Good thing I was sitting down. I was watching a replay of *Strictly Come Dancing*—I was quite distracted after that."

Avery laughed. "Sorry."

Claudia waved her apology away. "I live close to Perranporth, so I couldn't see the effects, but I hear you lit up the sky—magically, that is."

Avery gasped. Perranporth was on the north coast of Cornwall, so the blast must have been huge—although, no doubt those with magical powers would be far more attuned to it. "I saw it as an aura. It *was* quite impressive. I must admit, we had no idea it would be so large."

"You had no idea your magic was bound?"

"No! We didn't know we had missing grimoires, either. Did everyone know except us?"

"Only Council members knew—no one else. We insisted upon knowing the details if we were to support the

Favershams' request to keep you isolated. Many of us thought it extreme, but the Favershams are powerful. Or rather *were*, they have less influence now. But we didn't know *where* your power was bound, or where your grimoires were, either. That has been a mystery to everyone for centuries." She smiled in admiration. "Well done for finding them. Helena's power sits well on you."

"Thank you," she said, flushing slightly. "Before he died, Sebastian suggested we would attract creatures to White Haven, and that we put everyone at risk. What did he mean?"

"That's what we shall discuss at the meeting," Claudia said, her eyes clouding with worry.

Before she could say anything else, another flurry of activity interrupted them. Avery turned to see another few witches arriving, and she took a large gulp of gin and tonic to fortify herself.

Oswald tapped his glass and the sound echoed around the room, magnified by magic. "Welcome, everyone. Please, grab yourselves a drink and let's get this meeting started."

They made their way to the room next door and sat around a long, dark wooden table inlaid with arcane symbols.

Avery sat between Oswald and Claudia. Caspian sat opposite her, and she saw Genevieve Byrne enter and sit at the head of the table. She looked as imposing as she had the other night. The other witches were a mixture of male and female, young and old, mostly white, but there was also a black male witch, and young Indian female. As they all took their places, they glanced at Avery with curiosity, some welcoming, some not.

Silence fell and Genevieve spoke. "Welcome all. Thank you for coming today, I realise it is outside our normal meeting time, but events of the last few days made me act quickly." She glanced around the room, and as her gaze fell on Avery, she smiled briefly. "I'm sure you all felt the wave of power the other night. It was caused by the actions of the White Haven witches."

There was a murmur as heads leaned close together, and Avery was stared at with renewed interest.

She continued, "I'm sure you're all aware of our history. Helena Marchmont and the other witches of White Haven bound Octavia Faversham and her demon over four centuries ago, and then their grimoires were hidden to prevent them from falling into the hands of the Witchfinder General." A collective shudder seemed to run around the room. "These grimoires have now been found and the binding spell broken—hence, the wave of magic we all felt. With the breaking of that spell many things have now changed. I have formally invited the witches of White Haven back to the Council, and they have agreed. Avery Hamilton, the descendent of Helena Marchmont, is our new member, and as such I'm sure you will treat her with respect."

Genevieve looked at each and every one of them in turn, some longer than others, and Avery noticed a skinny, beady-eyed male witch squirm and drop his gaze to the table, as did a young blonde female. *Faversham supporters*, Avery presumed. Caspian glared at her and then stared defiantly at Genevieve.

Genevieve went on, undeterred. "The release of the magic has placed us all in danger. As you all know, many creatures wander our Earth, some friendly, others not, and they are also drawn to magical energy. Our role is to keep our communities safe from them, and fortunately, they mostly keep to themselves. But now…" Her words hung on the air and Avery felt a flush of guilt. She glanced at Claudia, and then kept her eyes firmly fixed on Genevieve.

Caspian leapt into the silence. "So, once again I ask why Ms Hamilton and the other witches should be allowed into our Council. They have caused enough trouble already."

Avery was just about to respond when Genevieve beat her to it. "Because, if they had been part of this Council in the first place, they wouldn't have been in the dark about the threat of releasing this magic. They would have understood their history."

"I agree," another middle-aged witch with grey hair sitting across the table said. "Nothing good comes of secrets, Caspian. And frankly, your family have had their own way for far too long."

There were a few nods of agreement, but the room was otherwise silent. Genevieve frowned at Caspian. "That's the last I want to hear of that, Caspian. The White Haven witches are here to stay. They now provide us with our thirteenth coven, and we have missed that over the years. We all know the significance of that number. Any powerful spells we need to do in the future will now have a far greater chance of success with thirteen covens. Agreed?"

Avery felt a strange realisation settle upon her as she looked around the table at those who nodded their assent. They were now part of a much larger collective, and would probably be required to be involved in decisions and spells previously unknown. That was daunting.

Genevieve hadn't finished. "On to the important question. Has anyone noticed anything untoward in the last few days?"

A young woman of about Avery's age nodded. She had long, dark hair that fell in dreadlocks down her back. They were kept off her face by a bright red scarf, wrapped around her head in a band. "St Ives has had several spirits manifest in the last twenty-four hours, most of them harmless, but a couple have been a little more malevolent. We've managed to banish most of them quickly. One, however, may need a little more time."

Avery wondered who '*we*' was, and presumed at some point in the future she'd find out.

"If you need any help, let us know," Genevieve said. "Anyone else?"

There were a couple more strange reports. The beady-eyed male witch said there had been reports of howls at night on Bodmin. "Something is there. We have no idea what yet, but we're monitoring it."

Almost everyone around the table had noticed increased spirit activity, and Avery felt she should share about the activities in White Haven and the sighting of the strange lights in the sea.

There was a gasp of concern around the room at her news, and Genevieve narrowed her intense gaze at Avery. "When?"

"Probably a couple of nights ago now. Just one report about lights in the sea, but there's some at the castle, too."

Claudia leaned forward. "Lights in the sea are very worrying, Avery. Sea creatures carry their own power that's very different from ours, and the power they exert on humans is significant. You need to start searching now."

Avery was confused, and slightly embarrassed. She felt out of her depth. "But what are we looking for?"

"Unexpected behaviours, such as people acting out of character, strange obsessions, and unexplained absences."

Avery nodded. "We had a few theories, but weren't really sure if we should take it seriously."

Rasmus spoke, his voice unexpected as he'd been silent so long. "Not many of you young ones will have experienced the lure of the Mermaid, but trust me when I say they are evil, dangerous creatures."

"Mermaids?" Avery asked. "Is that what this is? We thought of them, but also considered Selkies."

"Possible, but less likely," he said.

"Mermaids are very powerful, very frightening beings," Claudia said. "We all need to be on guard against them."

"There have been a few Mermaid encounters over the years in Cornwall," Rasmus continued. "Many are romanticised."

"The Mermaid of Zennor," Avery said nodding. "We've all heard of her."

"Yes, she entered the village of Zennor disguised as a beautiful lady, bewitched the men and ensnared young Mathew Trewella. He followed her and was never seen again. Then, many years later, a ship cast anchor off Pendower Cove and a beautiful Mermaid asked the captain to move his anchor, as it was blocking her way back home where her husband, Mathew, and her children were waiting. The captain weighed anchor and got out of there as fast as he could. And then of course there are Mermaids who lure men to their deaths with their singing, much like Sirens of the Greek myths. Also, there was the village of Seaton, which was cursed by a Mermaid because a fisherman insulted her. The sea rose and sand swallowed the whole town."

The table had fallen silent, and all were now watching Rasmus as his dry voice captured their attention.

"Have you ever met one, Rasmus?" a dark-haired witch sitting across from Avery asked.

"Once, as a young man, a teenager. I was poking about in the tidal pools, collecting seaweed and things for my mother's spells, when I heard singing and caught sight of a flash of silvered tail. I squinted, blinked, and then a woman appeared on the beach, literally just appeared out of nowhere, her eyes a shining green. She beckoned to me, singing all the while with her hypnotic voice, and without a second thought I followed her as she walked into the sea. And then my brother shouted, sending a well-timed curse at her, and she disappeared and I never saw her again." He looked up, his vision returning to the present. "Mind you, it was a long time before I went back there again."

"If Mermaids are returning to White Haven, it's likely they'll turn up in other places, too," Claudia said.

"Maybe not," Genevieve argued. "White Haven is the only place which has magic hanging over it."

"Children of Llyr," Oswald said, shaking his head, his eyes haunted. "They're always trouble."

"Llyr?" the young blonde witch asked, the one Avery presumed had sided with Caspian.

"The Celtic God of the Sea. He represents the powers of darkness, and fought the children of Don, the powers of light. Llyr's son is Manawdyan—or in Irish myth, *Manannán mac Lir*—Son of the Sea. They are dark, old gods, best left sleeping. Their children are the mythical creatures of the sea—the Mermaids, Selkies, water spirits, serpents, the Kraken, Leviathan, the Hydra, and others." Oswald turned to Avery. "Let's hope your magic has not stirred the depths of the ocean, or trouble will indeed come."

If Avery hadn't fully understood the threat of the magic they had released before, she did now, and she felt her throat tighten. The spirits that were now rising in the town could be just the beginning.

***

After the formal part of the meeting, most of the witches hung around chatting idly amongst themselves, and Avery had the chance to meet a few of the others.

It seemed the witches represented most of the major towns and some of the villages on the north and south coast of Cornwall. Avery knew that Claudia was from Perranporth, and she found that Rasmus was from New Quay, and due to the distance was stopping at Crag's End overnight, with Oswald. She gleaned he despised witch flight; it made him feel sick. Oswald represented the Mevagissey coven, and the young blonde witch represented the Looe witches, of which there were only two.

Avery met the young woman from St Ives with the dark dreadlocks, who had spoken about the spirits. Her skin was tanned and her smile bright, and she grinned and stuck her hand out. "Hi, my name's Eve. Good to finally meet you, Avery, you've created quite a stir."

Avery knew she'd get on with her straight away. "It seems so. Sorry."

Eve laughed. "Caspian's an ass. Serves him right. And Sebastian was an infuriating, superior nightmare." She lowered her voice. "I should be sorry he's dead, but I'm not."

Avery leaned closer, too. "I do feel bad about it, but then I remember everything he did to stop us, and that helps."

Eve looked at her curiously. "You really had no idea about the Council?"

"No. I feel we've been isolated for years."

"Well, the connections are useful of course, and the wider knowledge about what's happening in Cornwall, but to be honest, the politics are a bit of a drag."

"How many of you are in St Ives?"

"Two of us. Me and Nate." She rummaged in her bag for some paper and scribbled her number down. "Here you go, my phone number in case you need anything."

"Cheers, Eve. What will you do about your wayward spirits?"

"The usual banishment, but there's a lot of activity—it will be hard. But now I'm more worried about Mermaids."

"Yeah, me too. I feel a bit guilty."

Eve shrugged. "It's your magic, you were entitled to it. Don't let Caspian get you down. Or Zane or Mariah."

Avery looked at her blankly. "Who?"

She nodded discretely across the room to where Caspian stood talking to the beady-eyed man from Bodmin, and the blonde witch. "Those two talking to Caspian. Their families had strong links with the Favershams, but without the support of the others, they're no threat to you. Besides, they won't attack you, not like the Favershams did. They just like to suck up to them." She watched them for a few seconds more, and Avery wondered what they were talking about, but then Eve reached out to clink her glass with her own. "Cheers, Avery, welcome to the Council. Prepare to be called upon. Now that you're one of us, you'll be involved in lots of things."

3

Avery had been staring at the words for so long that they'd started to blur. She rubbed her eyes and glanced around, trying to refresh her concentration.

She was in the attic of her flat, and the long shadows of twilight were spreading across the room. The windows under the eaves were open, and the scent of dust, roses, and pollen drifted in, mingling with incense. She sighed, rolled her shoulders, and then looked back at the page, determined not to be defeated by the last few words.

The spell, like many of the others in her newly found, old grimoire, the one she now called Helena's, was written in tiny, spidery writing. The ink was faded in places, but was still just about legible. Avery pulled her own familiar grimoire towards her, picked up her pen, and continued the transcription. Although other witches had added notes to the spells over the years, she was reluctant to write in Helena's grimoire, worried about damaging it. It was far better preserved than it should be, having been protected from dampness and the effects of time by a spell; she could feel the tingle of magic every time she touched the book. In an effort to protect it from further handling, she'd found another spell that worked to cover the book's pages and binding.

Over the past few days, Avery had spent a lot of time examining Helena's grimoire and still couldn't get over the fact that she now possessed this precious item. The worn leather cover felt warm to her touch, and a faint smell of musk and vanilla drifted up from its pages. The first spell she was determined to read and master was the one that allowed flight. She wasn't sure if that was the right word for it, but it was the one she was certain Caspian used to wrap himself up in shadows and air and move from one place to the other. The spell was called the Flight of Spirits, but wasn't anything to do with spirit walking. She carefully transcribed the last few lines and copied the notes made in the margins, then put down the pen. Unlike many spells, there were no ingredients in this one, just repeated lines of incantation that she could only presume got easier with familiarity, as Caspian disappeared with undeniable speed.

She re-read the instructions, and then said the words.

At first, nothing happened, and then the air began to stir around her, gently to start, and then with increasing speed until she felt she stood at the centre of a tornado. Fear gripped her, but she fought through it, strengthened by everything she had experienced in the last few days.

I am a witch, a powerful witch, and I can do this.

She repeated the spell over and over again, her voice strengthening, and she varied the modulations in her tone and words, suddenly realising the meaning of one of the scribbled notes in the margin.

And then it happened. The wind whipped through her and she felt her body pull apart, and then she was standing in her living room and everything went black.

***

Avery stirred, feeling the rug beneath her cheek, and her hip pressing into the floor. *Ouch.* Her head felt like it had been trapped in a vice.

She was aware there was a soft, warm bundle of fur pressing against her arm, and as she moved, the cat stirred, meowing softly. It was Circe. She sounded very different to Medea. Avery patted her, comforted that she wasn't lying there completely alone, and then eased into a sitting position. Nausea washed through her. *How long had she been out for?*

It was darker now, the sky carrying only the tiniest hint of light, but she could make out the clock on the wall glowing with faint luminescence. It was after nine, which meant she'd been unconscious for just over an hour. Wow. But she grinned; she had moved from one room to another—a partial success, at least.

She dragged herself to her feet and headed to the kitchen, pouring a large glass of water that she downed in one go. That was a powerful spell. She hadn't felt that drained even after they'd broken the binding spell. All she wanted to do now was sleep, but she'd arranged to meet the others at Alex's pub, The Wayward Son, and she had lots to share. And besides, she wanted to see Alex again.

She downed another glass of water and decided now was not the time to try that spell again. She'd better walk instead.

***

The other four witches and Newton were already in Alex's flat above the pub when Avery arrived, and they looked at her in alarm when she entered.

El, tall and blonde, with legs up to her armpits, was dressed in her usual black jeans and rock t-shirt. She owned a jewellery shop called The Silver Bough, and silver piercings of her own design sparkled in the lamp light. She leaned against the kitchen counter, holding a bottle of beer, and frowned. "Avery! Are you all right? You look terrible."

"Do I? Why?" she asked, running her hand through her hair.

"You're white."

Alex was in the kitchen, placing some cheese and biscuits on platters, but he walked around the counter, frowning with concern. "What happened? Is it the Favershams?"

"No, I'm fine. Honestly, everyone relax. I wasn't attacked." She held her hand up as Reuben, Briar, and Newton all turned from where they sat on the sofa or the floor cushions. "I was trying a spell, and it was really hard."

"What spell?" El asked, coming closer to examine her.

"The flight spell, you know—swirly wind and mysterious disappearance and reappearance."

"Bloody Hell, Avery, you shouldn't be trying that on your own," Alex said gruffly. He pulled her in to a hug.

"Why not?" she asked, enjoying his unexpected display in front of the others and still feeling self-conscious about it. "We're all trying different spells on our own. Otherwise, how do we learn?"

"It's a fair point," Briar said. She owned Charming Balms Apothecary and sold lotions, soaps, candles, bath products, creams, and salves. She was dark-haired, petite, and very good at healing and Earth magic. "I've been brewing different potions solidly for the last two days. We can't accompany each other all the time."

"And you, Alex," Avery said pointedly, following him into the kitchen and grabbing a beer, "are always trying out spirit walking."

"Fair enough," he said. "But I don't look as white as a sheet afterwards."

"I admit, I passed out for an hour," she said sheepishly, "but I did move between rooms."

"Wow!" Newton said, looking shocked. "That's impressive!"

"I know!" she said, grinning. "Next time will be better. I'll be awake to enjoy it more."

"Pretty cool," Reuben said, nodding in agreement. Reuben, also tall, blond, and an avid surfer, was trying to master water elemental magic. "You'll have to teach us all when you've mastered it."

Avery joined them in the living room area, Alex and El close behind with snacks. "I will, and you guys will have to share some of your new skills, too."

"So what happened at the meeting, Avery?" Briar asked, leaning forward to grab a cracker and cheese.

"It was interesting. I had no idea that so many other witches were in Cornwall. I feel we've been missing out for a long time—but not anymore!" She related the events of the previous night. "I'd love you all to meet them. I'm sure it's only a matter of time."

Newton frowned. "But you say they're all experiencing some unusual supernatural activity?"

She nodded. "That's a very good way of putting it. Yes, they are. Every single place is having spirit activity at the moment, and it's probably only just beginning. And they gave us a warning about Mermaids. They're deadly. We have to be on our guard."

"Mermaids? Is that a joke? Have I missed something?" Reuben asked, a cracker halfway to his mouth.

"Sorry Reuben, I wasn't sure if Alex had told you. I had a visitor at the shop the other day." She filled them in on Caleb and the lights.

"Great. A few more risks with surfing, then," Reuben said. "I thought Mermaids were hot?"

"No. Not hot, just killers," she said, rolling her eyes.

"Shouldn't we warn people?" Briar said.

"Yeah, sure," Reuben said, nodding. "I'll let the Coastguard know, and we'll put a sign on all the beaches. *'Beware, Mermaid attacks, stick to the orange buoys.'*"

"Oh sod off," Briar said. "That's not quite what I meant."

"Seriously," Reuben said, looking at her incredulously. "What could we do?"

"I don't know," she answered, "but the locals are looking to us for advice. I've had several veiled questions already about whether I offer any other services. I wasn't sure what to say, if I'm honest. I just mumbled and said have a nice day. What are we supposed to do?"

"Well," El said, "the few charms and amulets I sell have sold out. A couple of girls who live in an old cottage said they keep feeling really cold draughts around the place. They're convinced they're being haunted, and I think they're right. I'm making lots of new charms and amulets, because as we all know, this is just the start. Unfortunately, Sebastian was right. We've started something, and we need to protect the town."

"Okay, I have to ask," Newton said, frowning. "Do some people know you're witches? Why did this old guy come to you, Avery? Why ask Briar and El for help?"

Alex shook his head. "No one knows anything. Some of the locals know of Avery's family history, and Avery, El, and Briar's shops trade on herbs, amulets, tarot, and the occult."

Avery added, "Dan and Sally told me that some locals suspect our magic—my magic—may be a bit more *authentic* than others, but it doesn't worry anyone, yet."

"We all know some of the other shop owners that trade on the supernatural, and there's the fake tarot reader at the back of the Angels as Protectors shop—they have had all sorts of enquiries," Alex continued. "It's that sort of town, Newton. Magic, or the pretence of it, is our lifeblood. Bloody Hell, we even have Stan from the Council dressing up as a druid for the pagan celebrations! Not many other towns openly celebrate those. Those rumours are what make White Haven so popular." He looked slightly rueful. "It just so happens that things may get a little more *real* for a while."

"You're right," El acknowledged. "I've always had the odd question about the extent of what I do, because some people really want to *believe*. I always kept it vague, because people love intrigue. Zoe, however—my shop assistant—is always honest about her Wicca activities."

"Well," Alex said, "I've been experimenting with scrying. I've had limited success so far, but I'm going to keep trying."

Newton frowned. "Scrying?"

"The art of divination using water, glass, or mirrors. A useful skill if I can master it. And it allows you a window into someone else's life."

"It sounds a bit stalker-y to me. Be careful," Newton warned.

"I'm not a peeping Tom," Alex said, annoyed. "I was thinking more about keeping an eye on the Favershams."

"Still sounds dodgy."

El interrupted. "Good luck, Alex. I understand it's a hard skill to learn."

Reuben put in, "I've been meaning to ask, how are the tattoos? Healing okay?"

"I forget I've got it," Avery admitted. "It's healing nicely."

"Good. I'll let Nils know. He was worried you'd been put off tattoos forever."

"I must admit, I quite like mine," Briar said, grinning. "I actually might get another."

Avery suddenly thought of something else from the meeting. "One more thing. We also make up the thirteenth coven of Cornwall, too. It means they'll call on us for big spells." She shrugged and grinned. "I think it's pretty exciting."

"Sod them," Reuben said, clearly sticking to his original argument. "They didn't care before, did they? We need to look after ourselves first."

"I'm glad you said that," El said, "because we have a job."

"We do?" Newton asked, looking at her over his beer.

"Maybe not you, but at least a couple of us. The lights up at the castle are getting worse. One of my regular customers told me today that she saw lights again last night and basically said, if you have any other mojo going on, sort out the castle because the town is going to freak out sooner rather than later."

"Have you seen them?" Briar asked her.

"No, anyone else?"

They all shook their heads.

Avery frowned. "I guess we've been too preoccupied. What did you say, El?"

"I merely smiled enigmatically, and told her I'd see what I could do."

"Interesting. And what are you going to do?"

"Rope you lot into a banishing spell, of course," El said. "We've been able to let some of the milder spirit activity play out, but I don't think we can ignore this."

"Spirit banishment seems to be my area of speciality, so of course I'm happy to go," Alex said, reaching forward to get more food.

"Me too," Avery agreed. "I'm trying to increase my knowledge in all sorts of stuff at the moment."

"Sounds like a great idea," Reuben said. "If there's more spirit activity in White Haven, we all need to be able to deal with it. Count me in."

"And me," Briar said.

"I'm coming, too," Newton chimed in. "I want to know exactly what we're up against, And I'll take the shotgun with the salt shells, just in case."

"Excellent. May as well go now, then," El decided, grinning.

4

Avery pulled her van into the castle's car park and frowned. "There's another car here."

Alex frowned. "Who the hell is here at this time of night?"

"Kids, probably," Newton shouted from the back where the others were sitting. "Kids love to spook themselves out with ghost stories."

"Kids who drive?" Alex said sarcastically.

"Well, teenagers then, Mr Pedantic," Newton said, annoyed.

"How're we going to banish spirits with kids around?" Briar asked.

"We're just going to have to glamour them," Alex said, as everyone exited the van and set off across the car park and up the path to the castle.

White Haven Castle sat above them on the hilltop, strategically placed to overlook the sea and the surrounding countryside. It was mostly a ruin now, but large sections of the outer walls still remained standing, and the local conservation group had reconstructed some inner walls creating rooms, although the roof had long since gone. A few trees had sprung up over the intervening years, growing both in and around the grounds. The car park had been built a short distance away so as not to mar the grandeur of the ruin.

Lights were placed at regular points along the wall, and were illuminated at various special times of the year, but tonight they were off. However, torchlight bobbed along at the base of the castle walls, and then disappeared.

"Bollocks," Reuben said, striding ahead with El, "this is going to make things more complicated."

"Are you sure you don't need your grimoire?" Avery asked Alex.

"No. I've been reading these spells and committing them to memory for days now," Alex explained.

Newton was walking alongside them. "What do you mean, 'spells?' Do you need more than one to do the same thing?"

"There are many different types of spells to dispel spirits," Alex said. "In fact, there are many different spells to do all sorts of things. Some work better than others depending on the situation, the witch who's saying the spells, tone, intonation—it goes on. Just as you need lots of ways to catch criminals, we have lots of ways to do things, too."

"Fair enough," Newton said. "What about spells to glamour people?"

Briar answered. "It depends how susceptible they are. It helps if the subject is already attracted to you, too. Men glamour women and vice-versa much more easily. Well, in general, anyway."

"I hope you haven't been glamouring me," Newton said, and Avery smiled to hear the tease in his voice.

"Newton! I would never do that," Briar said, and then she faltered as the implications of his words sank in.

Alex grinned at Avery, and then at Newton. "Nicely played, Newton."

If it wasn't so dark, Avery could have sworn Briar blushed.

"You're both so funny," Briar said, trying to brush it off.

Newton just laughed, and then changed the subject as the castle walls loomed above them. "Well, I know I don't need to say this, but we can't hurt them—whoever they are."

"We'll work it out," Avery said, trying to reassure him.

Reuben and El were waiting for them under the half-collapsed arch that was once the gated castle's entrance.

"There seems to be three of them," El said, pointing to the far side of the courtyard. "We can hear two male voices and one female, and we can see their torches."

"Any sign of spirit activity?" Alex asked, looking up and around.

"Not yet," Reuben said.

Suddenly, as if on cue, a scream pierced the night.

"Crap," Newton said, breaking into a run, the others following.

As Avery ran, she instinctively summoned her power, starting to ball energy into her hands. Torchlight flashed wildly from behind one of the walls, and shouts filled the air.

"It's okay, Cassie!" a male voice yelled.

"No, it's not!" Cassie yelled. "I felt something breathe on me, and it wasn't you or Ben!"

They slowed to a halt as they approached the broken wall. Peering around it, Avery saw three figures in the middle of a large room—although it was barely that anymore. Four partially erect walls encompassed a rectangular space. The floor was made of stone and grass, and broken stones were scattered everywhere.

The three figures carried an assortment of equipment, and they had a couple of lights set up, casting gloomy shadows in the area. First impressions suggested the trio were older than they'd initially thought; Avery estimated only a few years younger than themselves.

Newton stepped out from behind the wall, the witches close behind. "I heard a scream. Are you okay?"

The girl, who must be Cassie, screamed again, and the one of the boys shouted, "Shit! Where the hell did you come from?"

"Sorry, I didn't mean to startle you. My name's Newton, I'm a policeman." He gestured to the others, "These are friends of mine. What are you doing here?"

The man in the centre was holding a camera, and the big white light next to him cast his face into harsh planes and illuminated his dark skin. "Nothing!" he said belligerently.

Newton's voice became hard. "I think we all know that's bullshit. What are you doing with all this equipment?"

The second man answered. He was of average height and a stocky build, and he said proudly, "We're paranormal investigators—it's not a crime. We're not damaging anything!"

Reuben snorted. "Paranormal investigators! Is this a school project or something?"

"Do we look like we're at school? No! We're interested in the paranormal, and thought we'd investigate the lights that have appeared up here lately. It's not a crime," he repeated angrily.

Newton held up a hand to calm him down, which unfortunately drew attention to the shotgun he was holding in his left hand. "It's okay, you're not in trouble."

"Oh my God!" Cassie exclaimed. "Is that a shotgun?" She started backing away.

Avery stood next to Newton, hoping a female might calm things down. "It's okay, no one's going to hurt you. We came up here to investigate the lights, too. The shotgun is just for our protection. The shells are filled with salt."

The first guy, the taller one, said, "Oh, I get it! Very *Supernatural*. Cool. Wish I'd thought of that!"

"Well, unless you have a license, I suggest you forget about it," Newton said impatiently.

"Chill out. I didn't say I'd got one, did I?" He huffed dramatically.

Avery tried not to laugh. This was turning into a very interesting night. She strolled over to look at their equipment and introduced herself. "This stuff looks pretty impressive."

"It should do. It cost loads," the shorter, stocky one said. He reached out a hand. "I'm Ben."

"And I'm Dylan," the taller boy said.

"And you must be Cassie," Avery said, smiling. Cassie was short, with brown hair pulled up into a ponytail, and she looked nervous. "We heard you scream. What happened?"

Cassie glanced nervously over her shoulder. "I felt something breathe on me, over there. It was horrible."

"It's brilliant," Ben said. "That's what we came here for."

"But I didn't *really* expect it!" she answered him, annoyed.

"This is not our first haunting," he said, frowning.

"It's the first time something *breathed* on me," she pointed out.

Avery felt sorry for her. It probably sounded like a bit of a joke before they arrived, but it was very creepy up here. There was very little moon tonight, and the air was cold where the sea wind sliced through the nooks and crannies of the broken walls.

"Have you seen any lights?" Alex asked, glancing around the castle walls.

"No, nothing," Ben said.

"But," Dylan added, "the lights have been reported at hours later than this."

"How do you know?" Alex asked, curious.

"My mate lives on the hill, and he has a clear view from his house to here."

"Well, I suggest you go home now," Newton said in a very policeman-like tone.

"Why? We're not doing anything wrong," Ben said, becoming agitated. "What are *you* going to do?"

The witches and Newton all stared at each other awkwardly, wondering what to say.

"Mm, thought so," Ben said. "Something dodgy."

"Not dodgy at all," Alex said. "Why don't we help each other? We have an interest in ghosts, too. Why don't you show us how your equipment works?"

"Where's your stuff?" Dylan asked, suspiciously.

"I have slightly different methods than you," Alex said with a tight smile.

While the investigators huddled together for a brief second, consulting each other, Alex turned and made a quiet suggestion. "While me and Newton check out their stuff and see if they can help, why don't you check the rest of the place out?"

"Sounds good," El said. "Come on, Reuben."

They turned and headed to the other side of the castle, while Briar and Avery started to explore the room they were in.

"Can you sense anything, Briar?" Avery asked, heading to where Cassie had indicated she had felt something breathing on her.

"Not yet. Maybe an increase in energy in the atmosphere? Nothing concrete. What about you?"

Avery shook her head. "Nothing. It *is* creepy, though. Any idea when this castle was built?"

"Eleventh century, during the reign of William the Conqueror. After he was crowned, he arranged for the construction of many castles. I come here a lot. It's one of my favourite places in White Haven. I love the feeling of the age of the place just seeping around me."

Avery smiled. "I didn't know that! But wow, this is old, then. That's a lot of years, and a lot of ghosts."

"I normally find it such a peaceful place, though," Briar mused as she wandered around the shell of the room, stroking its walls.

"So no previous indication of spirits?"

"No, despite the rumours of a white lady walking the walls. But isn't there always, in these old places?" she laughed.

"I'm starting to think people are just imagining things," Avery said, half-disappointed that absolutely nothing appeared to be happening there.

"But if ghosts do appear, what are we going to do with *them?*" Briar asked. She looked over to where the three newcomers stood with Newton and Alex, showing them their equipment. The sound of static echoed across the space as they demonstrated a small, handheld device.

"They might prove useful," Avery said. "Maybe we should think about working with them. They're clearly open-minded about this kind of thing."

"Even witchcraft?" Briar said, her eyebrows raised. "I'm not sure we should trust our identities with people we don't know. We could end up on YouTube."

"I think we both know we can deal with that," Avery said.

"You know what I mean. I like remaining anonymous," she said, heading through a gap in the wall to explore other parts of the castle.

But then the unmistakable sound of an energy blast disturbed the night's silence.

Avery turned and ran, Briar hard on her heels, heading for the side of the castle where El and Reuben were exploring.

As they sprinted across the grounds, Newton and Alex ran past them, and the three investigators, after a moment's hesitation, followed.

As they rounded a corner, they saw El and Reuben backed up against the wall, as far as possible from an unearthly light in the centre of a large room, and everyone came to a skidding halt, Avery crashing into the back of Alex. Cassie, once again, screamed.

"Holy shit! That's a real, live spirit!" Dylan exclaimed.

"I don't think there's anything *live* about it," Alex said, dryly. He called over to El and Reuben, "Are you okay? Has it attacked you?"

"No, we're fine," Reuben explained. "It just appeared unexpectedly, and kind of gave us a shock."

El looked sheepish. "It appeared right in front of me, and I panicked. But, other than that, nothing. It's just floating there."

The spirit seemed to be just an amorphous blob, with tendrils reaching out around it like grasping fingers.

Briar turned to Ben, Cassie, and Dylan. "I think you three need to get out of here."

"No way!" Ben said, flourishing the monitor in his hand. It was emitting a whining, static noise that was very distracting.

Newton frowned. "I think we all know there's a spirit here, Ben. Turn your damn machine off—it's annoying."

"I can't," he said crossly, "I need to measure this."

Newton scowled, cocked his shotgun, and asked no one in particular, "What now?"

"Can anyone make out what it is?" Cassie asked, finally finding her voice.

As if on cue, the blob started to change, taking on a more human form.

"Looks like a woman to me," Alex said.

He was right. The blue glow made her shape hard to define, but it did appear to be a woman wearing a long dress—a very old-fashioned dress.

Avery snorted. "Crap. So much for us saying there's no such thing as a White Lady here."

The spirit turned in the middle of the space, her arms outspread as she seemed to watch them. Avery felt the hairs stand up on her arms as the woman met her gaze. And then the spirit looked up, over Avery's shoulder, to the top of the wall behind her. A horrible sinking feeling filled Avery's stomach, and she turned to follow her gaze.

There, on the top of the wall, was another blue, glowing ghostly figure. It was a man, and he was aiming an arrow directly at them.

Even though part of Avery's rational mind knew that he couldn't possibly hurt them, she instinctively yelled and ducked. "Move everyone, now!"

A glowing blue arrow sailed over Avery's head, landing at the feet of the ghostly woman with a distinctly solid sounding *thud*. A high-pitched keening sound broke the silence, and then everyone yelled and scrambled for cover.

Arrow after arrow thudded into the ground around them, one narrowly missing Avery's head. She felt it whistle past her ear.

"What the shit?" Reuben yelled, pulling El behind him. An arrow was headed straight for them and he swatted it away with a sweeping motion of his hand. "This feels scarily real, guys!"

Within seconds, at least a dozen ghostly men manifested around them, all wearing what looked like leather breeches, shirts, and cloaks, and all wielding swords or axes. The woman spirit ran from the room, trying to evade their clutches, but she was too late. The arrows finally found their mark as they thudded into her and she fell, facedown.

The men turned their attention to them, and Avery felt a trickle of fear run down her spine.

"Alex?" She looked at him from where they crouched behind a piece of broken wall. "We need to start the spell. We haven't got time to get rid of the ghost-hunters."

Newton was already standing. The men advanced menacingly towards them and he lifted his shotgun and took aim for the closest, releasing both barrels in rapid succession.

Then all hell broke loose as the spirits rushed them.

Avery stood with the others and released wave after wave of energy bolts, but for every spirit they sent whirling backwards, others appeared. Avery felt cold, clammy hands on her arm and looked up into the white eyes of a scarred man with an evil grin. He lifted her clean off the floor as she gasped in surprise. She should not be able to feel this, and he shouldn't be able to manifest that strongly, but...

Well, in that case, she decided, he could feel *this*. She punched him with a ball of energy straight at his stomach and he dropped her, disappearing only to reappear a few feet away.

Blasts of energy and fireballs ricocheted off the castle walls, and shouts filled the air. The earth trembled beneath her feet as tree roots shot up, grabbing at the legs of the attacking men.

45

Avery pulled the wind around her and then sent it through the ghosts like a hurricane. Although it scattered them, they didn't stop fighting.

"Cover me—I need time!" Alex shouted above the din.

He retreated as far as he could away from the fight, pulling the three hunters with him, who by now were wide-eyed with either fear, amazement, or both. Newton followed him, still firing, trying to keep the spirits back, while Alex started his incantation, his voice strong as it rose above the noise.

Avery glanced around and saw the scattered witches unleashing their magic in various forms on their attackers, and all managing to hold their own. *But how were the spirits so strong?* It must be the magic they'd released.

She heard a *whirring* noise and she ducked and rolled as an axe whirled past, thudding into the wall behind her. She grinned. *That's mine now.*

Extending her hand and her power, Avery pulled the axe out of the wall into her waiting palm and then turned, wielding her spirit-weapon viciously as she imbued it with extra magical energy. She rolled to the floor and struck out at the closest man's legs, feeling the horrible crunch of muscle and bone as he collapsed on the ground next to her. It was time to try a banishment spell. Her grimoire only had a couple, and she had never tried them before. She uttered the spell, but her incantation didn't seem strong enough, and the spirit just seemed to laugh at her as he dragged himself back to his feet.

Avery started to despair. These spirits were strong, too strong, and she could see the others struggling, too.

But then she felt Alex's power swell around them, and his voice seemed to magnify within the castle walls. As he completed his incantation, a wave of magic passed through the castle like a tsunami, sweeping up the spirits as it passed through, until every single one disappeared and the place fell into an eerie silence.

Now the spirits and their weird blue glow had gone, the place was plunged into darkness, a faint light from the stars overhead their only illumination. Someone sent up a couple of witch lights, and Avery sighed with relief as she saw that everyone was okay. She collapsed to the floor, her heart thudding wildly, and her hands shaking as her adrenaline ebbed away.

It was Dylan who spoke first. "Oh, wow." He stood on slightly shaky legs and gazed around, his mouth open. He grinned, "*Wow, wow, wow!* Guys, that was amazing! What the hell was that? Who are you? You have to teach me that!"

5

Avery gathered some wood from the fallen branches in the grounds and started a fire in the shelter of a reasonably solid corner of the castle, while the three paranormal investigators retrieved their gear. Then they sat and leaned against the castle walls, while Alex lectured. "Guys, we are not teaching you anything. In fact, you need to forget *everything*."

Ben laughed in a slightly maniacal way. "Ha! You're kidding, right? I can't forget that! *Ever.*"

Alex glanced at Avery, and she knew what he was thinking. *Should they try and glamour them so they forgot what they'd seen?* But they both knew that there was too much magical evidence to enchant away successfully.

Dylan looked excited, Ben looked shocked, and Cassie looked at them with fear in her eyes. She hadn't said a word.

Briar smiled at her. "It's okay, Cassie, we're not monsters, and we're not going to hurt you. I'm just sorry you were here to see it."

Ben made a strangled sound. "This isn't one of those times when we're made to *disappear*, is it?"

Reuben groaned from where he was lying flat on the ground. "We're not assassins, dude. Calm down. We're just aliens. We have extra-terrestrial powers." El laughed and poked him in the ribs with her toe.

"Not helpful, thanks Reuben," Avery said, laughing despite the horrified expressions on Dylan, Ben, and Cassie's faces. "He's kidding!"

"So what *are* you?" Cassie whispered.

"Can you keep a secret?" Avery asked her.

"And we mean, no blogs, Facebook, Twitter, YouTube chats, leaked camera footage, or *anything* else!" Alex said, looking each of them in the eye sternly.

They all nodded mutely.

"We have the ability to do magic," Avery said, reluctant to say 'witch.'

Ben snorted. "*Magic?*" He started to laugh, but it died on his lips as he saw that no one else was laughing. "Are you serious?"

Newton sighed from the shadows, where he'd sat next to Briar, the shotgun on his lap. "They are very serious. Why, Ben? What did you think that was?"

Ben stuttered. "I-I don't know, I thought maybe they had some sort of weapon. I mean, you have a shotgun!"

"That's because I'm not a witch."

Avery saw the newcomers all flinch at the word.

Reuben rolled over to look at them. "Guys, let them think we're aliens, it's probably more believable."

El sniggered again. "Shut up, Reuben."

He winked at her, grabbed her hand, and kissed it.

"Let me get this right," Alex said. "You're paranormal investigators, you believe in spirits and things that go bump in the night, but you don't believe in magic or witches?"

"Well, I admit to the possibility of them," Ben said defensively. "But we base our findings on rational and scientific investigation."

"Good for you," Alex said. "In that case, you can put this all down to a very active imagination."

Dylan glared at Ben. "Ben, stop being an ass. You wanted to see something tonight! Your EMF meter was off the charts. These guys are the real deal. I mean, look at that weird light thing floating above us."

Ben grabbed his meter from where it lay on the ground next to him, flicked it on, and pointed it at the witch light. He swung the device around and they could hear a low static buzz, steadily rising in volume.

Alex held his hand out and formed a small ball of fire. "Try reading this."

Ben's eyes widened and he leaned forward, pointing his meter at Alex. It started to whine with increasing intensity as Alex made the fire grow, and then decreased as Alex dissolved it again. However, the meter continued to pick up a low buzz from all of the witches.

"Wow. This is really happening, right?" Ben asked, his earlier excitement returning.

"'Fraid so," Avery answered, a trace of a smile on her face. "Are you going to keep our secret?"

All three glanced at each other and then nodded in agreement, and Dylan answered for all of them. "Deal. But you realise you want us to hide the very stuff we're looking for."

"Share what you want about spirits and other paranormal stuff, just not us," Alex said evenly.

Reuben added, "Think of us as your gateway into the unknown."

"I like that idea," Ben said, nodding.

"Good," Newton said, leaning towards them. "Now, tell me what else you know about weird ghosts and sightings lately. And what else do you do, apart from this stuff?"

Ben spoke first. "We all study at Penryn University. I'm doing postgraduate studies in parapsychology, looking at beliefs and experiences, precognition, ESP. I love this stuff—I just remain a healthy sceptic. It's good to have balance."

"Me too, but whereas Ben's background is physics, mine's psychology," Cassie said. "A while ago Ben posted a request on the university messages wall for someone doing psychology to join in his investigations, so I thought, why not? I'm curious. Life's all about experiences. I enjoyed it so much that when I finished my degree, I decided to do postgrad parapsychology, too. We're about to enter our second year. But, this is the first time anything so *obvious* has happened." She still looked wide-eyed and completely out of her depth, but at least she didn't look terrified. "If I'm honest, I thought it would be a load of rubbish and that nothing would happen, ever. How wrong could I be?"

"To be fair," Dylan said, "I don't think any of us expected this. Most of the things we monitor provide goose bumps and a bit of static. This is…unexpected. Anyway, I'm doing postgrad studies in English, focussing on folklore, and myths and legends. I'm an enthusiastic assistant." He grinned again. "This is awesome!"

Avery frowned as she remembered that Dan, who worked in her shop, studied English, too. "Do you know Dan Fellows? He's doing his Masters in something to do with folktales at Penryn."

"Tall guy, glasses, dark hair? I think he's taken a couple of tutorials. Why, do you know him?"

"He works with me in my shop, Happenstance Books."

"Okay," Dylan said, his interest piqued. "And does he know about you guys?"

"Yes, he does. I'll tell him to keep an eye out for you."

"So, how did you know to come here, and what other places have you been told about?" Newton persisted.

"I told you," Dylan said. "My mate lives in White Haven and he saw the lights. The other things have been reported to Ben through his website—it's just a simple one. There's a contact email."

Ben looked thoughtful. "My website's been up for months, but about ten nights or so ago, I picked up a really big EMF surge. It was totally off the charts and completely inexplicable. I was just playing around with the equipment at home, and *wow!* It was just so odd!"

Avery inwardly groaned and glanced at the others who looked as guilty as she felt. It must have been the night they released the binding.

Ben continued, "I thought I'd capitalise on it and put ads in the local papers, and I guess people saw them. I've had loads of reports in the last few days, especially of experiences at castles and other old buildings—you know, churches and stuff. There's no way we can check it all out straight away, but as this seemed to be one of the biggest, here we are. There have been a couple of reports in White Haven, actually."

"Where?" Newton asked.

"Old Haven Church. Apparently, there's a ghostly figure wandering the grounds, in the day as well as at night. Also the Church of All Souls, and the old museum on the hill. I'm going to check them all. Although, I am a bit worried now, after tonight." Ben turned to Alex. "What did you do to make them go? I mean, that was seriously impressive."

"It's my speciality," Alex said, shrugging.

"And harder than it looks," El added. "And you're not witches, so don't even think about trying."

"What worries me," Avery said, "is that these spirits seem to have an almost physical presence. They could grab me, with their horrible cold, clammy hands, and I was able to grab an axe that shouldn't exist in this plane. These are *spirits*. How can this be happening? We were attacked, and that means other people could be, too. And they can't banish them like we can."

Alex groaned. "Damn it. The magic we released has obviously strengthened spirits way beyond their normal means, and this could be only the start. We have to clean up—this is our mess."

Ben looked confused. "What do you mean about releasing magic?"

"Unfortunately, Ben, we're responsible for that EMF surge you picked up the other day. I'm hoping that only spirits that manifest in White Haven have become so corporeal. If you go spirit hunting elsewhere, be very careful."

6

It had been over a week since they'd met the ghost-hunters at White Haven Castle, and Avery had spent the early part of it chasing ghosts. The paranormal investigators had been right about the spirits at the churches, but fortunately they hadn't been as strong as those at the castle, and a few hours' work had banished them. Since then, she had caught up on sleep.

It was nice to settle into the normal rhythms of life again. Avery spent every day in the shop, selling and stocking books, and chatting to her customers. It was also a good way to get a feel for what was happening in White Haven. There were no further reports of weird lights at sea, and events seemed to have returned to normal. She was pretty sure the calm wouldn't last.

When she wasn't at work, she studied her new grimoire, and she knew the other witches were, too. Their individual strengths were growing in unexpected ways, and in every moment of their spare time, they honed their abilities. They all felt they were becoming more attuned to the details of their magic, and could wield it with greater precision.

Avery continued to try new spells, combining new with old, and practising witch flight—with slow but increasing success. She had managed to stop fainting, but it still seemed to take too long, and it was leaving her with headaches.

And of course she spent time with Alex. She could feel herself drifting around with a smile on her face, and had to shake herself out of her dreamy reveries. They had been practising some of their new skills together, and that seemed to be improving their magic, too.

However when Avery arrived in the small room at the rear of the shop on Friday morning, she knew she'd overdone it because Sally, the shop manager and her non-magical friend, looked horrified.

"You look terrible. What have you been doing?"

"Practising witch flight again. It's really hard. I think I'm missing something."

"Avery, I know you're anxious to do this, but you'll harm yourself if you push too hard. Can't you just put that spell aside for a while?"

Avery nodded, and headed to the cupboard under the coffee machine to find some paracetamol. "Yeah, I guess so. It'll be one of those things that will just fall into place—I hope."

Sally frowned, hands on her hips. "I think you should have a few days off from studying that grimoire. It's not going to disappear. You have time."

Avery found the pills and downed them with some water. "I know, but I'm just so excited to have found it—all of them. It's addictive! The spells, the history, the comments in the margins, it's just so…" She broke off, unable to really explain how life changing it had been.

Sally's expression softened. "I get it, I really do, but I'm worried about you. All of you, actually."

Avery smiled, feeling a rush of affection for her friend. "I know, but it's like I've just woken up after a long sleep. It's so cool!"

"It's not cool if you end up killing yourself. I popped into Briar's shop yesterday. She looked so tired. I don't even think she could concentrate. I think she needs some more help in there, she manages pretty much on her own."

"I think we're all trying really hard right now. We're worried about what might happen next, and we want to be prepared." She gave Sally a hug. "I don't know what I'd do without you and Dan. Thank you for being so great."

Sally patted her back. "It's okay. I'm glad to help. Now, come on through to the shop, I've got a few things to show you."

They spent the morning going over new stock and some changes in the store, and Sally ran though some promotions she wanted to implement, and then an unexpected voice interrupted them.

"Hey Avery, long time no see."

Avery looked up to find Ben and Cassie standing in front of the counter, each carrying a couple of books. Both of them looked different in the daylight—older, and less intimidated than the other night.

"Hey guys. Taking a break from ghost-hunting?"

"Are you kidding?" Ben asked. "We're snowed under with sightings. I wanted to let you know, and you're the only one I knew how to contact. And," he gestured to the books in his hands, "I thought I'd add to my collection. This is a great shop, Avery."

"You can thank my manager, Sally, for that," she said, introducing them to her.

"Oh, I don't know, Avery," Sally smirked. "You add a little something I can't."

"We also want to thank you for the other night," Cassie added, looking slightly embarrassed. "I'm not sure we thanked you properly at the time, it was all such a shock. But, you know, without you, things could have been really ugly."

"No problem at all," Avery said, smiling at her. She glanced around the shop and saw a couple of customers listening, and turned to Sally. "Do you mind if I head out the back for a couple of minutes?"

"Sure," Sally said, "just make me a coffee while you're at it."

Once they were safely away from prying ears and she had put the kettle on in the small kitchen, Avery asked, "So, what else have you heard about?"

"More of the same, really," Ben said. "Increased ghost sightings, abnormal noises, disappearing objects, electrical surges, cold spots. And it's happening all over Cornwall. A couple of people have even reported that they've spotted the Beast of Bodmin. You must have seen it on the news."

Avery nodded, remembering the evening news report from the day before. The Beast of Bodmin was a myth that had circulated for years. "I have, although if I remember correctly, there's no footage of it yet." She wondered if Zane, the beady-eyed witch from Bodmin, was having any success finding it.

Cassie continued enthusiastically, "At the moment, we're just trying to document everything, sort of create a database. But we've started to follow up on the more interesting ones."

"Follow up how?" Avery asked, frowning.

"Same as last week, really. We head out with our cameras and EMF meter and see what happens. We went to this old farmhouse a couple of nights ago, on the way to Helston. We picked up really strong signals, and one of the rooms was freezing!"

"Anybody in any danger?"

Ben shook his head. "No, nothing that manifested as strongly as at the castle. Just a really spooked family. They said it started a couple of weeks ago."

"That's good," Avery said, relieved no one could get hurt. "We've been catching up on a few other things." Avery pulled mugs from the cupboard above the kitchen counter. "Do you two want a drink?"

They shook their heads, and Ben said, "No, we've got an appointment at All Souls, actually. We thought you should know."

"All Souls? The Church in the centre of the town?" Avery looked up, coffee forgotten. "What have you got an appointment there for?"

"The vicar said that there's a spirit in the church, and he wanted us to check it out."

Avery felt her heart sink. "Did he give any details?"

"None. He was quite vague actually, other than that he thought there was *something unpleasant,*" Cassie said. She looked amused. "He sounded quite progressive. He wanted to know all about the equipment we used and everything."

"Do me a favour and let me know the details. I'll give you my number and I'll grab yours," Avery said, scribbling down her own and Alex's numbers before taking theirs.

Ben raised an eyebrow. "If something needs banishing, do you want me to pass on your number?"

Avery sighed deeply. If anything was happening there it was their fault, and they had to put it right. "I guess so. But keep things vague, okay? I don't need a modern day witch-hunt starting up in town."

"Sure thing," Ben said, grinning.

A thought struck Avery. "Have you heard anything about lights at sea?"

Ben frowned. "Lights? No, but there was a weird accident just out of Mevagissey a couple of nights ago. One of the crew of a fishing boat just disappeared. No shouts, no screams, he just vanished. The crew spent hours looking for him, and the Coastguard was called out, but they never found him. It's been all over the news, but it will be on the net if you missed it. They called off the search this morning."

Avery's heart sank. *Damn it. She'd hoped Caleb had been imagining things.*

Ben obviously caught Avery's expression. "Is there something we should know?"

Avery sighed. "This is going to sound really weird."

Ben laughed and looked at Cassie, incredulous. "Weirder than the other night?"

"Let me update you before you go," Avery said.

Halfway through the afternoon, Avery had another visitor. She was in the Local History section of the shop, seeing what books she had on myths and legends of Cornwall, when someone coughed politely behind her.

"Excuse me, may I have a word?"

Avery jumped, almost dropping the book she was holding. She had been so engrossed, she hadn't heard anyone approach.

She turned to see a man in his late forties, with short brown hair and a hint of grey at his temples. He was of average height and build, and wore smart jeans and a shirt, and a clergyman's dog collar at his neck.

Avery felt her stomach tighten with worry, but she tried not to show it. "Oh, sorry, you startled me. Yes, of course. Are you looking for something?"

"Only you. My name's James, and I'm the vicar of the Church of All Souls."

She forced herself to relax as she smiled, shaking his hand. "Nice to meet you, James. I'm Avery."

He smiled back, but his eyes were wary. "I'm sorry to disturb you, but I met Ben and Cassie this morning. They suggested I speak to you."

"Oh yes, the ghost-hunters. They mentioned they were going to see you." She glanced around and was relieved to find no one was within hearing range. "I gather you're having a few problems."

"If you call a spirit lurking in the church at night a problem, then yes. Is there somewhere more private that we could talk?"

"Of course, come this way."

Once again, Avery headed to the small room at the back of the shop, wondering if this was going to be a really uncomfortable chat. Dan was at the counter, and she saw his eyes widen with surprise when he saw whom she was with. She gesticulated to the back of the shop, and he nodded.

As soon as they were alone, James said, "This is an occult shop. You believe in witchcraft?"

"It's not *just* an occult shop, and I believe in many things, James. The world is a strange place, isn't it? You're here because of a 'lurking spirit,' after all."

He didn't answer straight away. He walked around the room, looking at the boxes of stock along the back wall, many of them new books for the shelves, as well as some second-hand editions, and then he picked up one of the boxes of tarot cards on the table. "Do these sell?"

Avery nodded. "Yes, they're very popular. So are the Angels Cards and the Dream Catchers."

He nodded abruptly. "Yes, people probably put more stock in these things than God now."

"Surely Angel Cards would suggest a belief in God?"

He looked at her sharply. "I guess so. So, what do Tarot cards suggest a belief in? The Devil?"

"Surely if God exists, then so does the Devil. You're the vicar, you tell me. But that's *not* what the Tarot is about, James, and I think you know that. There are many different beliefs in the world. Not everyone believes in the male omniscient being that controls our destiny. The Tarot cards tap into old magic. Or so some believe," she said, tempering her words.

"May I look at them?" he asked.

"Of course." She watched as he thumbed through the cards of the classic Rider-Waite pack, placing them on the table as he looked at their pictures. His gaze hovered over the Devil card before he quickly moved on.

The smell of incense drifted from the main part of the shop, and Avery was sharply aware of how the place would look to someone from the church.

James looked up. "And what do you know about ghosts and spirits?"

"Only that they exist. And you must believe that, too, or you wouldn't be here."

They were silent for a few seconds, assessing each other, and while Avery didn't think he was a witch hunter, he didn't seem as progressive as Cassie had made him sound. And then his shoulders dropped, and he sat abruptly in a chair at the table, worry etched across his face.

"Let me make a coffee," Avery said, moving to the counter, "and I think you need some cake."

James sat mute while she brewed a strong pot of coffee and put the carrot cake that Sally had made in the centre of the table. Half of it had already been eaten, mainly by Dan. It was a miracle he didn't have diabetes.

Avery sat down, pushed a cup of coffee in front of him, and then cut them both a large slice of cake. Before she spoke, she had a couple of bites of her own, hoping to relax herself as well as him. When she woke up that morning, she did not imagine she'd be having tea with the local vicar in her shop.

"So James, this is obviously difficult for you to be here. Why don't you tell me what's happening at All Souls?"

He rubbed his face with his hands, and then reached for his cake, taking a bite and chewing slowly, and all the time he watched her. "Before I tell you, I want to know if you're discreet. I don't want this all over the town."

She nodded. "I'm very discrete. Nobody wants panic in White Haven."

"Why did Ben and Cassie say you could help? They were very vague. There's no point to me telling you anything if you can't help."

"I have a friend who is good at exorcism. Very good, in fact."

James frowned. "Does he belong to the Catholic church? That's the sort of thing they do."

Avery almost choked on her cake. "No, he does not. He has independent affiliations."

James glanced around the room again and Avery felt sorry for him. He was obviously very conflicted.

"James, please tell me. I want to help. What did Ben and Cassie find?"

"Their EMF meter readings were high. They agreed that I was not going mad."

"I'm sure you're not, but I'm going to need more than that."

A small smile crept across James's face and she saw him start to relax. "Sorry. This is all very strange for me."

"I understand. Now, from the beginning."

"It started a couple of weeks ago. The energy in the church changed. It's quite odd, and I can't explain it, but it's like something *else* is there." He frowned as he thought. "Anyway, for a few days there was nothing but this strange feel to the place. I've worked there for years, so I know this is new. And then I was working in the sacristy and I felt as if I was being watched. I turned around and saw nothing, but the air got very cold around me. It was most uncomfortable. And then the next night, the same thing happened, and I saw a ghostly shape in the doorway—just for a second, and then it went. It was shapeless, amorphous, but I sensed intelligence and something malignant. I nearly had a heart attack and I left, right in the middle of writing my sermon."

"Why do you say malignant? What did it do?'"

"Nothing, but it just seemed to watch me—study me. I know that sounds strange, it didn't have eyes that I could see. But it was so uncanny. I had to force myself to go in the next day." He sighed, stealing himself to go on. "And then it appeared again, same time, same place, but this time for longer. It was like a dark presence just on the edge of my vision. It didn't hurt me, it was just there. But every night since it has returned, and although it sounds odd, I sense that it's growing stronger. The verger has also seen it, an older man called Harry, and despite his faith, he's very scared. And it's started moving things—the flowers, the Bible, the prayer books. We have to do something before it appears in a service, or at a wedding or a christening, or a funeral. Can you imagine?"

Avery nodded. "I would think you'd lose all of your worshippers."

"And the papers would come, and the archbishop would be involved," he said, his voice rising. "We need to do this quickly. I can't believe I'm even having this conversation."

Avery sat, thinking. They obviously had to help him. All Souls was at the centre of the whole magical release, and it had obviously disturbed a resting spirit. "Do you have any idea of who it may be?"

"I think it's a *what* more than a *who*." He shrugged. "I know that sounds stupid, but you were right earlier. I've come across restless spirits before now. Churches always have them, but this is different. Very different. That's why I called Ben."

"I think we can help, James. Would you like me to contact my friend? We can come tonight, if that helps?"

Relief swept across his face. "Yes, please. The sooner, the better. It appears to be most visible at about nine in the evening. Can you come then?"

"Of course. Probably best if you leave us to it, once you've let us in."

"Oh no," he said, shaking his head. "I need to see this, to know it's done. And I believe Ben and Cassie want to be there, too."

7

Alex leaned across the bar, looking incredulous. "Are you kidding me?"

"No. He's desperate, Alex."

"I get that, but he's a bloody vicar, Avery," he hissed, "at the place where we performed some very big juju."

"I know, Alex. I was there. The big juju is responsible for this," she hissed back. "*We* are responsible for this."

"But we'll be doing magic in front of the vicar."

"Catholic priests used to do this," she pointed out. "They might still, in fact. He asked if you were a Catholic, and of course I said no. But, can we make it look religious?"

"I suppose we'll bloody have to," he said, frowning. "Give me half an hour and I'll be with you."

Avery grinned and grabbed her glass of wine, perching on a bar stool to drink it.

It was 7.00 PM now, and she'd headed to The Wayward Son once she'd closed the shop and straightened up her flat. Having James visit reminded her that she had all sorts of magical things strewn around and she needed to take them up to her attic. If, for some reason, he'd come to her flat, things would have looked really weird.

As Avery sat looking around the crowded pub, she saw the main door swing open and Newton came in with Briar. She grinned and waved, wondering if they were on a date.

Briar looked flushed with happiness. *Maybe not*, she thought, as she looked at Newton's face. He was frowning. Again.

"Hi guys," she said, as they each pulled out a barstool. "How are you?"

"Annoyed," Newton said. "Since meeting you, my life has become very complicated."

Briar just grinned. "Hi Avery, lovely to see you. And Newton doesn't mean it. He enjoys it, really. He said so the other night."

"The other night?" Avery questioned, raising her eyebrow. "So you two have been spending some time together? How nice."

"He has asked me to go over the finer points of what we do," she said discretely as Newton turned away to order their drinks. "He feels it will enable him to help us better in the future."

"Of course it will," Avery nodded, trying to keep a straight face. "I presume you did this over wine and a nice meal. Sounds very pleasant. Of course, he does get the added bonus of your fabulous company."

"He's been the perfect gentleman, Avery. I think you're getting the wrong idea."

"Sure I am. Did you cook?"

"No, he did, actually." Briar squirmed slightly. "I went to his house. He said he wanted to repay me for looking after his burns and healing him. He's a very good cook." During their defeat of a demon a few weeks before, Newton had sustained some nasty burns.

"Really? That *is* nice, isn't it?" Avery started to smirk. "Did you enjoy it?"

"We had a lovely evening, thank you, Avery, and then I went home, so you can wipe that smirk off your face," Briar said primly.

"I'm not smirking."

"You so are," she said.

Avery glanced over to Newton, who was still pre-occupied at the bar. "But he likes you, I can tell. You must know, Briar."

"I don't know. I think you're imagining things." Briar looked slightly put out, and maybe regretful.

"He's playing the long game," Avery said, sipping her wine. "Just for the record, I'd like to say that I approve. I like him. He suits you. You'll make a lovely couple."

Briar was just about to say something very rude, Avery could tell from her outraged expression, when Newton slid a glass of white wine in front of her.

"What are you two looking all sneaky about?" he asked.

"Nothing at all," Briar said, breezily. She changed the subject deftly. "You'd better tell her your news."

Avery frowned. "What now?"

Newton leaned on the bar. "Have you heard about the man who disappeared from the fishing boat?"

"Unfortunately, yes."

"Well, it's been logged as an accident, but there's no sign of his body. It was a calm night, and we should have found his body by now, but I guess tides do strange things sometimes. He may turn up yet."

"Any suggestion of lights?"

Newton shook his head. "Nothing. One minute he was there, the next he'd gone. I wonder if there was some sort of Mermaid magic involved—apparently, all the crew looked a little dazed and glassy-eyed. We'll probably never know what truly happened." He gazed into his pint, depressed.

"Are you leading it?"

"No. It's not a murder investigation. I've just been privy to some of the details."

"Well," Avery said, "I have news for you." She filled them in on Ben and Cassie's visit, and then her afternoon call from James.

"I know James," Newton said thoughtfully.

"Do you?" Briar asked. "Is he okay? I mean, will he start pulpit preaching about demons and witches?"

"I hope not. He doesn't strike me as the superstitious type, but I suggest you keep your real nature to yourselves. Not many will like the fact that there are witches in White Haven. Especially the Church."

Avery grinned. "Alex is going to use a Latin spell—it's what they used in medieval times when the priests were involved in necromancy. Hopefully it will throw James off the fact that we're also using magic. I've told James it's an exorcism."

Newton frowned. "Priests were involved in necromancy?"

"Oh yes. In medieval times, the crossover between magic and religion was enormous. I mean, really, what's the difference between a miracle and magic?" Avery shrugged and laughed. "Nothing, except the Church endorsed one and denied the other. The saints replaced the pagan gods. That's how they managed to keep converting pagans to Christianity, by renaming pagan celebrations and incorporating them into the Church calendar. And then they converted everything to Latin—the language of Catholicism. Remember, this was way before Henry VIII and the Church of England."

Newton's mouth dropped open. "Really! I'd never thought about miracles and magic like that before. Sneaky."

"Very."

Briar asked, "Do you need any help?"

"No." Avery shook her head. "One spirit only. Should be manageable. And we want to keep this simple. I don't want to glamour the vicar. It should be pretty straight forward. I hope."

The main entrance of All Souls was closed, and Alex and Avery headed around to the side door where they found James waiting nervously. He looked at Alex with interest as Avery introduced them. "I understand you've done this before?" he asked, as he led them inside to the sacristy.

"Several times, and always with success," Alex said, reassuringly.

"Good. I really want this to stop. Harry said he wouldn't return again if I didn't sort it out soon. Like this is something I normally deal with on a daily basis!"

"Are Cassie and Ben here?" Avery asked.

James nodded and called back over his shoulder. "Yes, and their friend, Dylan. They are in the nave at the moment, taking readings."

They entered a small stone and wood-panelled room at the rear of the church. Vestments hung on the walls, and there was a small desk covered in a pile of papers beneath a high window.

"So, this is where you see your ghostly visitor?" Alex asked, looking around.

"Yes. As you can see, my back is to the door when I'm sitting here. The ghost appears in the doorway, and then from there moves to the rest of the church." He shivered. "I can feel it behind me. It's most unnerving."

Understatement of the year.

Avery could feel the magic they had released hanging in the still air of the church. Beyond that, she sensed a different energy signature, which must be the spirit. At the moment, it was faint.

"Let me take you through to the nave," James said, and he turned and led the way out through the chancel, past the entrance to the crypt, toward the pulpit and the nave where the paranormal investigators were setting up some of their equipment.

Cassie turned and waved. "Hi guys. Good to see you again."

"Sooner than I expected," Alex said with a wry smile. He dropped his voice so James couldn't hear. "Not planning on filming us, I hope?"

"Not you." She nodded to where James was chatting to Dylan. "Just the ghost. And James forbade us from mentioning the church on film. Didn't want this getting out on social media or the TV. And of course we honour that. Full confidentiality. But he did give us permission to monitor everything else. I think he's really interested in it all!"

"Good," Alex said, "or else I would have to fry your recording."

Cassie looked at him, wide-eyed. "I suppose you could."

"And would. Never forget that," Alex said, winking. "And it goes without saying that you keep our names out of your reports, too."

"No problem," she answered, almost stuttering.

"Try not to scare Cassie again, Alex," Avery said, patting his arm before looking at their equipment. It was a very impressive, professional set up. "You've got some pretty interesting stuff here, Cassie."

"We get funding through the university."

A shiver ran through Avery as she looked around the church. It looked so peaceful and unassuming. The pews were of polished wood, the flowers were fresh, late evening sunshine streamed thought the stained glass windows casting the interior in a rosy glow, and there wasn't a speck of dust in sight. But, the last time they were here, they had everything to lose—including her life. Somewhere below her feet was the secret space where Octavia and the demon had been bound and Alex had opened up the portal to cast the demon out of their reality, back to its own. And then a horrible thought struck her. When Alex had opened the portal, spirits of some sort had escaped. She had seen them when she spirit walked. *What if one of those was still here in the church, seeking to do harm?*

Avery pulled on Alex's arm and led him away to where they couldn't be overheard. "Do you remember me telling you that I had seen spirits exit through the dimensional doorway you opened?"

He frowned. "I think so. A lot of things happened that night."

"What if we're wrongly assuming it's a regular spirit that the magic has sort of re-energised, and actually it's something else far darker and malevolent? James said it was different from anything he's felt before."

"Like what? I mean, regular spirits can carry a lot of negative energy. It could just be very pissed at being disturbed after centuries of rest."

"I don't know. It can't be a demon, but maybe it's an evil spirit? Something cast in purgatory. Let's face it—we don't know what dimension you opened. Is there more than one? Are there hundreds? That could have been Hell itself!"

Alex's dark brown eyes were suddenly troubled. "As far as I'm aware, the only other dimension is the spirit or elemental world that exists alongside, but separate from, our own. I admit, I don't know the extent of what else is in there. Maybe it is Hell, but Hell is a Christian concept."

For once, Alex wasn't being sarcastic and cocky, and they stared at each other for a few moments, pondering the possibilities of the spirit world.

The scratchy whine of the EMF meter cut through the air and Alex and Avery spun around quickly. Ben held up his hand. "It's okay. We're just taking some basic measurements. We'll be finished soon."

Alex turned back to Avery. "Come on, let's see what they're doing. We can handle whatever it is."

Avery's heart was heavy. While she was pleased that Alex felt so confident, and she did have faith in his abilities, she couldn't shake the feeling that something was *different*—that this wasn't like the spirits they had encountered at the castle the other night.

She shook off her dread and listened to Dylan. "You see, Alex, we have to get base readings first to figure out what's normal and what's not. The great thing about a church is the low levels of electricity." He gestured around. "Sure, there are electric lights and heating, but it's minimal in such a big space. No computers help a lot."

Cassie added, "I'm recording our initial readings, and I've also recorded the temperatures in various parts of the church. Now, if anything happens, we'll have a concrete record of change."

Dylan lowered his voice. "Although, if it's anything like the other night, it'll be pretty freaking obvious."

Alex sighed. "That's very true. But, I think this is going to be a bit different."

"How do you know?" Ben asked, finally putting the EMF monitor down.

"It's my witchy senses."

"Is that a thing?" Dylan sounded doubtful.

"You'd be surprised."

Avery laughed, despite the odd situation. Alex never failed to amuse her. He was so confident and so funny, and yet he never once patronised the others. Alex caught her gaze and smiled, and she felt her stomach somersault.

James joined them. "Have I missed anything? I was just trying to contact Harry."

"No," Alex reassured him. "I was observing these guys. It's pretty fascinating. How is Harry?"

James paused and ran his hands through his hair. "I'm a little worried, actually. I haven't seen him at all today, and he's not answering his phone."

Avery glanced worriedly at Alex and then said to James, "Could he be ill at home?"

"Not as far as I'm aware. He was due in this morning, but maybe he was too spooked to come. However, he hasn't phoned, and he normally would."

Avery felt a dread start to creep though her. "Maybe we should search the church."

"I've been all around it, and he isn't here."

Before they could say anything else, the light dimmed in the church as the sun dropped below the windows, and cold seemed to seep through the nave. Every single one of them glanced nervously around, and James hurried to put on some side lights.

And then Avery felt the energy change. Something else seemed to be with them in the space. Ben obviously felt it too, because he whipped around, pointing his EMF meter around the nave, and the whine of the meter started again. He swung it backwards and forwards, the high-pitched whine intensifying when he pointed it towards the far corner of the church.

"It's over there," he said, advancing cautiously forward.

Alex and Avery joined him, Avery subconsciously summoning a ball of energy into her hands until she remembered that James was still there.

Avery's skin prickled. Keeping her eyes on the corner, she said to Alex, "Can you feel it?"

"Yes. It feels different from what we've experience before. Even Helena."

"It's very different from what we've experienced before, too," Ben agreed as the whine intensified. "This reading is very strong."

The electric lights suddenly exploded above them and glass shattered everywhere, making Avery cover her face for a split second.

In that moment, the EMF meter whined like a wounded animal and then fell silent as the energy signature vanished.

"Where's it gone?" James called out nervously from behind them.

They turned slowly, looking for any sign of the manifestation. Avery pushed out her magical senses, but whatever it was had gone for now.

Alex's shoulders dropped a fraction as he released some tension. "I don't know. Stay together in the centre of the room."

James's voice shook as he looked around. "It feels different again."

"In what way?" Cassie asked, her pen poised over the paper she'd set up to record the events.

"Stronger. More malevolent, somehow. It was…palpable."

The energy had felt malevolent, but more than that, it felt old, like when Avery had sensed the age of the dimensional doorway they had opened in the witch museum. *Very old.*

74

Moments later, the spirit manifested again, this time on the far side of the church, near the side-chapel where Avery and Newton had hidden before they entered the crypt on the night they broke the binding spell.

"Over there," Avery pointed. "I can feel it again."

Even before she'd finished her sentence the EMF meter exploded into life, and Ben almost dropped it. "Wow. This is vibrating up my arm!"

Before Avery could comment further, Alex stepped forward and started his incantation, his words loud and powerful, echoing around the nave, but he was barely a sentence in when once again the spirit disappeared, and the EMF meter fell silent.

"It's toying with us," Avery said.

Alex nodded. "This thing has time. It's waiting. It has intelligence."

"What do you mean by intelligence?" James asked.

"Most spirits act out repeated events from their previous lives—an experience we had in the castle a week ago. We witnessed old events replayed, caused by a spike in energy in the local area. " He didn't elaborate about the energy, and James didn't ask. "Spirits don't think as such. They exist, lost, drifting around in an existence that isn't their own."

Dylan agreed. "Except for Poltergeists, which are very disturbed spirits."

"But even then, they don't have *intelligence*," Alex said. "This does. I can feel it."

"I agree," Avery said.

Ben headed into the side-chapel, his EMF monitor hissing with low static, and Dylan followed him with the camera.

"Has the basic reading changed?" Cassie asked.

"It's slightly higher than earlier," he said, reading out the levels for Cassie to record.

Avery turned to Alex, lowering her voice. "What are we going to do?"

He shrugged. "Not much we can until it reappears, but I have a feeling it knows exactly what we want to do."

Then, for a third time, the EMF meter roared into life, and this time Avery and Alex turned in unison, looking up high into the vaulted roof of the church. In a split second, the spirit—or whatever it was—charged them, and Avery and Alex fell to the floor, rolling to avoid its attack.

A wave of freezing cold *something* passed through Avery and she struggled to breathe, but Alex had started his incantation again, causing the spirit to disappear as rapidly as it had arrived.

Alex pulled Avery to her feet. "Are you okay?"

She nodded. "I'm fine. You?"

"Pissed off."

"Please tell me you recorded that?" Ben asked Dylan.

"I'm recording, but I don't know what I got," he said. "Not 'til I analyse it later."

"I thought you weren't filming us?" Alex said, annoyed.

"Sorry, dude," Dylan said. "It was instinct. I swear I won't release it. But it could be really useful."

Alex narrowed his eyes as he weighed up his options. "Don't let me down, Dylan."

"I swear, I won't post this anywhere."

James was watching the exchange with interest. "You value your privacy too, Alex?"

"Yep," he said, not elaborating. Alex looked around the church once more and then turned back to James. "I hate to tell you this, but this is no ordinary spirit."

James was pale. "Yes, I'm getting that. I think I need to find Harry."

"Have you checked the crypt?" Avery asked.

James frowned. "No, why? We hardly ever go down there."

"Well, I think we should."

James pulled a bunch of keys out of his pocket and then led the way back to the chancel, down the stairs to the heavy sealed door of the crypt, everyone trailing behind him.

He went to unlock it, and then frowned. "It's already unlocked."

"Let me," Alex said, and he pushed James behind him, entering the crypt first.

The crypt was filled with candlelight and it smelt of blood. In the middle of the floor was the broken body of a man wearing religious clothing.

James released a strangled cry. "Harry!"

8

"What did this?"

Newton stared at the scene in front of him and turned his troubled grey eyes on Avery.

"We don't know," Avery said, feeling more helpless than she'd felt in a long time. In fact, she felt sick at how they had been joking about it earlier, like banishing a spirit was a game. This was a horrible return to reality.

"You don't know?" he said, incredulous. "Your last words to me were, 'one spirit only. Should be manageable.' And now *this*?"

They stood alone in the entrance to the crypt. Everyone else was upstairs in the nave being interviewed by Officer Moore, Newton's red-haired police colleague who worked closely with him, and another uniformed officer.

"I'm sorry, Newton. I feel terrible about this. A man has lost his life because of our actions here only weeks ago. And no, we don't know what caused it, other than some sort of spirit."

Newton was furious. "Shit. Well, you better fix this. The verger is *dead*."

Instinctively, wind began to build around her as she became annoyed. "Of course we're going to fix it," she hissed. "What the hell do you think we were doing here in the first place? We didn't come here to have a chat and a night cap!" Avery turned and started to pace off her anger. "Seriously, Newton. I think you know us better than that!"

"All right, all right," Newton said impatiently. "Get out of the crime scene."

"I'm not in the bloody crime scene! It's over there," she said, pointing to where the body still lay in a broken heap, Harry's head slanted at an unnatural angle.

They had given it a brief examination before calling Newton, desperately hoping Harry was injured and not dead. But his blank eyes had stared up at the roof of the crypt, and they knew it was too late. They were now waiting for the Scene of Crimes Unit.

Newton's face was etched with sorrow. "I'm sorry. I'm just upset and annoyed. It doesn't matter how long you've been doing this, finding a dead body is never easy."

Avery's anger vanished as quickly as it had arrived. "I'm sorry, too. I'm scared, as well. This is different, Newton."

He shook his head. "Not here. We'll talk later. Or tomorrow," he said, looking at his watch. "It's late now."

The thump of footsteps on the stairs heralded the arrival of SOCO, and Avery stepped back to give them space, and then joined the others in the nave.

***

"So, what killed him?" Briar asked.

It was the following night and all five witches were in Avery's attic space, surrounded by spell books, herbs, magical paraphernalia, pizza boxes, and beer.

Alex was sitting on the floor, leaning back against the sofa, sipping a beer. "It looks like his neck was broken. And other bones. Like he'd been smashed like a doll. But he was pale, too, and his skin looked dry, as if the life had been drained out of him." He shrugged. "Of course, it could have been the light."

The room fell silent as they thought through the implications, and then Reuben spoke. He sat on the floor, leaning against the wall under the window, his long legs stretched out in front of him. "So, like the other spirits, it has physical capabilities."

"I guess it must," Avery said. "Although, we couldn't feel it when it attacked us. It was like a really strong wind had rushed us."

"But you think it was intelligent," El said from where she sat nestled on the couch. "Maybe it chooses who to be physical with?"

Briar sat next to El, looking thoughtful. "I forgot you'd said you'd seen spirits escape, Avery. I guess I was just so happy to have broken the binding spell that I forgot everything else."

Avery nodded. "I'd almost forgotten as well. Whatever it is—or they are—it's very old."

"Which could explain why it feels different," Reuben said thoughtfully. "It's much older than the spirits we've encountered before, and something different from demons— which are fundamentally elemental."

Avery collapsed against the back of the couch, sighing loudly. "Crap. I better hit the books to try and work out what this could be."

"We all should," Briar agreed. "Do you think we should involve the Witches Council?"

"Not yet," Avery said. "Although, I have a feeling they'll involve themselves when this gets out."

"You know this will hit the papers," Reuben said.

"Yep," Alex agreed tersely. "Exactly what we didn't want to happen. James wants to keeps the whole ghost-hunting thing out of this for as long as possible, and so do the police. And of course the police will not believe a spirit did this—except for Newton. They're looking for a real person."

"Which it may prove to be," Briar pointed out.

"Maybe, but highly unlikely in the circumstances," Alex said. "We're saying we were at the Church doing historical research. We'll look less freaky," he said, encompassing Avery in his statement. "Of course, the press has a way of finding stuff out."

"Well, James is more upset than us," Avery said. "Not only has he lost a friend, but he didn't want to alarm the congregation. It's too late for that. The church will be closed for the next few days while SOCO complete their investigation. I have a feeling Newton is going to be busy."

And then Reuben said something that Avery had thought, but hadn't voiced. "What if the spirits that you saw escape, Avery, were the same—all ancient and intelligent. They could be lurking all over White Haven, or anywhere in Cornwall—or even further. What did the Witches Council think about them?"

"I didn't tell them," she said, feeling guilty. "I forgot! The news about the lights in the sea made me forget everything else."

"Great, we'll be outcasts again." Briar sighed and reached for another slice of pizza.

"Good," Reuben said. "We don't need them, anyway."

"I think we will before this is over," Alex said.

"So now we have ancient malevolent spirits of something, and lights in the sea. Just brilliant," El said.

"But we have our grimoires, and we're stronger than we've ever been. Don't forget that," Avery reminded them.

"I think our lives were easier without them though," Briar said sadly.

***

The first person Avery saw in her shop the next morning was Caspian Faversham. The doors had been open for only seconds when he strode in, dressed in his customary dark clothes, setting the wind chimes ringing. Sally saw him and went pale, heading straight to the back of the shop.

"What do you want?" Avery snapped, watching Sally go. "You're not welcome here, and if you touch her, I'll kill you."

"My, my. Aren't we pleasant? We're supposed to be working together now."

Caspian leaned on the counter, looking around her shop in his easy, dismissive manner that made Avery want to smash him right between the eyes. And not with magic, either. She wanted to feel the physical pleasure of actually assaulting him. And it was such a shame, because she'd woken in a great mood after spending the night with Alex. Unfortunately, her warm glow had now gone.

"You made it very clear in the meeting the other day that you didn't want me there. So, why are you here?"

"You haven't seen the morning news, then?" he asked, his eyebrow rising in an infuriatingly superior manner.

"No."

"You don't know about the death in All Souls?"

"Yes, I was there when they found the body." She frowned. *Where was he going with this?* "What's that got to do with you?"

"Humour me. Why were you in All Souls?"

Avery really wanted to tell him to get lost, but she had a feeling there was more to this early morning inquisition than sheer nosiness. She glanced around the shop and, seeing it was still empty, headed to the front door and locked it, reluctant to take Caspian to the back room with Sally there. She turned to find Caspian watching her with narrowed eyes.

She leaned against the door, keeping distance between them. "It's haunted. We were there with a paranormal crew."

He sneered. "Don't you keep interesting company now? Planning to do some ghost-busting?"

"Yes."

"And how did that work out?"

"Caspian, can you please get to the point and then get out of my shop?"

He leaned back against the counter and folded his arms across his chest. "How did the man die?"

"It looked as if he'd been shaken violently. And, his body looked…drained," she said, for want of a better word.

"So you think the spirit did it?"

"It's possible."

He filled his voice with a dangerous tone. "Avery?"

She glared at him. *Why did he have to make her feel like a child?* "Probably. The spirit was strong, malevolent. It was toying with us."

He fell silent and watched her, the seconds stretching between them before he finally spoke. "It seems we have the same problem."

Her annoyance drained out of her, only to be replaced by a sinking feeling. "What do you mean?"

"We have a lurking spirit in St Luke's Church in Harecombe, and it killed the verger last night, too." He watched her, waiting for her reaction.

Avery's heart started racing. "What? How do you know it was the spirit and not a person?"

"Because the body was found in the same manner as the one you found in All Souls. I heard an early report on the radio about both deaths and made a discreet visit to our church. I can feel the spirit there, and it did not like me being there one bit. It's lurking there, like a toad. Unfortunately, I could not linger for too long, there are police everywhere."

"It could be completely unrelated," Avery said defiantly, reluctant to admit that Caspian may be right.

He lowered his voice menacingly. "I think we both know there's no such thing as coincidence, Avery. The news knows that your vicar had paranormal investigators there, too. Speculation is only just starting, and it will get a lot worse. I suggest you tell me what's going on."

She inwardly groaned. *So the historical research ruse hadn't worked.* As reluctant as she was to share anything with Caspian, she knew she had to. It was only a matter of time before the Council was involved. "When we released the binding spell, Alex had to open a doorway to the spirit world to send the demon and Octavia through. Spirits escaped from it. I don't know how many exactly, maybe a half dozen. I think it's these spirits that are causing the problems."

Caspian's face immediately hardened. "Spirits escaped? Then we are in big trouble, Avery."

She swallowed. "Why? Surely we can banish them just like any other spirit?"

"But they're not just any other spirit, are they? They have escaped from one of the dimensions of the Otherworld. And that makes them mean. And strong."

As much as Avery didn't like to agree with Caspian, she knew he was right. And he seemed to believe there were different dimensions. While she was spirit walking, she had seen other spirits trying to get out and failing, which *did* mean these were stronger. "Did you sense intelligence when you were at St Luke's?"

"Yes." He shifted his position slightly as he made himself more comfortable. "Why do you think they're in churches?"

"I don't know. I would think they'd hate churches if they're from some level of a demonic Otherworld."

"Some spirits may feel very comfortable in a church. All those souls to feed on," he speculated. "Something else to think about."

"We'll deal with it," Avery said, sounding more confident than she felt.

"Will you? Sorry if I doubt you," he said, not sounding sorry at all, "but I'll deal with the one in Harecombe. Do you even know what spirits they are? Are they all the same, or did several different types escape?" He stepped closer, closing the space between them. "We need to know, if we're to deal with them properly."

"I'll find out."

"Good. Do it quickly." He smirked. "And I'll inform Genevieve. This matter needs to be brought before the Council."

9

Avery sat at the table in her attic surrounded by her grimoires and books on all things myth, folklore, and magic, quietly fuming. As soon as she could, she had left Sally and Dan minding the shop, and then headed upstairs to her flat to do some research.

She was furious with Caspian, but she was more furious with herself. They had been arrogant when they retrieved their spell books. Arrogant and overconfident. Yes, the grimoires belonged to them, and they had every right to them, but right now, she wished she'd have looked at the possible consequences. Ever since Anne had left them the box, and all of her research that led to their grimoires, there had been death and destruction. And no, not all of it had been their fault, the Favershams were definitely responsible for some of it, but they had to accept some of the blame.

And they had to clean up this mess.

She had many old books that listed varieties of spirits and demons, and something must be in there somewhere. And then a thought struck her. *Maybe Alex could help with his psychic abilities? Maybe they should spirit walk?* But she had a feeling that would be too dangerous when they had no idea what these spirits were.

She thought back to the night when they broke the binding spell and tried to remember what the spirits looked like. The room beneath the church had been chaotic, the witches wielding their magic in huge bursts of action just to stay alive. The demon had been dangerous, and she'd been trying to get back in her own body, which Helena was enjoying being in a little too much. She'd noticed the spirits as an afterthought, really. They were vague and shapeless, with only the barest suggestion of having a human-shaped body; it was the spark of animation and the sense of a soul that marked them as human rather than demon. But whether they were fully human in origin was another matter entirely.

She pushed away from the table and crossed her arms, annoyed. *How could they find out what they were? And if they could manifest at will, how could they trap them long enough to banish them?*

Avery leaned over her grimoires again with determination, summoned a witch light to float above her just in case there were hidden runes and notes, and then uttered a searching spell to look in the books for anything related to identifying spirits. She felt the air shift around her and then the pages started to ruffle in the breeze, as if unseen hands were turning the pages. After a few seconds the pages fell still and she marked the page, but then the pages kept on moving, and Avery marked another page, and then another, until she had almost a dozen spells spread across both books.

Pulling a notepad towards her, she started to make notes on the spells, dismissing some quickly, while deciding to try others, but it was the final spell she looked at that seemed the most promising. She'd left it until last, because it was close to the front of the oldest grimoire—Helena's grimoire—and completely invisible without the use of the witch light. It had been written within another spell, the lines interspersed within the visible spell. The writing was minute and cramped, a scrawl across the page that required time and energy to decipher. Immediately, her pulse began to quicken. This looked interesting. And chilling. There was a line of runes down the side, denoting a warning to only use with protection. It also required objects that Avery didn't have, but she knew Alex did, like a crystal ball for divination. But the thing that interested her most about this spell was that it seemed to offer a way to talk to the spirit in question.

She reached for her phone and called Alex. His warm voice made her smile. "Hi, gorgeous. How are you?"

"I'm fine, how are you?" she asked.

"Busy—it's the lunchtime rush. I shouldn't complain."

Avery could hear the chatter of the pub in the background. "Well, I have a quick question. I've found a spell that should allow us to talk to spirits, but we need a crystal ball. Are you interested?"

He paused for a heartbeat. "Who are we talking to?"

"Our unknown visitor to the church."

"Ah. That sort of thing is dangerous."

"It is?"

"Yes. Opening up a direct line to a spirit can come with a powerful backlash."

She groaned. "Yeah, I sort of got that impression."

"But, I'm always up for a challenge. I'll catch you later—someone's glaring at me for a pint."

"Sure, and thanks," she said as he rang off.

She started to assemble the ingredients for the spell, reaching for a variety of herbs, and wondered if they needed to perform the spell in the church, or would anywhere do. Probably the church would be best. It was where the spirit lived—for now.

She was halfway through the preparation when her phone rang, and she saw Ben's name on the screen. "Hi, Ben? How are you guys after last night?"

"Absolutely psyched," he said excitedly, and then added, "and of course feeling really bad about Harry's death. But we've found something on the camera footage. You need to see it."

"Why? What?" she asked, her own excitement mounting.

"I can't explain it. You just need to see it."

"Can I bring the others?"

"Sure. We'll come to you. What time?"

"Seven?" Avery offered, hoping she'd get everyone by then, and still leave enough time for her and Alex to do the spell.

"Great. Laters," he said, hanging up.

As soon as he rang off, she felt the tingle of magic start to fill the attic. Avery looked around alarmed. *What was happening?* It was like an itch that she couldn't locate, but a strange hyper-awareness started to spread across her skin and beneath her skull. And then Genevieve's voice spoke from somewhere around her, disembodied and surreal.

"Avery. It is Genevieve. We have convened another meeting. Please be at Crag's End tomorrow. 8:00 PM. Do not be late."

Avery groaned. It was like being summoned by your mother. *And why couldn't she just use the phone?* Thank the Goddess it hadn't happened in the shop. That would have been tricky to explain.

It was now late afternoon, the wind had dropped, and it looked hot out. She needed to get out of the attic and get some air in her garden. She could collect some herbs and roots, and do a reading. She grabbed the tarot and her cutting knife, and headed down to the garden.

***

Avery's living room seemed very full by half past seven that evening. All five witches were there, along with Newton and the three paranormal investigators.

The smell of take-out curry filled the room, and foil containers covered the dining room table, alongside naan bread, beer, and wine.

Most of them had come directly from either work or home, but Reuben had been surfing. His hair was still wet, and a fine crust of sand dusted his skin. They had all helped themselves to a selection of different curries, but Reuben's plate was piled especially high.

Avery looked at it, and then at Reuben's lean form. "Where the hell do you put all that, Reuben?"

He grinned. "I surf it off, Avery."

"Wow. Your food bill must be immense."

"It is. Thank the Gods I'm rich, eh?" he said, winking, and then went to sit on the end of the sofa, facing the TV.

Avery grabbed her own food and then sat on a large floor cushion, watching Ben as he finished finding the downloaded file he plugged into her TV.

He turned around, excited. "Guys, I can't wait for you to see this. It's one of the best thermal images we've ever had!"

El grimaced. "Explain. I don't get this stuff."

"Spirits or ghosts work on different levels of existence than us. We usually can't see them or hear them, but we use equipment to try and see what's there. We use EMF meters to read for different electrical signatures, like varying energy levels. But we have to exclude existing phone, radio, and electricity. We've got a Trifield Natural Meter, which we can set to a magnetic setting, and it excludes most electrical interference—but we take baseline readings anyway. Then we have audio equipment, a regular camera, a thermal camera, and a temperature monitor. I've got a motion sensor, but didn't take it, which was stupid, but next time…" He shrugged. "It sounds complicated, but it really isn't. We're just trying to get as much data as possible. And of course, this isn't an exact science."

El looked impressed. "So, you set all of this up at the church the other night?"

Dylan answered while Ben turned back to the TV. "Yep. I got some audio, but it was just static, a sort of hissing that changed in tone, but was inconclusive, and Cassie got some temperature changes. I'm pretty sure we'd have got some motion stuff, because that thing seemed to be moving around the room a lot, but as Ben said, we didn't bring it. But the camera footage was the best."

Everyone nodded, and Avery felt a chill start to run up her spine in anticipation.

"I'll show you the regular camera recording first."

They saw a dim image of the interior of the church fill the screen, the image panning around the entrance, then the nave, the side-chapel, and the choir. The footage recorded Cassie and Ben setting up the other equipment, and the sounds of their low-voiced discussions were only slightly audible. Then the footage stopped, and when it restarted, the camera was pointed to the far corner of the room. Avery could hear her voice and Alex's before the electric lights exploded above them, showering glass everywhere. A faint, white shape seemed to fill the corner before it fled upwards.

Briar gasped. "Is that it, the spirit?"

"Probably, yes," Ben said, nodding. "But it's not clear."

"I switched cameras then," Dylan explained. "The exploding glass was pretty intense, and I thought I might get better results."

Ben then pulled up the thermal imaging footage, and the next thing they saw was a grey image of the church interior and Cassie and Ben looking like photographic negatives. Then they saw James, Alex, and Avery. After some stopping and starting, the footage of the small side-chapel appeared. There was a glimpse of a white image that looked human, but it appeared to have huge shoulders, and it floated off the floor and then disappeared. Then the camera was pointed up at the ceiling, the vaulted roof clearly visible, and there was the most chilling image. A huge, winged creature hovered above them before speeding down in a blur, so fast that it disappeared from view altogether in the jerky footage.

Ben and Dylan looked triumphant, but everyone else looked at each other in stunned silence.

"What the hell is that?" Newton asked, turning to the others in alarm.

Avery felt the blood drain from her face and she struggled to find her voice. "It didn't look like a regular spirit."

"It looks like a bloody great Angel of Death!" Newton shouted. "Why are you all looking at me like that? What is it?"

Alex's usual confidence had gone, replaced by utter confusion. He looked at the others before he finally turned to Newton. "I don't know."

They watched the footage over and over, each of them throwing in suggestions, but unfortunately, no one had a better idea than Newton, which in the light of day, seemed ridiculous.

Reuben turned to Avery. "Is that what you saw flying out of the doorway under All Souls?"

"Absolutely not," she said determinedly. "I would have remembered that. What I saw were formless shapes, small, insubstantial. Although, I was trying to avoid a demon, and struggling to get back into my own body."

Briar leaned back against the sofa looking thoughtful. "But whatever that is had already killed the verger, Harry, at this point. Is that right?"

Avery glanced at Alex and then said, "Yes, I guess so."

Briar looked at the frozen image on the screen and shuddered. "Then maybe the fact that it had fed on Harry— sorry for the choice of word, but you did say he looked drained— had made the spirit, or whatever it is, more powerful?"

Newton leapt off the sofa and started pacing. "Then why hasn't it killed again? And what happens when it does?"

"The Church was sealed by the police," Alex said. "No one is going in or out at the moment. Before we left yesterday, we placed wards of protection around the building—very rudimentary ones, there were too many police around. We hope we've contained it, but honestly, it's unlikely." He looked at Avery. "We should head back and do it properly."

"What about the death at St Luke's in Harecombe?" Reuben asked, finally putting aside his empty plate. "I saw it on the news. Is it the same?"

"First impression says yes, but I'm waiting for the Coroner's report," Newton said, pausing at the window to look out onto the street below before turning back to face them. "However, there's no sign of a break-in."

"Any other suspicious deaths in the last twenty-four hours?" El asked.

"No. But if there are more spirits, and they're linked, then maybe there will be."

Avery mulled over her visit from Caspian, wondering whether to cast more doom on their gathering, but she knew she had to share his visit. "Caspian's already been to see me about that," she said, explaining what he'd said. "And there's another Council meeting tomorrow. I expect to get shouted at."

"Damn it," Alex said, looking concerned. "I'm working, or I'd come with you. I don't like you going alone, especially with vengeful spirits around."

Despite the circumstances, Avery smiled, feeling a now familiar warmth spread though her. "I'll be fine. Besides I have protection—a tattoo and *magic*!"

"Which reminds me," El said, turning to Cassie, Dylan and Ben. "I have amulets for you guys. Wear them always! Strange things are happening, and you are up close and personal with some of it. And don't take any chances."

They all nodded and thanked her profusely, as they took the small silver amulets on chains and examined them carefully.

"Well, guess who's going to come with you tomorrow?" Reuben said, grinning.

Avery felt her stomach drop. "I said I'll be fine. I don't need anyone to come with me. Especially *you*, at the moment. You have a lot of *attitude* going on. I don't think it will help."

"Tough shit. I'm coming anyway. I want to see who these jokers are."

"They're not jokers, Reuben," Avery corrected, sensing conflict already. "Some of them are lovely and welcoming. They're witches. Our friends. We can't afford to alienate them. I don't want to, either. This is our chance to be accepted into the magical community. There's a whole other world of stuff going on out there that we need to know about."

Reuben rolled his eyes. "I know. I'm not an idiot. But two are better than one. I'll tell them I'm nosy."

"You better behave, or we'll fall out," she said, starting to get annoyed.

El snorted. "Good luck with that."

10

Avery drove up the somewhat familiar twists and turns of Crag's End drive, arguing with Reuben. For the entire journey he'd been updating her about his grimoire and his experiments with the spells, and he was teasing and joking constantly, but underneath, she could sense his tension.

"Seriously, Reuben, you need to behave tonight. I will be really pissed off if you deliberately antagonise them."

He dropped his bantering tone. "I'll behave, I promise. Ever since Gil died I've been struggling to deal with this whole magic thing. I thought I'd turned my back on it forever, and now I'm up to my eyeballs in it." He sighed and rested his head against the back of the seat. "Don't get me wrong, I'm glad it's who I am and I've accepted that, although I wish it hadn't taken Gil's death to make me see it."

Avery slowed down and glanced at him, feeling suddenly mean for giving him a hard time. "I know, and I'm sorry, Reuben. You're handling it really well. I wish the circumstances were different. Gil would have been the perfect representative for us, better than me."

Reuben shook his head. "You're doing fine, Avery. I don't doubt you. But, Alex is right. We don't really know these guys, and you being here on your own *is* worrying. If they turned on you, you couldn't fight them all."

She slowed down as she saw a passing bay on the left, pulled to a stop, and then turned to face him, desperate to reassure him. He seemed so fragile sometimes, which frankly was ridiculous, considering the size of him. "This isn't the Wild West, and I'm sure that won't happen. I actually think you'll like them—well, most of them."

He swallowed, and looked out the window, unable to meet her eye. "But, the fact that there are lots of us now—it's really making me question everything. Who I am, who witches are, what other types of things are going on we never knew about. You, Alex and the others, seem to have a handle on it. Even Newton does! I don't think I do. It's too vague— no, too *big*!"

Avery reached out and touched his arm, and he turned to face her, his eyes full of doubt, and she wanted to cry. "It *is* big, you're not alone in thinking that. I feel terrible, Reuben. I started this whole thing off. And look what's happened! With my headstrong insistence that we find those grimoires, I've unleashed something hideous into White Haven…well, the world, actually." The feelings she'd been trying to subdue for weeks suddenly flooded out, triggered by Reuben's heartbreaking honesty. "People are dying, and this time it's not Caspian's fault, or Alicia's. It's mine. I've been so arrogant." She started to well up, a tear trickling down her cheek, and she sniffed, fumbling in her bag for a tissue. "Fuck it. I'm so annoyed with myself."

"We followed you, Avery. You didn't do this on your own."

She wiped a tear away and blew her nose. "You're just being kind. And I'm supposed to be comforting you."

He laughed weakly. "You are. Thanks. Although, making women cry seems to be my speciality lately."

"Have you talked to El about all this?"

He shrugged. "Sort of. I feel I'm being a bit of a crap boyfriend. Have you talked to Alex?"

She smiled wryly. "Sort of. I've been trying to bury all of this guilt, actually. Sex helps."

He laughed, throwing his head back. "Yep, it really does." He pointed to the back of the van. "You're not suggesting anything, right?"

"No, you dick."

He grinned at her, a cheeky glint in his eye. "I'm kidding. Besides, Alex would kill me. And so would El."

Avery pulled the visor down and peered in the mirror. "Wow. I look like crap." She tried to adjust her makeup and took a deep breath. "Well, this is not a good way to enter the Witches Council. Look at us. I'm puffy-eyed, and you look sad."

"By the time we get to the top of this massive drive, we'll look fine. Come on. United front."

She turned and smiled. "United front."

***

The atmosphere in Oswald's meeting room seemed to be frostier than the last, and Avery looked around the table, trying to get a feel for who would be allies.

The room was dark. The clouds were gathering outside and the evening light was dim. A few lamps brightened dark corners, candles were lit down the centre of the table, and incense smoke was unfurling on the air, giving everything a slightly hazy quality.

They had arrived a few minutes late, so everyone was already seated around the long table, engaged in muted small talk. Oswald had greeted Reuben enthusiastically and found an extra chair for him, and Avery and Reuben now sat together towards the end of the table, just inside the door to the room. Oswald was again wearing a velvet jacket, this time with plaid trousers, and Reuben raised a questioning eyebrow at her and glanced towards Oswald's clothes. Avery flashed him a warning with her eyes and hissed, "Behave."

Claudia, the older witch from Perranporth, gave Avery a welcoming smile, as did Eve, the witch from St Ives with the dreadlocks who'd been so friendly at the last meeting, and Avery started to relax. Caspian merely narrowed his eyes at both of them and gave a barely-there nod. If Avery didn't know better, she thought that nod almost denoted grudging respect. But she must be imagining things. Zane, the witch from Bodmin, and Mariah from Looe, were seated either side of him in a show of solidarity, and they barely glanced at her.

Genevieve was once more seated at the head of the table, authority emanating from her in waves. Her long hair was loose tonight, and it cascaded down her back, softening her sharp, refined features. "Right, let's get on with it," she said, the softness of her Irish lilt belying her brusque manner. "There have been three deaths in a very short time, and all of them seem to be the result of spirits or Mermaids." She turned her piercing gaze to Avery, her glance brushing across Reuben. "What happened in All Souls?"

Avery explained about the spirits she had seen escaping from the dimensional doorway, James asking for help and using the ghost-hunters, but held back about the thermal imaging for now. She had every intention of telling them, but wanted to see what the general consensus was first.

Genevieve frowned. "You didn't mention these escaping spirits before. Why not?"

Every single witch around the table was focussed on her, and Avery felt a little embarrassed. "If I'm honest, I forgot about them with everything else that had happened. We were fighting for our lives that night. It was chaotic, crazy—the escaping spirits seemed the least of our worries with that enormous demon in the room. And I was spirit walking at the time. I had to get back into my own body."

"Perhaps," Rasmus said, his rasping voice slightly impatient, "this would be a good time for us to learn what happened that night. We didn't fully talk about it last time. I'd like to know."

"I agree," Eve said, smiling with encouragement. "We all know you had to break the binding, but we have no idea how. What happened?"

"You don't have to discuss this." Genevieve gave a warning glance around the table before looking at Avery and Reuben again. "Our magic and our rituals are private."

"I think we're fine with it," Avery said, looking at Reuben, who nodded in agreement. She saw Caspian shuffle uncomfortably, but ignored him. "I'll try and summarise the lead up. Things got complicated." She relayed the whole story as best as she could, and then described the events that led to them using Helena in her body, and the ritual. She held back from the specifics of the spell—she knew what Genevieve meant. Spells were power, and sharing the details wasn't in their best interests. Witches weren't averse to stealing magic to gain power, Caspian's family was proof of that, but she told them enough to understand the set up. By the time she'd finished relaying the events at Faversham Central, there were more than a few open mouths around the table, and Caspian was seething.

A chorus of exclamations, general swearing, and a huge amount of sympathy and understanding flooded the room. Avery glanced at Reuben in surprise and a smile crept across his face.

Eve's voice broke through the noise. "I had no idea that things were so complicated and dangerous, Avery. I'm sorry you had to deal with that. And Reuben, please accept my sympathies for Gil's death." She shot a look of pure venom at Caspian. "What were you thinking? It's outrageous that you should ever put another witch in such a position. You're a disgrace. I had no idea that things were so bad." Eve then rounded on Genevieve. "Why didn't you explain this before? You gave us a very watered-down explanation of events."

"I didn't know the full details," Genevieve explained, not looking completely surprised at the annoyed faces around the table, but also uncomfortable at the attention.

Avery suspected that was why Genevieve has never asked them for specifics, and didn't give her the opportunity to share the last time. The sympathy she now felt was enormous. She risked a glance at Caspian, and found he was staring at her with grim respect and a challenge flashing in his eyes.

Caspian turned to Eve; he knew he had to make public amends. "You're right, Eve. I and my family must take responsibilities for our actions." Caspian turned back to Reuben and Avery. "We were put in a difficult position by my father. And Reuben, I meant what I said—I did not intend to kill Gil. I'm sorry."

"I'm afraid I really don't believe that, Caspian," Reuben said softly. "Remember, you nearly pulled my family's mausoleum down on my head. Your father cannot accept all the blame. But, I will move on from this, if you can."

Avery tried to hide the shock from her expression. She could not believe Reuben had just said that. She reached her hand under the table, found Reuben's hand and squeezed it, feeling him return the gesture.

Avery had the satisfaction of seeing Caspian's shocked reaction, too. He nodded. "Of course."

For the next five minutes, the table buzzed with questions, either for Avery, Reuben and Caspian, or chatter to each other, and then Genevieve called them to order. "Although this has been very illuminating, I think we should discuss the next death. Caspian, I understand you had a similar experience in St Luke's Church?"

He nodded. "Yes. Another death, another spirit." Caspian relayed the story of the verger's death. "It's almost identical, and that means even more police interest. Your friend, Newton, has already been asking too many questions," Caspian sneered.

Avery tried to bite back a retort. Caspian could not help himself. His sneer was on default. Reuben was not so polite. Their temporary cease-fire was over swiftly.

"He's a detective, that's his job," Reuben shot back. "You should be grateful he understands about this—us—or things would be a lot worse."

"Is that right?" Caspian said, his eyes hard. "So glad he's looking out for *us*. I'd rather he keep his nose out of Harecombe business altogether."

"Enough," Genevieve said, her voice icy. "The police are a necessity. Reuben is right. Better Newton than anyone else. And the death at sea?" she said, turning to Oswald.

"No signs of suspicious activity as far as human intervention goes. The crew are bewildered and understandably upset. Ulysses was able to chat with them. They trust him."

Avery wondered who Ulysses was, but fortunately, Claudia saw her confusion. "Ulysses is the other witch in Mevagissey."

Oswald nodded. "He has strong water elemental magic, and has his own boat. The sailors and fisherman are used to him being around. Of course, they have no idea he's a witch."

"And what does he think of the possibility of Mermaids or Sirens?" Genevieve asked.

"He thinks Mermaids are involved. In fact," Oswald paused and looked around the table. "He is convinced that some are already on land."

Genevieve gripped the table and leaned forward. "What makes him think that?"

"At the moment it's just instinct, but I don't doubt it. He has *very* good instincts," Oswald said.

"Has he any suggestions for what we should do?"

Oswald shook his head. "Not at present, other than to be watchful, and look for unusual activity, especially among men."

Genevieve glanced around the room. "Any other incidents?"

The general feedback seemed to be more wayward spirits, and Genevieve dropped her shoulders and sat back. "So, any suggestions about the spirits in All Souls and St Luke's?"

Avery was about to speak, but Caspian beat her to it. "These spirits broke out of the other dimension, the spirit dimension. That means they are strong, and getting stronger. They seem to be feeding on these bodies."

"I agree," Avery said. "From the brief glance I had at Harry's body, the verger appeared to be drained, and many bones were broken. We wonder if that's why the spirit was so strong when we encountered it in the church."

Eve leaned forward. "What makes you think it's stronger?"

"James, the vicar, said he had only been aware of its presence before. It was watchful, and obviously creepy, but not threatening. Harry's death was a shock for many reasons." Avery shrugged and looked at Reuben. "I must admit, I didn't think spirits could manifest quite so strongly. But we also had an encounter with quite a few ghosts up at the castle grounds, and they were also strong."

"You didn't mention that," Genevieve said, frowning. "When did that happen?"

"Just after the last meeting," Avery said. "The ghosts at White Haven Castle seemed to be re-enacting some kind of event."

Reuben agreed. "It was as if the magical surge we released had jolted them into action again. But they were almost physical...it took a lot for us to banish them. That's where we met the ghost-hunters."

Caspian frowned. "Are you actually trying to advertise the fact that you're witches?"

Avery glared at him. "Stop being a drama queen, Caspian." A few witches smirked and then tried to hide it. "They saw the spirits and would have been hurt if we hadn't intervened. They're trustworthy. In fact, they've also been helpful." She looked around the table, gauging everyone's reaction. "They managed to film the spirit in All Souls with a thermal imaging camera."

Everyone leaned forward now, some frowning, some curious, and the silence around the table seemed to intensify.

"And?" Genevieve asked.

Avery glanced at Reuben, and he nodded almost imperceptibly. "The image appears to be of a large, winged spirit. It rushed down from the vaulted roof to us, and then disappeared."

"Winged?" Rasmus questioned, eyebrows raised. "Like an angel?"

"Or a demon," Claudia said. "They come in many forms."

The black witch that Avery remembered from the first meeting spoke for the first time, his deep voice as rich as treacle. "Or, it could be a Nephilim."

Reuben looked as puzzled as Avery. "What's a Nephilim?"

"They are the children of fallen angels who fled from heaven and mated with human women. They were supposedly giants who dominated other men."

Zane, the weasel-faced witch sitting next to Caspian, looked and sounded annoyed. "That's a Christian myth, Jasper."

Jasper laughed, incredulous, and he spread his hands wide. "Have you learned nothing, Zane? So are angels and demons, but they exist, don't they? As do Mermaids, Sirens, ghosts, Poltergeists, Vampires, shape-shifters, witches, and all manner of other strange, mythical creatures that either exist here or in other dimensions. And there are still other creatures, according to other myths. Many of these spirits or creatures are the same the world over. It's just that they are named differently according to each culture. We were talking about the Children of Llyr the other day. A Celtic myth, but they exist nonetheless."

Zane looked down at the table, but Avery could tell he was angry at being lectured.

"Jasper, what made you suggest Nephilim?" Avery asked, immediately liking him. She estimated he was in his thirties, his dark hair shorn close to his scalp, clean shaven, and wearing a smart blue shirt, open at the neck.

"I research myths and legends, and the legends suggest that the Nephilim were once winged, which makes sense as the children of angels, but they walked among men without them. As I said, they were tall and powerful. It is suggested by some that God sent the deluge to rid the world of them once and for all. And that is the last time they walked the Earth."

"The deluge?"

"The Flood. There's one in every world myth. The one Noah had to build the ark for."

Avery's head was spinning. Old myths of creation, and monsters that walked among men. But, she reflected, some people considered witches to be monsters.

"Were they giants, or just tall?" Reuben asked.

Jasper shrugged. "It's hard to say. Adults were much shorter centuries ago. Poor diet, harder life, shorter life expectancies. Anything approaching six feet would be seen as giant."

"And why did God want to rid the Earth of them, according to myth?" Avery asked.

"Because they were violent, they dominated men, and more importantly, the Earth was not where they should be. They were the mixed offspring of mortal and immortal. It was considered an abhorrence. But, many things are considered to be abhorrent, and they still exist. *We* know this to be true. But humans do not like to accept the stranger things that walk among us. That's why there are so many fairy tales and myths—to try to explain the inexplicable. We must not be so blind." Jasper allowed himself a wry smile.

Jasper was right. As much as witches kept to their own kind, so did other creatures, but they all knew they existed, even if they didn't mix.

"Avery," Genevieve asked, "would your friends the ghost-hunters be interested in setting up their investigations at St Luke's?"

"No!" Caspian exclaimed. "I forbid them to get involved."

"You are in no place to forbid anything," Genevieve said forcefully, causing Caspian to look furious, again. "We need to know if this is the same type of spirit, and if they're linked to what happened beneath All Souls. I hold you partially responsible, and therefore you will cooperate. Avery?"

"I'm sure they'll be happy to help." *Ben would probably give his right arm to get in that church.*

"Good. Arrange it. And Caspian, be helpful, or you'll find yourself banned from the Council."

11

"In light of what we now think this spirit may be, is it wise you try to speak to it?" Newton asked.

Newton, Briar, Alex, and Avery were sitting around a small table in the back room of The Wayward Son; they had almost finished eating, and Newton was frowning over his pint.

"Yes, it's still important. Nephilim or not, it's still a spirit, and we might be able to find out something," Alex insisted before he almost inhaled his final forkful of rare steak.

Briar sighed. "It is risky, I know what you mean, Newton. But I also agree with Avery and Alex. It would be good to try to get some insight into what's going on."

"But two spirits, two churches, two deaths. It's *very* risky. And since the deaths, they've been locked in by your spells. They might be feeling pretty angry. If they experience any kind of emotion," Newton said, trying to be rational.

Avery smiled and pushed her empty plate away. Newton's protective instincts were strong, and she had a feeling that although some of this was due to his profession, it was also because they were friends now. And on the positive side, Alex and Newton's initial testosterone battles seemed to have settled down.

"We'll protect ourselves well, I promise." Avery said, trying to reassure him.

Alex nodded. "Salt circle, spells, the whole thing. Trust us."

Newton continued to frown. "I don't want any more deaths."

"Neither do I. Especially mine. Or of course Avery's," Alex said with a wink.

"Nice to know, thanks," Avery said.

"Are you going now?" Briar asked, sipping her white wine.

"Half an hour or so," Avery explained. "James will meet us at the entrance and let us in. We wanted to make sure he felt involved in this. But, he stays outside."

"How did you explain that one," Newton asked, curious.

"I said Alex had psychic abilities, as part of his talent for exorcism. He bought it," Avery said with a shrug. "And it is true—I just omitted the witch part."

"Did you see the headlines in the local paper this morning?" Briar asked.

Avery sighed and quoted the headline. "*Unnatural Death at All Souls. Is a violent ghost to blame?* How do they hear about these things?"

Newton answered. "Unfortunately, the press hang around police stations and hospitals, and talk to ambulance staff. They pick up stuff we don't want them to know. If anyone gets in touch with you, deny everything. I've told Ben the same thing."

"I bet it would be good publicity for Ben," Briar said.

"It might well be, but I've ordered him to keep his head down for now."

"Well, he's pretty excited about going to St Luke's in Harecombe," Avery said, recalling their earlier conversation. "Caspian is not."

"I like this Genevieve woman," Alex declared. "She doesn't put up with Caspian's shit."

"Not many do, actually," Avery said, thinking about the previous night's meeting. "It was interesting going to the meeting again. I got more of a feel for the atmosphere and associations. Who likes who, who doesn't. While Caspian has a couple of allies, most people are pretty indifferent, if not annoyed with him. I just get the general impression that everyone's over his grand pretensions. Oswald, Claudia, Genevieve, and Rasmus are too old and too wise to put up with him. I think it was good taking Reuben, too. He's less annoyed now. And of course, we had an opportunity to share what *did* happen recently. They had no idea."

"Well done," Briar said, smiling brightly. "I knew you'd do a great job. And I'm glad Reuben enjoyed it, too."

"He really did," Avery agreed. "It gave him perspective, and me too. I know what our place is in all this now. We really are part of a much bigger thing. Our town, or coven, has been in the dark about so much. No wonder our ancestors left town and abandoned witchcraft. I think it would have been less likely if they'd been part of a bigger community. It explains a lot," she mused.

"Just think," Briar said, "my family may never have left, or El's."

"At least you're back now," Newton said, "and hopefully not planning to leave again."

Avery suppressed a smile as she saw Briar's slightly startled expression. "Absolutely not, Newton. Especially with my shop doing so well."

"Good," he said, swiftly downing his pint. "Must be time for another."

James met Avery and Alex at the side door to the church. In the few days since they'd seen him, he looked as if he'd aged by several years.

"Are you all right?" Avery asked, as she watched him fiddle with the keys. Not that they needed them, but they couldn't tell James that.

"Not really. Harry is dead in extremely suspicious circumstances, the church is locked down, and now the Bishop's becoming involved." He looked up, harassed. "Did you see that headline?"

"We did," Alex said sympathetically. "In a few months, this will be old news. Don't worry."

"But where do I see my congregation? Can I come in now, just to see what's going on?"

"No," Alex said firmly. He leaned against the door frame, his arms crossed. "It's too dangerous."

"You can't possibly believe it really was the spirit?" James asked, although doubt filled his eyes.

Avery felt sorry for him. Although they'd all been together when the spirit attacked, James was clearly trying to play the whole thing down. It wasn't unusual. To admit that there was a violent spirit in the church was one step too many for some. Although James had been willing to investigate, the proof now seemed daunting.

"James, let us do what we need to. Who knows, it may have gone?" Avery said, trying to be positive, even though she didn't believe it for a second.

"But if it's not? How long could this take? This Bishop could well insist we re-open."

"We have no idea how long. And if the Bishop does insist, all future deaths will be on his head. Now, can we go in

111

please?" Alex said, pointing at the keys that James still held loosely in his hands.

"What are you going to do?"

"I come from a long line of psychics," Alex explained. "I'm going to try and communicate with it, that's all."

James paused for a second, and then opened the door. Alex and Avery slipped inside, hefting their backpacks with them.

Avery turned to thank him, blocking the doorway. "Thanks. Can you give me a key? We'll lock ourselves in and return the key later."

"I can wait."

"Please don't. Go home, relax. We'll see you soon."

James looked as if he would argue, but then turned and disappeared, his head down and shoulders bowed. He looked defeated, as if every ounce of his energy had been sucked from him. And maybe also his faith. *James would be okay*, she reassured herself. *At least he wasn't a zealot.*

Avery carefully locked the door, leaving the key in the lock, and turned to find Alex had already gone. She looked around and concentrated, feeling with her magic to see if she could detect anything, but the church felt eerily silent. It smelt musty after days of being locked up, and a heavy dampness hung on the air.

She headed down the corridor and found Alex in the nave, already setting up in the space in front of the altar, the noises he made echoing sullenly around the church. "Feel anything?"

"Nope, you?"

"No." Avery paced around, feeling for changes in temperature, or electrical static and pools of energy. She looked at the vaulted roof. "Weird, nothing at all. You'd think we'd feel *something*."

Alex pulled the salt from his bag and poured it out on the floor, making a large circle, big enough for him and Avery to sit in. "We need to encourage it to appear. Come on, jump in."

Avery stepped inside, carrying the bags with her. She pulled out twelve candles, all black for protection, and placed four of them at the compass points, and the rest in between all along the inner edge of the circle of salt, lighting them with a spark from her fingers. Then, while Alex uncovered the heavy crystal ball, she pulled a bundle of incense out, the combination designed to aid with communication and concentration.

She ran the ends of the incense through the flames and watched them spark in an even red glow, and the spicy-sweet smell of incense filled the air; along with the soft light of the candles, Avery felt herself begin to relax and her senses heighten. Her magic started to build as she began to focus in this cavernous space.

She pulled a heavy cotton scarf from her bag, folded it, and then sat cross-legged, watching Alex prepare himself.

Aware he was being watched, he looked up and smiled, his teeth gleaming in the dusky light of the church. The last rays of the sun were setting behind him and falling through the stained glass windows, casting a rosy glow around them. "Glad you're here, Avery."

"I wouldn't miss it," she said, her pulse quickening. She wasn't sure if it was because of the situation or just him. Probably just him. Every time he looked at her she felt his gaze like a caress across her skin.

"We should protect the circle first."

"You lead," she said, as he took her hands in his warm, strong grip. Together they uttered an invocation, reminding her of the first time they had done this together in her attic.

Avery felt a rush of energy and the magic of the spell soared around them, effectively sealing them within its protective embrace. The candles flared, and as the daylight diminished, the church filled with shadows.

And then she felt something stir in the blackness.

A shiver ran across her skin, which was not caused by Alex. "Can you feel it?"

He nodded, scanning the room. "I can't pinpoint where it is."

"No, me neither. It hasn't gathered itself yet."

"It feels old."

Avery reconsidered the spell she'd suggested as a way of communicating, and doubted herself. "Maybe bringing the crystal ball was pointless. If it's here, you won't need it."

"I'll need it," Alex assured her, still searching the room. "It will help me focus."

"What if it's too strong and hurts your mind?"

"You'll have to break the connection."

"How?" she said, worry flooding through her.

"You'll think of something," he said, his calm voice soothing her.

Now that they were sitting there, the candles blazing, with something manifesting in the dark, she realised how ill-conceived their plan was, and how vulnerable they were.

This spirit had killed a man.

Alex seemed to have no such doubts as he confidently reached forward to the crystal ball sitting between them and grasped it with both hands, closed his eyes, and began the spell.

Avery felt his power build and watched the ball at the same time as she sensed movement of the spirit around them. It had drawn closer and she felt a prickle between her shoulder blades. She fought the compulsion to turn around, and continued to watch the crystal ball. For a few seconds nothing much seemed to happen; she could see the distorted images of Alex's crossed legs though the glass, but then it started to darken, and a swirl of smoke filled the centre, until it was completely opaque.

Alex's chanting slowed and he opened his eyes, staring into the depths of the ball. His pupils looked huge, his skin burnished in the light of the candles, and his hair fell around his face, giving him the look of a mystic. "Show yourself to me," he commanded, his voice lowered.

The air seemed to thicken around them, and Avery had never felt so thankful to be within the circle.

Alex continued. "Tell me what you want." The ball within his hands was now impenetrable, and while Avery could see nothing, Alex stared into it, frowning. "Talk to me. You bring fear and death. What do you want?"

Sparks appeared within the smoky interior, and Alex gripped it harder, his knuckles whitening. "That is not possible," he said. "This is not your dimension. Leave! Find peace."

Avery was startled. Alex must be talking to it. She felt the spirit draw closer, circling them slowly, and Avery looked up, trying to see beyond the bright bloom of candlelight into the darkness beyond. For a second she thought she saw something and her heart rate rocketed. The protection spell responded and the flames from the candles flared, shooting several feet into the air to create a wall of fire around them. Immediately the spirit fell back, and it seemed as if there were footfalls in the darkness.

Alex continued to talk in his low monotone, reasoning and coaxing. "Tell me what you are. How many came with you?"

She heard another sound like a sigh, something she couldn't quite identify, and the ball flickered with light again. Alex became more insistent. "Let us help you return, you do not belong here."

Avery watched, mesmerised as the lightshow within intensified, like small lightning strikes hitting the glass. She didn't need Alex to tell her that the spirit was angry, she could feel it. It wanted to escape, but Alex's will was too strong.

Suddenly, the spirit surged, the white light within the ball became blinding, and Avery looked away, but Alex didn't move. He was transfixed, his hands like claws around the glass.

"Alex!" Avery shouted. "Release it, *now!*"

But Alex wouldn't, or couldn't. Was it drawing power from Alex? He wasn't speaking anymore; instead, he seemed locked in his own private battle.

Crap. This was just what they'd feared. If Avery also touched the ball, would she become locked within it, too? Instead, she reached over and held Alex's face within her hands, talking to him urgently but softly.

Nothing happened. The light grew brighter, the spirit grew stronger, and Alex's hands started to shake.

She must destroy the ball.

Avery said the first suitable spell that came to mind, holding her hands above the ball, but not touching it, and sent a powerful shot of energy down through the crystal like a punch. It shattered, chunks of glass flying out in all directions, and Alex fell forward into Avery's lap.

Alex's weight pinned her to the floor. She could see blood trickling down his arms from where he'd been cut. The smell of blood filled the air, and Avery bit back her fear. The circle would protect them. The spirit beyond the flames weakened suddenly, as if a howling wind had suddenly stopped, but she still felt it watching them, and then a second later it vanished, and the church was empty again.

"Alex, wake up," she said, shaking him violently. They needed to get out of there before it came back. "Wake up, now!" She sent a burst of energy across his skin and she felt him stir. He groaned and she sighed in relief. "Alex, are you okay?"

He grunted something she didn't understand.

"Sorry, I didn't get that, but you're alive, so that's good. We need to get out of here." She tried to lift him up, but he was a dead weight. "Alex, please. That thing has gone. We need to go before it comes back."

He rolled his head slightly, his eyes tightly closed, muttering something in a guttural language she didn't understand. *What the hell was going on?*

"Stop being funny. I can't understand you."

Alex sat up suddenly, his eyes opened, and Avery almost shouted with shock. His eyes were white and blinking blindly as he turned his head. His voice rose in panic, and then he fell forward again, the words tumbling out one after another. *Damn.* She had to get him to Briar.

"It's okay, take deep breaths," she said, trying to calm him with her most soothing voice. She stroked his arms, trying to avoid the shattered glass that lay between them, but he tried to throw her off, still muttering, becoming almost hysterical. *Was he possessed?*

She knew a few healing spells, and she tried one then. For a few anxious seconds that felt like hours, she watched him uneasily, hearing the old building settle around them; the squeak and crack of old wood, the eddy of a breeze from ill-fitted windows. And then she felt Alex start to relax, his words slowing.

"Okay. Time to go." She eased away, and started to collect their few belongings, placing them into their packs. She wanted to turn the lights on, but was worried it would damage Alex's eyes even more, so she conjured a witch light before extinguishing the candles. She used a spell to collect the glass from the crystal ball, and the pieces hung in the air before she dropped them into a pocket.

Alex groaned as she hauled him to his feet. "Come on, time to see Briar."

12

Before they headed to Briar's house, Avery needed to return the key to the church. The vicarage was an eighteenth-century house, a few steps from the church. She left Alex sitting in her van, still muttering to himself, and rocking gently backwards and forwards. She didn't want to leave him, but she had to return the key, so she headed up the path to James's front door.

James appeared in seconds, his eyes filled with questions. "What happened? Did you get rid of it?"

Avery shook her head. "We weren't trying to, James. We were trying to find out what it is."

"And did you?"

"I don't know yet. I need to ask Alex." She hesitated. "He's not very well at the moment. I need to take him to a friend."

"Can I see him?" he asked anxiously.

"Not now. Look, I know you're worried, but we need to be careful. Do not go back in that church—whatever the Bishop says."

He looked at the floor for a few seconds, and then looked her in the eye. "Do you believe in the Devil?"

"I believe in many things. The world is not as black and white as some would like it to be. Do you?"

"I believe in God. I believe he cast out his brother angel, and I believe he tries to lure us into evil."

Avery nodded, not sure where James was going with this. "Well, you're a vicar, that figures." *Wow. That sounded lame.*

"Is he in my church, Avery?"

She stared at him for a second. "The Devil?"

"Is he?" he repeated.

"No, I'm pretty sure it's not the Devil, but I don't know what it is yet."

James sighed and passed a hand over his face. Avery could hear the TV in the background, and someone talking. James had a family and a congregation to worry about. Avery felt as if the safety of the whole town rested on her shoulders.

"I have to go. Stay safe, and I'll be in touch."

***

Alex started to become agitated again on the drive, and Avery pulled over and managed to subdue him again, and then made a quick call to Briar to check that she was in. Avery was relieved it was a short trip. By the time they arrived at Briar's small cottage it was after eleven o'clock, but Briar met them at the door, and led them into the small conservatory at the back where they had eaten dinner only weeks before.

The walls of the conservatory were mainly glass in wooden frames, the lower half solid wood. A sagging couch sat under one of the long windows, stacked with cushions, and she led Alex to it.

Rattan blinds covered the windows, but the double doors were ajar, letting in a warm night breeze. Candles filled the space, and incense coiled on the air. Books and papers were stacked on the long wooden table, and it was clear Briar had been working there. An old, battered case that she used for transporting her herbs, gems, and potions was sitting on the table, open in readiness, her grimoires next to it.

"What happened?" Briar asked, once Alex was lying down.

"Well, it worked. Alex could speak to it, I think. I have no idea what it said," Avery explained. "But then something happened. The crystal ball went white and Alex just stared into it. I had to destroy the ball to release him, and now he's talking in some strange language, and his eyes…" She paused as he opened his eyes and started to yell, and Briar cried out in surprise.

"Avery, what the hell?"

Avery could feel herself welling up now that she was with Briar and her adrenaline was wearing off. "I don't know. I managed to subdue him, but the spell doesn't hold for long. Is he possessed?"

"I'm not sure until I examine him. Have you got your phone?"

When Avery nodded, she said, "Start recording, I want to listen to what he's saying properly later."

"That's a brilliant idea," Avery said, pulling her phone from her bag. She sat on the floor and leaned closer to Alex, trying not to get in Briar's way, and then pressed record.

Although they had managed to deposit Alex on the sofa, he was far from settled. He twitched all over, his hands were clenched tight, and he continued to chant and groan, a sheen of sweat visible on his face. Avery watched Briar's deft hands moving over his forehead, and then she did as Avery had done, taking his head within her hands. Every now and again she turned to her case to collect various stones and herbs. She placed a large amethyst on Alex's forehead, held her hand on it, and started a spell, her lips moving quickly.

Avery tried to tune out everything else and just listened to Alex, the way his breath was rushed and shallow, the words falling from his mouth in a torrent. She realised as she sat quietly that he was repeating the same thing, over and over again, but she couldn't work out what it was. Maybe she should call Genevieve or Rasmus, or Oswald. They were older, more experienced. They should know what to do. But as she watched Briar, Avery's thoughts calmed, too. Avery could feel her magic binding around Alex, drawing out whatever it was that was inflaming his brain.

Alex's face turned white and for a brief second he looked terrified, his eyes staring and fixed, and then his eyes closed and he fell into a deep sleep, his head falling to one side as his breathing became deeper and slower.

Avery released a long-held breath she hadn't even realised she was keeping in, and leaned her head on Alex's arm, comforted by his warmth. Exhaustion now washed through her, and felt she could sleep for a week, but there was more to do. She sat up and looked at Briar, taking in her appearance properly since she'd arrived with Alex.

Briar's long hair was tied up loosely on top of her head, and stray strands tumbled down on either side of her face. Her face was stripped of makeup and she looked young and fresh-faced. She was wearing some loose cotton trousers and a t-shirt and it looked like she was ready to go to bed. "Sorry, Briar. I didn't mean to disturb your evening."

Briar pursed her lips. "Don't apologise, you know you can come anytime. And besides, I was doing some reading in here. You didn't wake me up."

"I'm just relieved you're here. You might have still been at the pub, or with Newton."

"He's gone home—he's really busy at work right now. So what happened?"

Avery relayed as succinctly as possible what had happened in the Church. "It was super scary. I could feel it prowling round us." She changed tack. "Is it over? Have you cured him?"

Briar shook her head. "I doubt it. I've just calmed him enough to relax for now. Do you know what language that was?"

"No. His eyes. Is that permanent?" Avery felt her chest tighten with fear. "Is he blind?"

Briar placed a hand on Avery's arm. "I don't know. It's hard to say until we understand what really happened tonight. Sometimes, when the eyes turn white, it denotes the Seer—a vision state. I'm hoping it's that. The crystal ball will intensify such things, and it sounds as if the spirit, or whatever it was, trapped his gaze within the ball. The spell I've used is fairly general, just to calm him for now, but there's another spell I need to check."

Briar rose swiftly to her feet and started searching through her grimoire, while Avery pulled a floor cushion over and made herself comfortable on it, turning her attention back to Alex. She took his warm, strong hand in her own, and stroked it as she watched him breathe. His colour had come back, and he looked healthier in the warm light of the candles. His hair was loose, and stubble grazed his chin and cheeks. She'd always thought of Alex as being unassailable. He was so strong and his magic so powerful, she'd always believed that nothing would get the better of him. And now look at him. She reached out and laid a hand on his cheek. All she wanted him to do was wake up, so she could hold him and tell him how much he meant to her. He would be okay. He had to be.

Avery heard Briar whisper a spell behind her, and heard the pages of the grimoire swiftly turn. A finding spell, similar to one she'd used before.

"There it is," Briar exclaimed triumphantly.

Avery turned. "What?"

"A spell to rid the mind of a forceful vision. It's not perfect, but if I tweak it…"

Her voice faded as she started to assemble the spell's ingredients, and Avery turned back to Alex and thought about the events of the night.

The spirit was old and powerful. It had wings, like an angel or the devil. She paused as she thought of James's question. It wasn't the Devil. Not if there were two or more of them. A shudder ran through her as she thought of the spirit's watchful presence stalking the outside of the circle. *What did it want?*

A cool breeze eddied through the room, and she shivered, looking for a blanket. She rose to her feet, and pulled the door shut. "Do you mind if I close it, Briar?"

Briar shook her head and went back to her spell. Avery locked them in, pulled a blanket over Alex, and then grabbed one to wrap around her shoulders, sitting on the floor cushion again. She noticed her phone on the floor. *The recording. What would it say?*

She played the recording at a low volume so as not to disturb Briar, holding it close to her ear. The words were clear enough, but they meant nothing to her. However, there was a pattern to them. She had been right earlier. It was the same phrase repeated over and over again. *Was there a spell she could use to help her understand it?* She ran through the spells she knew, but none of them would work on this. However, there may well be something in either her own or one of the other grimoires. If—no, *when*—Alex awoke, maybe he would know.

Avery's throat felt like sandpaper. *I need a drink.* Leaving Alex sleeping, and Briar working on her spell, she headed to the kitchen and turned the kettle on. After making chamomile tea, in a vain effort to calm her racing mind, she headed to the living room and idly flicked on the TV, scrolling to the news. She needed a distraction. She collapsed on the couch, filtering through the events in her mind. The Witches Council, the lights in the sea, the threat of Mermaids, the restless ghosts, the church spirits, and the deaths. The magic they had released, their magic, had created so much unforeseen trouble. And then a news bulletin flashed across the screen and she stared in horror.

There had been yet another death, in another church in St Just.

A young woman had been in the church that evening to clean, and the vicar had found her dead. There were no details on how she had died, just the death, but it was clear to Avery that this death was linked to the others.

Could this night get any worse?

"Avery!" Briar's voice broke her reverie, and she ran through to the conservatory.

"What? Is Alex okay?"

"No, but he's talking again."

Alex was still lying down but he was restless beneath his blanket, and half of it was on the floor. A sweat had broken out again on his face, and his eyes were open wide, a wild look to them. His eyes were still completely white.

Avery ran over and held his hand. "It's okay, Alex, you're fine. You're not in danger. Can you hear me?"

Alex's grip was tight on her hand, but there was no hint of recognition in his behaviour.

"I have a potion ready, so it's good that he's awake again," Briar said. "Help him sit up, or even just raise his head," she directed, seeing Avery struggle with him.

Briar knelt next to Avery, holding a small chalice with a thimbleful of liquid in it. With Avery supporting Alex's head, Briar tipped the liquid into his mouth, one dribble at a time, and as he drank, Briar said a spell.

As soon as the spell was completed he fell back, unconscious, and Briar placed a lapis lazuli gemstone on each closed eye. "Good." She smiled at Avery. "That should do it. Now we let him sleep. I'm pretty sure that he's been gripped by a powerful image or vision. His mind is trying to process it, probably replaying it over and over again. This spell will banish it for good—hopefully without him forgetting it completely."

"Thank you, Briar." Avery said, hugging her. "I was so scared. But," she hesitated a moment. "There's been another death. In St Just."

Briar's triumphant expression faded. "There'll be more, Avery. I can feel it. The earth itself is unsettled…it trembles. This is far from over."

13

It was a long night.

Briar had offered Avery a bed, but she didn't want to be so far from Alex, so, like Briar, she slept on one of the sofas in the lounge. Unfortunately, the lounge was small and one sofa was only a two-seater, which Briar insisted on having because she was shorter, but they both hardly slept anyway, woken every hour by an alarm to check on Alex. Not that they really slept in between either.

By the time dawn arrived, Avery felt grubby, her neck ached, and her eyes were gritty. But Alex was better. His breathing was regular and deep, and he had rolled over in the night, pulling the blanket close. The stones had slipped off his head and eyes and Briar collected them up. She smiled at Avery. "I'm pretty sure this is a normal sleep now, Avery. You can go if you want."

"No. Dan will open up. What will you do?"

"My shop can stay closed for a couple of hours," she said, reassuring her. "Let's have some breakfast and coffee."

"Really strong coffee," Avery said, blinking back tiredness.

Briar headed for the fridge. "And really crispy bacon. And eggs. And crusty bread."

Briar had only just brewed the coffee, and the smell of bacon was filling the air, when there was a knock at the door.

Briar raised an eyebrow at Avery. "I can feel him from here. Can you?"

"Not like you can, but–" she raised her head and called the air to her, filtering the smells of the morning, "I smell Newton, and determination. I'll go let him in."

When Avery opened the door, Newton looked at her in shock. "What are you doing here?"

"Long story. Come in," she said, turning and heading into the kitchen, Newton on her heels.

"Bacon!" he said, his eyes gleaming. Avery wasn't sure if it was the smell of bacon or the sight of Briar that had given him the bounce in his step. "Morning, Briar. How much you got there?"

She smiled at him over her shoulder. "I've got plenty. Want some?"

"Yes, please. I left the house in a rush, but suddenly I'm hungry."

He reached over to grab the coffee pot, searching in the cupboard above for a mug at the same time, and Avery tried to subdue a smirk as she realised just how familiar Newton was with Briar's kitchen. Despite the early hour, he had dressed with care. His dark grey suit and light grey shirt were pristine, and he smelt of shower gel and was clean-shaven. *Someone was making an effort.* Although, to be fair, he was always impeccably dressed for work.

Avery leaned against the kitchen units. "Well, you're here early and quite jaunty."

"Not jaunty. I'm clinging to normality like a mad man." He leaned back on the opposite counter, watching her. "You look like death. What happened?"

Avery ran her hands self-consciously through her hair, and whispered the tiniest of spells to give herself a little beautification. *Vain? Maybe.* "We had a very unpleasant encounter last night with the spirit. Alex linked with it a little too strongly, so here we are."

Newton stood straighter. "Is he okay?"

"We think so, now. Thanks to Briar." Avery hesitated a second. "We saw the news late last night. There's been another death."

Newton exhaled loudly. "Yes. I was out until two this morning. It looks the same as the others."

"Two!" Briar exclaimed. "And you're up already?"

"It's the job, Briar. So, another broken body, drained, pale, found in the nave of the St Andrew's Church in St Just. It's one of the oldest churches in the town, just like here and Harecombe." He paused for a second, thinking. "And there's no sign of a break-in, no stolen items, and according to the vicar, an uncanny sense of something strange in the church in the last few days."

Briar turned away from the cooker where she'd been preparing eggs and sipping her coffee. Her expression was bleak. "There'll be more. I can feel it in the earth, I told Avery last night. It's like the earth is trembling, from either fear or because power is stirring. I can't quite tell what yet. Maybe both." She looked at Avery. "Take some time if you can today, Avery. See if you feel change in the air."

Before Avery could answer, they heard the door to the sunroom open and suddenly Alex was leaning on the frame. "Do I smell bacon and coffee?"

Avery broke into a broad smile and rushed over, reaching up to hug him. "Alex! You're awake! Are you all right?" She looked at him carefully, relieved to see his eyes had returned to their normal dark chocolate brown. "You scared the shit out of me."

He hugged her, too, releasing her reluctantly. "I scared the shit out of myself, too. My mind was gripped by…something…" he trailed off.

"Coffee and breakfast first," Briar said decisively. "It's ready now, go sit," she commanded, shooing everyone into the sunroom.

Sitting at the wooden table with a strong coffee in her hands, Avery started to feel human again, especially now that Alex was all right. His experience certainly hadn't damaged his hunger; he ate like he hadn't been fed in months.

"Thanks, Briar," Avery said, finally finishing her bacon and egg sandwich. "That was awesome."

"Yeah, thanks Briar. But I have to get to work to investigate a murder, so tell me. What did you see last night?" Newton asked, narrowing his eyes at Alex.

Alex paused for a few seconds, gazing at the table while he gathered his thoughts. When he finally looked up, he sighed. "The spell worked. The crystal ball helped to focus on the spirit and provided a way for us to communicate. It didn't want to at first. It shied away, prowling around on the edge of my consciousness, until its curiosity got the better of it. I think the fact that we were locked within the protective circle annoyed it. So, I found out that it's old, thousands of years old, and it's been trapped beyond our plane for a long, long time. When we opened the door to their dimension, they saw their opportunity and forced their way out, as you saw, Avery. The rest of us were too engaged with the demon to notice."

"And I *was* spirit walking," Avery reminded him. "That allowed me to see things you couldn't."

"True. Anyway, unlike the other spirits there, they were powerful enough to break free. I don't know how many of them crossed. It wouldn't tell me at first. It liked having knowledge I didn't, I could tell."

Briar leaned on the table. "You were talking in some strange language last night we couldn't understand. Avery recorded it. It was as if you were repeating something over and over, like it was locked in your brain. Do you know what you were saying?"

Alex didn't answer straight away, instead picking up his cup and drinking more coffee.

"You found out something bad, didn't you?" Avery asked, her heart sinking into her stomach.

Alex met her eyes and nodded, and then glanced at the others. "I don't know if it's bad or good, but Jasper was right. It *is* one of the Nephilim. Or rather *they* are. No wonder it feels old. It's bloody ancient."

"So, what does this mean? What now?" Newton asked.

"I have no idea. It was curious as to what I was, what we were. It didn't like our power, but it respected us. And so, after this battle of the spirits, for want of a better word, it revealed its name."

"What do they want?" Avery asked. "I could sense you arguing with it."

"They want to return to what they see is their rightful place on Earth—to walk amongst men again."

"That's ridiculous," Newton said, colour draining from him. "They're old, they don't belong here."

"That's not what he thought," Alex explained.

"So why the deaths?" Avery asked, fearing she already knew why.

"They need the energy. They need more to make them corporeal."

"And why stay in the churches?" Briar asked.

"For our particular spirit, it was convenience, since it was where he escaped. But churches carry spiritual energy, which as we thought, is good to feed from. Plus, they're also generally quiet places. The others fled to find their own churches to lurk in."

"So, what were you saying that had been blazed on your brain?" Briar asked.

"We are the Nephilim, we are seven, and we will walk again. Try to stop us and you shall die."

***

When Avery got to work, all she wanted to do was crawl into bed and pretend last night had never happened, pretend one of the Nephilim did not inhabit her local church. At some point she would have to tell James, the vicar, but not now. She couldn't face it. To top it off, Sally had taken a few days of annual leave, as it was now the summer holidays and her kids were off school.

Dan was behind the main counter, his back to the room, leaning his tall frame over the music system when she walked in carrying two steaming lattes and two large, sticky pastries. He was wearing jeans and his university t-shirt, and he turned as she arrived, looked bright-eyed and rested. *Ugh.* That made Avery feel even worse.

Dan took a coffee appreciatively as the sounds of John Lee Hooker filled the room. "Cheers, Ave. You're up early." He looked confused. "You've already been out and it's barely nine. Are you really Avery Hamilton?"

She grinned, despite her crappy night. "Funny. I do get up early sometimes."

"Sure you do. You keep telling yourself that." He grabbed a pastry and took a bite. "So, go on. Why?"

Avery groaned and looked around to make sure the shop was still empty. "We had an eventful night. Alex and I were trying to communicate with a spirit and it gripped Alex in some sort of Seer state. Anyway, thanks to Briar, he's okay now."

"Wow. Your life is anything but boring lately. What spirit?"

She briefly considered not elaborating, but Dan knew what she was and what had happened beneath All Souls, so it seemed only fair to come clean. "I'm not sure how much Sally told you about the death at the church and the spirits I saw escaping when we released our magic—"

"I know it all," Dan said, interrupting her.

"Good. Well, one of the spirits is lurking in All Souls. It turns out that it—*he*—is a Nephilim."

Dan paused, mid-bite, and stared. "Isn't that some biblical something?"

"Yes," Avery said, and explained what it was. "There are seven of them, three deaths in three churches so far, and no doubt more to come. And we have no idea how to stop them. They're very powerful, far more than normal spirits. I need to talk to the Witches Council."

"I hate to tell you this, but there are more than three deaths, Avery. There were another two reported in breaking news only a few minutes ago. I heard it on the radio."

"What?" They must have been reported after she left Newton, or he'd have said so. "Where?"

"Bodmin and Perranporth."

"More old churches?"

"I think so. There weren't many details."

Avery's legs felt weak and she headed around the counter and sat on one of the chairs next to Dan. "This is awful."

Dan cradled his coffee as he watched her. "Yes, it is. Pretty scary, too. There must be a spell you can use, with all your juiced-up magic."

"There are lots of spells...it's just finding the right one."

"Isn't that what the Council is for? You all work together, pool your power. You're not alone, remember that." Dan smiled, trying to reassure her.

"I think I'm feeling very overwhelmed right now." She sipped her coffee again, enjoying the hit of caffeine.

"That's because it's big and it's new, but you'll get your head around it. You always do."

She smiled at him. "Thanks. I'm just tired, I think. Sleep will help."

"Guess who I saw yesterday?"

Avery considered him for a second. "Dylan?"

"Bingo! I saw at him at the Uni library. You've made quite an impression. All of you, actually."

"Have we?"

"Oh, yes," he nodded. "He tells me they're heading to St Luke's tonight."

"Yes. I'm going, too. I'm not leaving them alone with Caspian."

Dan nodded, relieved. "Good, I was hoping you'd say that. Now, go and catch up on some sleep, I'll manage here for a few hours on my own."

"Are you sure? Because that sounds wonderful."

"Yes. Come and relieve me for lunch."

Avery stood gratefully, walking towards the rear of the shop. But before she headed up the stairs to her flat, she strengthened the protective wards on the shop, just in case.

14

"Another night, another church."

Alex leaned on the low wall that edged St Luke's Church. Unlike All Souls, this church was slightly out of the town, and there were no neighbouring shops or houses to witness their activities. "This is becoming quite a habit."

"Not one I'm enjoying," Avery said. She studied Alex's face again, worried that he hadn't yet fully recovered from last night.

He saw her worried expression and laughed. "I'm fine, Avery."

She reached up, cupping his cheek with her hand. "I hope so. I was really worried last night."

He grabbed her hand, pulled it to his lips and kissed her palm. "I know. You're gorgeous, you know that?"

"So you keep telling me." She smiled, warmth spreading through her.

"I mean it." He looked as if he was about to say more when they heard cars arriving, and they looked around to see the three investigators arriving at the same time as Caspian.

Dylan, Cassie, and Ben shouted their hellos, and then started to wrestle equipment from their van, but Caspian grimaced when he saw them. He slammed the door of his sleek Audi, and his sister, Estelle, emerged from the passenger seat.

Avery's only contact with Estelle had been on two instances. The first time was when she had been attacking Reuben at Old Haven Church, and in defence, Briar had half-buried her in soil and Avery had knocked her unconscious with a fallen branch. The second time had been at Faversham Central, their name for Sebastian Faversham's mansion, where Estelle had attacked them in the corridor and Reuben had managed to better her. Today, Avery reflected, was the first time they had seen her and they hadn't been attacking each other. Unfortunately, she looked like she wanted to attack them right now. That was fine. Avery wanted to wipe that dismissive look right off her face.

"Nice to see you, too," Alex said, smirking.

"We don't need you here," Caspian said, turning his back on them as he opened up the church. Estelle stood next to him, glaring at them.

"Well, they do, so get over it," Alex said, joining Caspian at the door. He nodded at Estelle. "Estelle, always a pleasure."

Estelle narrowed her eyes. "Do we need both of you?"

"Safety in numbers. Especially with you two here. Besides, if this is anything like the spirit in our church, it's very mean." He hesitated a moment. "We found out what it is. What *they* are."

"And?" Caspian drawled. "Do you want a drum roll?"

Alex ignored his sarcasm. "They *are* Nephilim."

Estelle released a barking laugh, throwing her head back. "Really?" Her voice dripped with doubt.

"Really. So watch your step, Estelle. It might get all biblical on your ass."

Caspian and Estelle paused on the threshold of the church, staring at each other for a few seconds, and then

Caspian looked at Alex, clearly annoyed. "How do you know?"

"I communed with the one in All Souls last night, through a crystal ball." Alex shrugged. "He said there were seven of them. The question is, do we really want to try to record this one, now we know what it is?"

That was a good question, Avery thought, and one they had debated on the way over. They could all be put in more danger than they needed to be. The whole point of allowing the paranormal investigation was to see if the spirits were linked, and it seemed they were.

Ben spoke from behind them. "Yes, we do. The more we film, the more we know."

"And besides," Caspian put in, "you might be wrong."

"I didn't think you wanted them here?" Avery asked sharply, referring to the parapsychologists.

"Let's not upset Genevieve," Caspian said, turning away from her. "Now, let's get this over with."

They followed Caspian into the nave, the dim electric lights throwing shadows everywhere.

Like All Souls, this church was medieval in design, and the high, vaulted ceiling stretched above them. Unlike All Souls, it was much smaller, a country church, similar in size to Old Haven. And it had been smashed to pieces.

Over half of the polished wooden pews had been destroyed, the altar overturned, and candles were scattered on the floor. Set in the walls were small, arched niches that had contained icons, flowers or candles, and all but two of these were now empty, their displays strewn across the floor.

"Bloody Hell," Ben murmured, looking around in shock. "What happened here?"

Avery felt as shocked as he looked. This spirit had actually destroyed objects. Big, heavy objects. Some of the pews were now only splinters of wood.

Caspian rounded on them, eyes blazing. "I presume this hasn't happened at All Souls?"

"No," Alex said, taking in the damage. "Not last night, anyway. It might have by now."

Estelle's cool, clipped tone resonated through the church and she glanced dismissively at Avery and Alex. "Well, so much for it just being a spirit."

"Maybe," Avery began, just as coolly, "the spirit has gained a lot of power from killing its victim. Where was the body found?"

Estelle dropped her eyes and pointed, a glimmer of regret on her face. "Here in the nave, next to the altar. You can just about see where the blood was."

Dylan and Cassie were now behind Ben, and rather than looking dismayed at the damage, they actually looked excited. "Wow. Brilliant," Dylan said. "I wish we'd caught this on camera."

"Be careful what you wish for," Alex said, raising his brows. "Let's get this show on the road."

Cassie, Ben and Dylan worked quickly, falling into well-practised routines, and soon they had their equipment set up, and Cassie had taken her initial temperature readings. Dylan was already prowling the perimeter with his thermal imaging camera, while Ben set up the audio.

While the team organised themselves, Avery and Alex righted the candles and Avery lit them with a word. Estelle and Caspian stood in the centre of the room, and Avery knew they were doing what she and Alex were doing; trying to feel the spirit and locate its presence. So far, Avery sensed nothing, but she knew it must be here.

"You know what?" Alex said, frowning. "I'm going to make a very big protective circle. Guys!" he shouted. "Be prepared to get your ass over here quickly."

Ben, Cassie and Dylan turned and nodded, but Estelle sneered. "Scared, Alex?"

Alex just smiled thinly. "You'll thank me for this later."

Working quickly, he withdrew all the necessary things from his pack, including a large silver dagger, and he used salt to outline the circle, just as they had done before. Avery worked with him, speaking softly. "I think this is a great idea. And it worked well last night."

Alex nodded. "I have a bad feeling about this."

For the next 15 minutes nothing happened, other than their own pacing and waiting.

"It doesn't want to play," Caspian murmured, annoyed.

"Could it have escaped?" Avery asked.

"No. I know how to seal a building, thank you," Caspian said sarcastically. He turned his back to them and watched the ghost-hunters.

The spirit may have been refusing to appear, but the tension in the room increased anyway. Being in such close proximity with Caspian and Estelle was annoying.

Ben and the other parapsychologists ignored them, focussing solely on recording the damage, and Ben even provided some walk-through audio.

Then, without warning, the electric lights that weren't that bright in the first place started to buzz and crackle, the light pulsing.

They all spun around, and Avery threw her senses wide, trying to identify where the spirit was. A large, dark mass started to manifest behind the altar. The EMF meter started to whine, and then one by one, the lights shattered around the room, the candles now their sole source of light.

Alex grabbed Avery's hand and pulled her into the circle. "Everyone, get in here *now*!"

Cassie ran to them straight away, standing close to Avery, but Ben continued to use the meter, and Dylan continued to record. Caspian and Estelle ignored them too, stepping closer to the spirit that had started to manifest.

The dark mass rose taller and taller, its bulk filling out.

Cassie shouted, "Dylan. Ben. Please come here!"

They glanced at them, and then looked back at the spirit, and seemed to decide that retreat was wise. They edged back, step by step, continuing to record all the while.

Caspian and Estelle, however, had poised themselves for attack, their hands raised, balls of energy visible in their palms.

Without warning the spirit grew, becoming more human in shape - except for the wings spread wide behind it. It lunged at Caspian, one large wing sweeping him off his feet and sending him crashing into the wall.

That was enough to make Ben and Dylan run.

Estelle had no such fears, and Avery wasn't sure if she was brave or stupid. She threw ball after ball of energy at the spirit, but instead of retreating it grew in size, its enormous wingspan now reaching halfway along the wall. Avery couldn't work out if she was seeing its shadow from the candles, or the spirit itself. *Would it even have a shadow?*

Alex yelled, "Estelle! Stop! You're giving it power!"

She ignored him, instead conjuring flames and hurling them at the spirit. Caspian, meanwhile, staggered to his feet, and added his power to hers.

Avery looked at Alex bewildered. "Can't they see what they're doing?"

"Blinded by stupidity," Alex muttered. "Caspian! You're not helping. Get back here!"

The spirit continued to change, forming two legs and then arms, but the wings remained. It again lunged at Caspian and Estelle, catching them both with its wings this time, and sending them flying through the air. Caspian landed awkwardly on the top of the broken pews, and Estelle on the stone floor in a crumpled heap.

Avery glanced at Alex and they instinctively had the same thought. They both darted out of the circle, Avery yelling at the ghost-hunters, "Don't move!"

Avery headed for Estelle where she was lying dazed, but still conscious, and summoned air. The gust lifted Estelle up, clean off her feet, enabling Avery to pull her back into the safety of the circle. At the same time, Alex pulled Caspian to his feet, and dragged him away.

The Nephilim, now more creature than spirit, advanced towards them across the nave, but its features were still unformed. A voice filled the air, almost deafening, and Avery recognised the language that Alex had been repeating over and over again the previous night.

Caspian resisted Alex's help, but Alex had clearly had enough and punched him, obviously the last thing Caspian expected, because he collapsed in a heap and Alex dragged him along the floor. Avery helped lift him into the circle, and then uttered the spell that would seal them in.

The flair of magic was palpable and the Nephilim paused, watching them. It then began to circle them, its strange, guttural language still filling the church.

"I did not expect *this*," Ben said. His eyes were wide and his hands shook. The EMF meter buzzed wildly. He asked Dylan, "Are you still recording?"

"Yep. Not sure quite how steady the footage will be."

Estelle rose shakily to her feet and hissed at Alex, "You punched Caspian."

"And I'll punch you, too if you try anything," he said, rounding on her. "Normally I don't like violence towards women, but I'm willing to make an exception for you."

Caspian sat up groaning, clutching a hand to his nose. Blood streamed down his face and he glared at Alex.

"We saved your life," Avery said pointedly, before he could start to argue.

The heavy slap of feet on the floor made them turn back to the Nephilim, but instead of advancing further, it laughed—if that's what it could be called. It was like a howl that sent goose bumps along Avery's skin and lifted the hairs on the back of her neck.

The Nephilim turned away, lifted its wings, and soared towards the closest window. It didn't hesitate, crashing through at speed, sending glass shattering everywhere and splintering the frame. And then it disappeared into the night.

"Great. Just great. So much for sealing the bloody church," Alex shouted. He clenched his fists and with visible difficulty took deep breaths and tried to calm down. He looked at the ghost-hunters. "Are you okay?"

"I think so," Cassie mumbled, while the others nodded.

Avery sank to the floor, depressed and unsure what to do next.

"It was stronger than I anticipated," Caspian admitted. He was still sitting on the floor, and like Avery he seemed deflated, sinking into himself. He whispered a spell and his blood flow stopped, and then he lifted his t-shirt, wiping his face with the hem.

"It will be going after the others," Alex said. "They'll all be out within the hour, and then who knows what will happen."

"Death and destruction. We need to tell Genevieve." Avery looked resolute. "Who knows, with some warning, she may be able to stop the others?"

Caspian shook his head and stood up. "I doubt it, but it's worth trying. Drop the spell, Avery, we don't need to stay in the circle any longer."

Avery nodded and released the spell, watching Caspian as he stood beneath the shattered window. He raised his hands and the broken glass and frame started to reassemble itself, until seconds later the window was fixed.

"Wow," Dylan said admiringly, "that's so cool."

Caspian turned to him, narrowing his eyes. "I trust you will keep our secrets?" His tone didn't invite refusal.

"Absolutely. We value our clients' privacy," Dylan said emphatically, Ben and Cassie nodding vigorously next to him.

"Good." Caspian looked at Alex and Avery. "You better go and check All Souls and repair any damage there, too. We'll stay behind and fix this." He gestured to the destroyed pews. "This is all about damage control now. The less anyone, including the police, knows about this, the better."

15

After the cold and dismal atmosphere at St Luke's Church, Alex's flat was a warm and welcoming haven.

Avery sat with a glass of red wine, curled in the corner of Alex's soft and luxurious sofa, watching the dancing flames of the candles. The blinds were closed, shutting out the night, and Alex was sitting on the floor, turning the pages of his grimoire in a vain attempt to do something useful.

Avery had just taken a call from Genevieve confirming that the others had escaped, too, leaving broken glass and damaged window frames behind. What was worse was that she hadn't blamed her, and Avery felt that if only she had shouted at her, she might be feeling slightly better.

Before Alex and Avery returned to Alex's, they had stopped at All Souls, but that too had a smashed window, fortunately at the rear of the church, away from the road. They had repaired it, and checked the interior to make sure nothing else had happened inside, but unlike St Luke's, the interior was intact.

The ghost-hunters had returned home and Avery reminded them to wear their amulets, just in case. Dylan had pulled his out of his shirt, saying, "Are you kidding? I wear this *everywhere* now!"

That had given Avery some comfort, but she felt more depressed than she had in a long time. She swirled her wine and took a large sip. "I feel helpless."

Alex looked troubled. "Me, too. But the spirits have escaped, so now we have to figure out what to do."

"What was it like the other night, to have that *thing* in your head?"

He shuddered at the memory. "Intense and unpleasant. It was strong, maybe more than it should have been because of the crystal ball, but," he shrugged, "it worked. We know what it is. And it knows what we are, too."

Avery leaned forward. "What do you mean?"

"Well, the whole protective circle meant it recognised magic, but I felt it brushing across my thoughts. I'm sure it knows we're witches, and I'm sure it knows what that means." He smiled softly. "Let's face it—witches have been around a long time, too. Magic is at the root of everything."

"Do you think that frightened it?"

"No. But," Alex looked thoughtful, "I think it respected me. *I think.* Let's hope that works in our favour, eventually. We might even work out what to do with them."

"I don't even know what day it is, never mind how to work out what to do with errant Nephilim."

"You'll be pleased to know it's Saturday, which means a lazy lie-in and Sunday brunch."

"Good, that's something," she said, collapsing back on the couch. "I'm not sure when my Saturdays turned into full-on spirit hunting in collaboration with the Favershams."

"Since *someone* decided to find grimoires, that's when." He caught her foot in his hands, and started kissing her calf, all the time watching her with his dark eyes.

"That's nice," she groaned, feeling like she might melt into the sofa.

"Only nice?" He continued up her inner thigh.

"Very, *very* nice." She watched him, wondering if he was going to stop, and hoping he really wouldn't.

He looked up at her with a wicked grin and took her wine glass out of her hands. "I think we've had enough of grimoires and ghost-hunting don't you?"

***

The next morning, there was nothing on the local news about the churches, which was some relief. Their efforts to disguise the spirits and their escape had been successful.

Avery sipped her coffee and watched Alex move competently around the kitchen. "Where do you think they've gone?"

"Good question." Alex pushed a plate of Eggs Benedict under her nose and sat down next to her along the breakfast bar counter. "Somewhere dark and protected."

"A cave?" she asked, through a mouthful of food.

"A deserted building, somewhere inaccessible? But," Alex said, pointing his fork, "so far, no deaths."

"That we've heard of."

"But they're clearly together, and maybe with the other two. Remember the Nephilim I communicated with? He said, '*We are seven.*'"

Avery nodded absently, slightly side-tracked by the fantastic brunch Alex had cooked. "Do you think there's a guidebook on Nephilim? Like, how to destroy them and send them back to the Otherworld?"

"Mmm, unlikely, Ave. But maybe you could write one after this? Or, of course, you could cause it to rain for forty days and forty nights. Isn't that what the flood was for?" He smirked infuriatingly at her.

She groaned. "I don't think my weather magic is that good. And neither is your boat building."

Before Alex could tease her any more, his phone rang. "Hey Reuben, how you doing?" He continued to eat as he talked, grunting occasionally, while Avery watched, curious.

She hadn't seen Reuben or El for a few days and she wondered what they'd been up to. She didn't have to wait long.

"Sure," Alex continued. "See you at the harbour in half an hour."

He hung up and Avery looked at him expectantly. "What are you going to do at the harbour?"

"You mean, what are *we* doing?" he corrected, raising his eyebrows.

"We? Can't I go back to bed?" she said, wishing she could summon the energy to feel even vaguely enthusiastic.

"No. A boat's been found out at sea. Empty. Like the Marie Celeste. Reuben heard about it while he was surfing. He's persuaded Nils to take us out to the area."

"Nils, the tattoo guy? He has a boat?" The last time Avery had seen him was when he was putting her protection tattoo on her hip in his shop, Viking Ink.

"He's a Viking. Of course he has a boat."

***

"Morning, guys!" Nils yelled in his slight Swedish lilt from where he stood on the deck of his old fishing boat. He waved and grinned. "Come aboard. I'll give you a tour of my baby!"

It was hardly a baby, Avery reflected as she looked at it. The varnish was peeling, and it had a battered quality to it that suggested it had seen better days. But clearly, Nils loved it. He leaned over the side and extended his hand to Avery, clasping her hand in his very large one. She'd forgotten just how huge he was.

She gingerly walked up the narrow gangplank onto the boat, and looked into Nils's pale blue eyes. He winked. "Great to see you, Avery. Hope my tattoo is looking good. Reuben is inside making tea." He jerked his hand over his shoulder to the cabin, and then looked at Alex, who had followed Avery onto the boat. "Alex! My tattooed friend!" He clasped him in a huge man hug. "We having trouble again, yes? Missing people. It's bad news. I'll go check the engine. As soon as the others are here, we go."

He disappeared to the far end of the boat, leaving Avery bewildered. "Wow. He's a force of nature."

Alex grinned. "He's great though, right?"

Reuben emerged from the cabin at the sound of their voices. His blond hair was slightly damp, and he was dressed in his board shorts and t-shirt. He didn't look anywhere as near as enthusiastic as Nils. "Morning, guys. What a crappy night."

"You too?" Alex said. "You haven't even heard *our* news."

"Does it involve missing fisherman and a drifting boat?"

"No. But there are missing Nephilim."

"Shit," Reuben said, leaning against the side of the boat and cradling his steaming cup. "This keeps getting worse."

"You got any details on the boat?" Alex asked.

Reuben nodded. "Yeah, some. It doesn't sound good. When I had my morning surf, the guys filled me in on the news. One of them had spotted the Coastguard heading out early. You know this place. News spreads. After that, I caught up with Connor, one of the crew." He exhaled with a heavy sigh. "Said it was weird. It was a calm night. There were no distress calls, but the boat was deserted. No missing gear, no signs of damage. The nets were still out. Small family business, too. Dad and two sons. How crap is that?"

"Who was it?" Avery asked, sure she'd know them. Most people in White Haven knew each other by sight, even if they didn't know each other well.

"The Petersons," Reuben said, watching her.

Avery closed her eyes briefly. *Yes, she knew them.* "Damn it."

She turned away, leaving Alex and Reuben talking, and leaned against the side of the boat. Looking out at the harbour and the sea beyond, she reflected on how such a bright morning could exist when there was so much darkness out there. Several women were missing husbands, boyfriends, sons, and fathers. And it sounded as if the Daughters of Llyr were to blame.

The harbour was still mostly empty of boats, many of them still out fishing. Some of the bigger vessels were lined up, ready to take tourists out for a few hours, and queues of people were already getting ready to board.

Beyond the harbour, the town sparkled in the sunshine. Bright splashes of colour marked the plants and hanging baskets outside of shops and pubs, and the smell of salt was strong in the air. It was late July and the tourist season was in full swing; families were everywhere. This was a terrible time to have Mermaids and Nephilim stalking the coast.

Avery heard a shout, and she looked around to see Briar, Newton, and El clambering on board. She waved, unable to summon a smile. "Hey, guys."

They shouted their greetings and crossed the deck to join them.

Nils must have heard them arrive, and he appeared from the engine room, streaked in oil and wiping his hands on a ragged cloth. "Everyone ready?" he asked.

They nodded.

"Great, grab a lifejacket and we'll go."

***

Once they were out of the harbour, a brisk sea breeze ruffled the waves, and they bobbed across the water, heading to the site where the boat had been found. It took them almost an hour to get there, and on the way, they updated everyone about the Nephilim. They stood at the stern of the boat, well away from the wheelhouse so that Nils couldn't hear them.

"Great. Seven Nephilim spirits loose in Cornwall. Just brilliant," Newton said, pacing up and down the deck. "And potentially, they might not even be spirits anymore."

Briar squinted against the sun and lowered her sunglasses. "I can still feel them—not so much on this boat—but I can on the land. They're growing stronger."

"Can you pinpoint where they are?" Newton asked eagerly.

"No, unfortunately not. It's more like I have a subtle awareness of their presence in the atmosphere."

"Well, no further deaths have to be a good thing, right?" El asked.

"I guess so," Avery said. "I really wish we knew what they were up to, though."

"Did Caspian look the slightest bit apologetic for giving the one at St Luke's enough juice to get out of there?" Reuben asked.

"Not really," Alex answered, "but I did enjoy punching him."

"And he didn't retaliate?" Newton asked, shocked.

"There was too much going on there already. A fight would have been dangerous. And besides, I did it to stop him from struggling. God knows what that Nephilim would have done if it had got to us."

"And what about today?" Briar asked. "Other than seeing where the crew disappeared from, what's the plan?"

"I want to see if we can find the Mermaids," Reuben explained. "I have a spell that should work."

"Then what? I mean isn't that dangerous?" Briar asked. "There're five guys on board, and you will all be susceptible to their call. How can *we* stop that?" She gestured toward Avery and El. *It was a great question*, Avery thought. She'd been wondering that herself.

"You're presuming you won't be at risk, then?" Newton asked, confused.

"In theory, no," El explained. "Me and Reu have been doing some homework on Mermaids, and it seems they only target men. We're hoping that means their call won't work on us. Of course, we could be wrong. We can spell you all and tie you to the boat if we have to, but we don't think they'll be around today. This is more of a tracing spell."

Reuben elaborated further. "Oswald was convinced that they were walking the land in Mevagissey. Maybe they're here. I want to see if we can find if they've come ashore."

"Can we detect them on land?" Newton asked. "I mean, will they look different to humans?"

"Folklore suggests they look the same," Reuben said. "That's part of their success, but there should be fundamental differences. If we can detect a signature *something*, we may be able to make a spell to help us find them. I mean, I would imagine there's a strong water elemental nature to them, even if we can't see it."

Avery rubbed her face, frustrated. "So, they won't have bright green eyes or webbed feet or something?"

"Pretty sure not, no," Reuben said, grinning.

"What about Nils?" Newton asked, glancing towards the wheelhouse. "What does he know about us?"

"Not much. He knows I tinker with a bit of witchcraft, but he has no idea of the extent of it. He hasn't asked too many questions about today. He's clever that way."

Avery nodded, knowing what he meant. Like Sally and Dan used to be, he probably knew more than he let on, and sensibly kept out of it. He may not have that luxury for much longer.

As if he'd read her thoughts, Reuben said, "I'd appreciate it if someone distracted him while I'm performing the spell."

"No problem," Newton said.

At that moment, they felt and heard the engine throttle down and their speed drop, and Nils yelled across the boat. "We're coming up to the spot now. It's not one of the common fishing spots—they'd have been on their own here for quite a while."

"Maybe they were lured out here in the first place," El speculated.

Avery peered overboard, wondering where below them the Petersons might be. "Do you think they knew they would die?" she asked.

"They're probably not dead," Alex said, wrapping his arm around her. "Remember the old tales. They could be Mermen by now."

Avery shivered. "Do you think they'd have memories of their life on land? Their loved ones, their friends?"

"Let's hope not," Alex said softly, and kissed her on the forehead. "It would be easier that way."

Newton headed to the wheelhouse to talk to Nils, leaving Reuben free to perform his spell. He pulled a few objects from his backpack, and handed them to El. Avery watched him, curious as to the type of spell he had in mind.

Briar caught on quickly. "You're going to harness elemental water, aren't you?"

Reuben nodded. "Much like you harness the earth and feel its energies, I feel water flow through me. I try not to use it when I surf—it feels like cheating—but I think I'm kidding myself. I probably use it subconsciously, anyway. I can feel it now. And as the earth feels a disturbance, I'm hoping I can feel the Mermaids here."

"You didn't notice anything different when you were surfing?" El asked.

"No. But I'm too busy focussing on surfing and catching that perfect wave," he grinned sheepishly. "It's pretty distracting."

Avery, Alex, and Briar backed away, giving Reuben some space. "So, how are you holding up, Briar?" Avery asked her.

"Not bad. The shop's busy, which is good. When I have spare time, I've been trying to weave some protection into my potions." She looked guilty. "I feel it's the least I can do. I want to protect the town, the people who live here. It's okay for El, she makes protection amulets, but women mostly come to me for creams and potions that have more to do with skin and smells than protection."

"That's a great idea. What about making bundles of herbs for drawers and wardrobes? They could have protection spells woven into them. Or welcome herb bundles for front doors and porches?"

Briar's face brightened. "That's a brilliant idea! I could do that! I've got so many herbs and flowers now in the allotment, it will be perfect. And I could dry them for the winter."

Avery smiled, pleased to have thought of something useful. "I'm happy to help. Why don't you make up a few and I'll sell them in my shop, too? They'd go well with the incense and tarot cards. I'll ask El for some amulets as well, and some gemstones. That way we can try to protect as many people as possible."

Alex frowned. "We have lots of foot traffic coming through the pub. Lots of locals and visitors. I'll ask the bar staff to keep an eye out for suspicious activity, and any strange news or gossip."

Briar looked relieved. "This is great. For the first time in days, I feel like we can make a positive difference."

"The thing is, though," Alex warned, "I think this is our new normal. There'll always be something happening now. If it's not this, it will be something else."

"Cheers, Alex," Avery said, looking at him in disbelief. "Just as we were feeling good."

"But this *is* good," he said. "We're finally awake and aware of the possibilities of the paranormal world. We just need to up our game."

They were distracted by Reuben's shout and he pointed overboard. They turned to see the sea churning behind them, and a strange, silvery trail started to spread from the boat towards the shore. "Nils!" Reuben yelled. "Follow the trail!"

Nils heard his shout and the throttle picked up, and they followed the trail towards the coast.

Reuben and El headed to the prow of the boat, the others right behind them. They followed the trail to the west of White Haven, a small cove out of town. As they neared the coast, Nils slowed down and they entered a deep bay, with high cliffs on either side.

"The Devil's Canyon." Reuben pointed to where the cliff face hollowed out, becoming a cave. "And that's Hades Cave. It gets pretty deep there on a full tide, and it's always dark in daytime."

The boat idled and Nils joined them, his eyes squinting against the light and looking almost icy blue in the full sun. He nodded in agreement. "No one ventures in there, except stupid kids who try to dare each other. They risk drowning. The undertow is massive."

Avery nodded. They'd all heard about this cove and the dangers of the cave. It looked ominous, even in the sunshine. The town council had attached a notice on the side of the rock face, warning of the dangers at high tide. "The perfect place for those who don't care about powerful currents though, isn't it?"

"Can you take us further in?" Reuben asked Nils.

"Entrance only," he said. "The tide's ebbing already. In fact, we really need to get back to the harbour."

"Just a quick look, then."

Nils nodded and headed back to the wheelhouse, and then they eased forward to the cave entrance, nudging just inside. Immediately, the sunshine disappeared and the temperature dropped. The heavy *glug, glug* of the water as it eddied around the cave filled the air. The back of the cave was in darkness.

Reuben reached into his pack and pulled out a huge torch. He flicked it on and trained the powerful beam on the back of the cave. The water looked dark and forbidding, and the walls were slick with moisture. A tiny strip of rock edged the back of the cave, and something on it glistened in the light, but it was unclear what it was, and Avery had the strongest sensation of being watched. She shivered, desperately wishing they could leave. And then she heard something; the lightest splash—something different than the *glug* of the water.

And then another, and another.

Alex must have heard it too, because he said softly but urgently, "Time to go."

Reuben nodded, turning off the light. He turned to Nils and gestured to go, and they eased back, out into the sunshine, heading toward the safety of White Haven.

However, Avery noticed that with the exception of Nils at the wheel, the other three men turned and looked back longingly at the cave.

16

All five witches and Newton were subdued as they sat in the courtyard of The Wayward Son, soaking up the sunshine.

They had barely spoken on the journey back to White Haven, and only Nils seemed unaffected. Avery presumed, and hoped, that in the wheelhouse he'd have been protected from what they had heard and felt. It was only now, with a pint of beer or a glass of wine in front of them, and the promise of food on the way, that they all started to relax.

"I know we've faced some pretty weird shit recently," El said, staring at each of them as if challenging them to disagree, "but that has to be the absolute worst."

"You're right, and I know we didn't see anything, but something *was* there. I could feel it. It gave me goose bumps," Avery said, shivering. "*Something* was watching us."

Briar nodded, looking into her white wine as if the answers to the universe were in there. "It felt different from anything else—demons, ghosts, dark magic, the lot. It felt … Other." She shivered as she finally settled on a word.

Alex, Reuben, and Newton remained silent, and Avery looked at them, concerned. It was Briar who had ordered the drinks, and Avery and El who had sorted seats. The guys had been suspiciously quiet, meekly doing as they were told. "Are you all right? Alex?"

He looked up and finally met her eyes. "I heard something. Something wild and inexplicable, just as we were heading out of the cove. I can't explain it. It was haunting, and—"

"Compelling," Newton finished for him. "I can still hear it." His eyes had a slightly glazed look and he glanced absently around the table. "Maybe we should go back?"

Shocked by his statement, El turned to Reuben, "And what about you?"

"I heard the soft sounds of water, and I had images, sort of, of something beneath the surface, something…" He trailed off, unable to focus.

El acted quickly. She glanced around making sure no one was close enough to witness her actions, and then flashed a short burst of fire to all three men. A jolt of flame flashed across their hands and up their arms, and they shouted in pain.

Newton yelled, "What the hell?"

"Feel better?" El asked, narrowing her eyes.

Reuben shook his head and rubbed his arms. "Wow. Ouch! What the hell was that for? It seems unnecessary."

"Was it?" El asked incredulous. "Because you were all in thrall to something. Not fully, but definitely not your normal selves."

Alex and Newton seemed to focus on their surroundings for the first time since they had arrived.

"I do *not* remember getting here," Alex said, looking around with confusion and concern.

"Me, neither. I just felt really sleepy, actually," Newton said. "Did I doze off? Did someone just burn me?" he asked the table in general.

"Oh, crap," said Avery, incredulous. "In the space of seconds at that cave entrance, you were all enthralled to Mermaids. I mean, seriously. How can that happen? I didn't hear a thing."

Briar agreed. "It's reassuring that we didn't, but worrying that you did. Thank the Gods you didn't dive in."

El frowned, still playing with the flames at the end of her hands. "We need to protect you from their call."

"But how?" Alex asked, bewildered. "I'm not particularly thrilled by it, either. I don't want to become a bloody Merman."

"Does anyone?" Reuben asked, looking around the table. "It's making me think twice about surfing. In fact, I can't believe surfers haven't been attacked yet, but I guess we don't surf in deep water."

"That's a good point," Avery said, frowning. "Maybe deep water is their preferred way of luring men, but then why would they walk on land?"

"There's just too much about them we don't know," El mused. "But so far, both of the boat attacks were at night, so maybe they're put off by daylight. And maybe that's what protects the surfers."

"We must search our grimoires," Reuben said. "There has to be something we can use. And maybe the Council will have some suggestions, too."

Avery looked at him, surprised. "I really didn't expect to hear you say that, Reuben!"

"I know. I've changed my mind about them. You were right. We should learn from them. How else do we grow?"

At this point, the whole table looked at him in shock. He laughed at their expressions and shrugged. "I've been doing some thinking, that's all. And I don't want to end up as a Mermaid mate, no matter how much I love the sea."

From the depths of her bag, Avery's phone started to ring, and she fished around in the bottom quickly, surprised to see Eve's name. "Hey, Eve," she answered quickly, leaving the table so as not to disturb the others. "How are things?"

"So, so," she answered, her voice strained. "I just thought you should know that we've found some dead cattle at Zennor Quoit, the Neolithic burial chamber on the moors just outside of Zennor."

"Dead cattle?" she asked, puzzled. *What on Earth was Eve telling her about cattle for?*

"We're pretty sure the Nephilim have killed them. There were seven of them, all drained of blood, their bodies covered by bracken. The farmer, Carrick, noticed some of his cows were missing, but obviously had no idea to look there. One of the locals was up at the Quoit earlier on a walk, and contacted him."

Avery felt faint and slightly nauseous, and heard her pulse booming in her ears steadily. She pulled a chair out from an empty table and sat down. "Cattle? At least they're not killing humans. Is this a good sign?"

"I don't know, yes and no. That they're not killing people is good, of course, but it means they're gathering power and growing."

Avery thought quickly. St Ives wasn't that far away. It would probably be useful to go take a look. "Would you mind showing us where? I mean, is it worth us looking?"

"Sure, I thought you'd want to. I'm going, too. I know the farmer. He keeps me informed of any unusual things happening, and this *is* pretty unusual. He hasn't called the police yet, but he will. He has to. We have a small window on time, so…"

"I get it. I can come now."

"Great, I'll meet you there," Eve said. It was only when she rang off that Avery realised that Zennor was the place that had been visited by a Mermaid, too.

***

El's old Land Rover bounced along the lanes and roads to Zennor. It had taken just over an hour to get there, and she pushed the aging motor to move as quickly as possible.

In the end, four of them decided to go. Briar was working on some protection potions for her shop, Charming Balms, and Newton didn't want to interfere with the police investigation, although he really wanted to join them, so Alex, El, Reuben, and Avery made the trip without them.

Avery was lost in thought as she gazed at the moors. They had crossed to the north coast of Cornwall, and after passing through St Ives, had travelled past cultivated fields and meadows for grazing cattle. And then the fields fell away, replaced by wild moorland covered in bracken and heather, an undulating ripple of purple unbroken to the horizon, and the sea to her right.

"What does this mean, then?" Reuben asked, raising his voice so that Avery and Alex could hear him in the back.

"I hope it means they're not going to become cold-blooded murderers," Alex answered.

"Again," Avery tempered. "Five deaths are enough."

"But, it would have been easy for them to kill humans again," Alex argued. "It suggests they have a conscience."

"I suppose so," Avery said reluctantly. "I'm not exactly going to start celebrating, yet."

"Interesting that the cattle were slaughtered at Zennor Quoit though," Alex said, raising his eyebrows. "It's an old burial ground, with a long history of death and spiritual significance to the area."

Avery nodded. "True. Do you think it has significance to them, though?"

"Well, they're old. It may mean something to them to kill at such a place. They are the children of angels, after all, if we're to believe the myths."

"Didn't you ask them about their lineage during your little one-on-one?" Reuben asked Alex, smirking.

"Not really, no," he answered, dryly. "I had other priorities. Plus, I really didn't dictate the conversation."

"Maybe they ritualised the deaths," Avery mused.

"Let's hope this place will tell us something, then," Alex said.

"It's quite a long way to take cattle," El chipped in. "They must have flown them there."

"And I doubt the cattle would have been quiet, either," Reuben added.

They fell silent, and it wasn't long before they passed through the small village of Zennor, and then headed onto a tiny lane that led to the moors. Miles of bracken and heather now surrounded them on either side, and it was only a few minutes later that El pulled to a stop as the track ended at a tiny car park. An old estate car was the only other vehicle on site, and a notice pointed the way across a winding track. Avery could just make out a jumble of stones in the distance.

"It's on foot from here," El said, leaving the car and pulling on her jacket to protect her from the brisk wind that blew from the sea.

The track wasn't long, and in a few minutes they passed large rocks, some of the many that were strewn across the landscape. This land was steeped in history, marked from years of human habitation; the surrounding fields systems were pre-historic and the rocks marked ancient barrows and old settlements for miles around. Eventually, on a slight rise of land, they saw the huge jagged rocks that made up Zennor Quoit, a Neolithic burial chamber. It was quiet and eerie, the landscape all moor and sky, the only sound the wind brushing through the heathers, gorse, and bracken. It was ancient, and Avery felt the weight of the years around her. This land was special.

Two figures had their backs to them, and they turned as they approached. Avery recognised Eve, waving. She could already smell the blood and stench of decay as she led the others over.

"Hey, Avery," Eve greeted her, smiling weakly. "Great to see you. I just wish it wasn't for this." She gestured behind her to the slaughtered remains of cattle visible under the bracken. She nodded to her companion. "This is Nate. He's another witch from St Ives. That makes a grand total of two of us."

Nate muttered a soft "Hey," and shook their hands as everyone introduced themselves. In that brief word Avery thought she heard a northern accent, and estimated he was in his forties. He had short dark hair, streaked with grey. A section above each ear had been shaved, giving him a slight mohawk, and he had a short beard and light brown eyes. He wore old blue jeans tucked in biker boots, a t-shirt, and an old pilot's jacket—brown leather lined with fur. Eve wasn't dressed that differently from him, but a bright blue scarf bound her hair up and off her face, her long dreadlocks visible down her back.

Eve added, "Carrick, the farmer, was here earlier, but he's gone to the farm to get his truck. He won't be long." She looked sad, regretting the deaths for him. "He really didn't believe the cattle were his. Thought he was being told wild stories. He's pretty gutted, actually."

"Where's the person who found them?" Avery asked.

"It was a local walking his dog. He left when we arrived. He didn't want to hang around, understandably," Eve explained. "Anyway, come and look. We haven't disturbed them."

The slaughtered cattle were strewn across an area several metres wide. An attempt had been made to cover them with bracken, but they clearly hadn't meant to hide them properly. All of the cows had their throats slit and their hearts removed. Flies were buzzing around, and Avery felt bitter bile rising in her throat. But, there was very little blood anywhere. She turned into the wind and took several deep breaths before looking back at the carnage.

Alex looked at them thoughtfully. "They've been drained completely. Seven Nephilim, seven cows."

Nate whirled around. "How do you know there are *seven* Nephilim?" His accent was more obvious now, his deep voice betraying a softened Geordie tone.

"We set up a little psychic one-on-one the other night in the church, and that's what it told me."

"That's a pretty cool trick," Nate said, narrowing his eyes.

"I wouldn't recommend it," Avery said, looking at Alex, exasperated. "He scared the shit out of me. Started talking in a foreign language, probably ancient, and his eyes went white."

"It was *your* idea," Alex pointed out.

El and Reuben had left them talking and were strolling around the site, when El called out from the dolmen. "This stone has been moved. The capstone had fallen years ago, if I remember correctly."

Eve walked over, the others trailing behind. "You're right. The large, flat stone on top of the jagged one is the capstone. They put it back in place."

"Impressive lifting," Reuben said. "They've used it as a sacrificial table. There's blood all over it."

At that moment, a wild wind keened across them, and they all shivered, pulling their jackets closer. Avery eyed the table uncertainly and wrinkled her nose; the tang of blood was sharper here. The press would run wild with this, if they ever found out.

Nate hunched his shoulders and asked Alex, "So, what do they want? Did they share that with you?"

"They want to walk the Earth again. The spirit I spoke to thought they'd been cheated from life."

"So these sacrifices, what will they achieve?" Eve asked.

"We think they want to manifest in physical form, and that's why they killed those people in the church, to give them the power to change."

Avery continued, "And then Caspian and Estelle managed to give the spirit at St Luke's an extra boost the other night, and that's when it escaped."

Nate snorted. "Typical bloody Caspian. Arrogant prick."

El laughed, but without humour. "So, you're a fan, too."

"As much as anyone is on that bloody Council," Nate said, exasperated. "Eve said you made quite an impression."

"I don't know how," Avery said, confused. "I thought we'd annoyed everyone."

"Not everyone," Eve said. "Yes, you've made our life complicated, but it's shaken the Council up, and Sebastian has gone. He was a bully. That's a good thing." She shivered and looked around. "Is there anything else you want to see here? Carrick will be back soon."

Avery shook her head. "I don't think so."

While she was talking Alex leaned forward, touching the capstone and drawing his finger across the dried blood. He immediately cried out and fell to his knees, and then rolled backwards, unresponsive. His eyes were closed, but fluttering wildly.

Reuben ran over. "Shit. What now?"

Avery dropped next to Alex, the springy earth cold through her jeans. She shook his shoulder. "Alex!"

Nate pulled her hands away. "Let it run its course. He's made a connection."

Alex groaned and once again, started speaking in the strange language he had uttered the other night. For what seemed an age, but was probably only seconds, Alex muttered and writhed, a sweat breaking out on his forehead, and then he passed out.

"He needs water," Nate directed. "Anyone?"

"Here," El said, passing her bottle.

Nate lifted Alex's head carefully, and trickled some water around his lips. He then brushed his hand across Alex's brow. Alex immediately stirred and blinked a few times.

"What did you do?" Avery asked Nate.

"My mother had the Sight," he explained. "I've learnt a few tricks over the years."

Alex sat up slowly, breathing deeply. "Wow. That was intense."

"Care to share?" Nate asked, still supporting Alex's back.

"It was a warning to stay away. It knows we're here—that *I'm* here. But also some unwelcome advice. They warn that the Children of Llyr have arrived, and the Nephilim aren't happy about it." He rubbed his head. "Has anyone got any paracetamol?"

Eve crossed her arms in front of her decisively. "Right, you better come back to mine."

17

El followed Eve back along the B3306 towards St Ives, and then on through the town towards Porthmeor Beach and the small nub of land called The Island.

The streets here, like many small Cornish towns, were narrow and edged with a variety of old stone houses built over the centuries, and because of their size, some of the roads were one-way only. St Ives was known for its colony of artists and art galleries, and the streets hummed with pedestrians weaving in and out of shops, restaurants, and pubs. It had been years since Avery had visited, and she looked out of the windows curiously, noting the changes, while keeping half an eye on Alex. He was subdued, lying flat on the back seat, his head in her lap, and Avery stroked his hair and face.

Eve led them through a warren of lanes until they were on the coastal road overlooking Porthmeor Beach, and pulled into a tiny car park at the back of a row of cottages.

Eve lived in an attic studio flat above an art gallery, and while the back view was of the streets and houses, the front looked out over the beach and the wide expanse of the sea, over which was the southern coast of Ireland.

Avery had not realised Eve was an artist, but it was obvious as soon as she entered her flat. The walls were covered in artwork, either finished or in various stages of completion, and paints, pencils, brushes, pastels, canvases, books, and easels were everywhere. The windows were huge, allowing lots of light in.

Avery looked at some of the paintings, noting they were of brooding landscapes overshadowed by large expanses of sky. Close up, she could see faint images of faces skilfully disguised in the trees and hills.

Avery smiled as she looked around, feeling a kindred spirit. If possible, Eve was even more untidy than she was. The far end of the studio was set up as a living area, and three couches had been arranged around the fireplace on the end wall. It was here that Eve escorted them, settling Alex into a seat, before heading to make some tea. The kitchen was open plan, tucked in the far corner next to the living area, where there was space for a small round table and four chairs. There was a single door in the wall, which Avery presumed led to the bedroom and bathroom.

Avery sat next to Alex who had stretched out on the sofa, while Reuben looked out of the window, and Nate disappeared through the door to the side. El went to find painkillers.

"How are you?" Avery asked softly, her voice low.

Alex squinted, his eyes creased with pain. "I've been better."

"You should stop communing with spirits, then."

"He started it," Alex muttered.

El came over with a glass of water and some paracetamol. "Here you go. Nate's in the back fixing you up something a little more potent."

Alex groaned, sat up, knocked back the pills and some water, and immediately lay down again.

"Is he making a potion?" Avery asked.

El nodded, folding herself gracefully onto the floor, her legs crossed. "I believe so. He has a recipe for something that worked wonders for his mother." She nodded towards the back of the room. "Eve's spell room is back there, beyond her bedroom."

At that point they heard the kettle boil, and Eve came to join them, carrying a huge tray filled with mugs, a teapot, and a coffee pot. She placed everything on a worn wooden coffee table and sat next to El on the colourful rug on the floor.

"I wasn't sure what everyone wanted, so I made everything. And I've got biscuits."

She opened a packet of cookies and offered them around, before sorting out their drinks.

"Awesome," Reuben said, taking a handful of biscuits. "My blood sugar was dangerously low."

"You are a wonder woman," Avery declared, reaching forward to take a mug of coffee. "Thank you. It's great we didn't have to drive straight home."

"No problem. It's good to finally have a chance to talk to you properly." She grinned and looked at the others. "And to meet some more of the famous White Haven witches."

Reuben let out a short, barking laugh and sat on the other sofa, stretching out his long legs. "That's funny. Don't you mean *infamous*?"

"Maybe that would be a better word," Eve said, laughing for a moment before becoming serious again. "We live in strange times, though, so it's good to finally meet you. I'm worried about what your friend said." She nodded at Alex.

"Me, too," he agreed, groaning. "I don't think we're enemy number one anymore."

"Wait until Nate is back with his miracle cure, and then we'll talk more," Eve said. She made herself more comfortable and took a sip of her tea. "Instead, you can tell me about what you all get up to on the south coast."

For the next ten minutes they chatted idly about what they did, and then Eve explained about her work. "I do watercolours mainly, and exhibit in a few places about the town and in various shops. I rent this place long-term. I love it, the light's fantastic."

"And what about Nate?" El asked. "Is he an artist, too?"

"Yes, but he sculpts in metal mainly. He has a place across town."

"So, are you two…?" Reuben asked, meaningfully.

Eve laughed. "No. He has a girlfriend, and I'm between boyfriends right now."

"Are there any other witches in St Ives?" El asked.

Eve shook her head sadly. "No. There were three of us, but Ruth left town years ago. Neither of us are originally from here. Nate's from Newcastle, but moved down here in his early teens with his mother. She married a local after Nate's dad died when he was only a child. His step-father died, too. Nate's mother was a powerful Seer, but she passed away last year after a sudden illness. My family is originally from Glastonbury way, but I moved here on my own. St Ives is the next best place to Glastonbury, in my opinion."

Eve looked a little sad as she said that, but didn't elaborate, and Avery wondered if there was some reason she'd had to leave Glastonbury. Or some reason she wanted to.

They were interrupted then by Nate, who came out of the back room carrying a steaming cup of something fragrant. He knelt next to Alex, who was still lying down, his eyes closed.

"All right, mate. Sit up. I have something for you that'll sort you right out."

Alex squinted at him, and slowly sat up. "I'll believe it when it works."

"It'll work all right," he said, passing him the small, steaming cup.

Alex took a tentative sip and grimaced.

"What is that?" Avery asked, inhaling deeply. "It smells delicious, just like summer."

"I can assure you it does not taste like that," Alex said, wrinkling his face in distaste.

"Interesting you think that," Nate said, addressing Avery and ignoring Alex. "It's called Summer Lightning. It's been fine-tuned for centuries."

"You should share that with Briar. She's our healer— she'd love it."

"Sure. I don't jealously guard my spells like some," Nate said evenly.

"Are you a Seer, like your mother?" El asked him.

He shook his head. "No. That has skipped my generation. Probably a blessing." He looked at Alex. "It's not easy to bear. Especially when your Sight wakes fully."

Alex looked at him. "What do you mean, wakes fully?"

"Yours is just starting, mate. I can tell. The Sight can lie dormant for years, or just turns on and off in fits and starts. But then, for some, something triggers it, and when that happens, it's a battle to stop it."

Avery felt a thread of worry start to run through her, and Alex stopped drinking his potion and looked at her, and then back to Nate. "You mean these things will start to happen more often?"

"Have they been more often lately?"

"I guess so," Alex said thoughtfully.

"I thought so. I can tell. Maybe it's the tail end of my mother's sense. Things might get rough for a while. You'll need to learn to close it off."

"I will?"

171

"Unless you want to go nuts," Nate said. "Which, I presume, you don't."

"Great. Just great," Alex said, and forced himself to take another sip. "Any tips?"

"I may have a few," he said. "When you feel better, we can talk some more."

Avery liked Nate and Eve. They were friendly and down to earth, and didn't seem to harbour any resentment towards any of them, despite the fact that they had released a cloud of powerful magic and caused some degree of havoc across Cornwall. She felt she knew Eve a little from their brief meetings at the Council, but despite knowing a little bit about Nate from Eve, he still seemed a mystery. He'd shed his leather jacket, revealing an old New Model Army t-shirt full of holes, and up close she could see a slight singeing to his jeans. *Sparks from fire for his sculpting*, she presumed. He wasn't aloof at all, but she couldn't read him as well as Eve.

"And what about you, Nate? What's *your* strength?" Avery asked, looking at him curiously.

He fixed his light brown eyes on her. "Fire, which makes sculpting easier, and telekinesis, of all things. And of course, potions."

There was a brief second of silence in which even Reuben stopped crunching. "Telekinesis?"

Nate nodded. "I barely have to think it, and…" He held his hand out towards the collection of brushes on a nearby table, and in seconds they had lifted into the air, whizzed across the room, and landed in his outstretched hand.

Reuben swallowed loudly. "Wow. It takes a lot of effort for me to do that."

"I have to summon air to do that," Avery said, agreeing with Reuben.

Nate shrugged and looked mildly embarrassed. "What can I say? It's a gift."

"Impressive." El turned to Eve. "And what about you?"

Eve's expression was bright and slightly mischievous. "I'm a weather witch. Of course, I have elemental powers, but they combine to manipulate weather particularly well. However, I don't do that often. It plays havoc everywhere." She gestured to the artwork spread around the room, and Avery suddenly realised why all of her artwork was of stormy landscapes.

Avery had never met a weather witch. It took great control to manipulate huge systems of water, wind, and fire, and weather was a combination of all those things, particularly storms. The chance that they could get out of control was magnified on a huge scale.

"Wanna do swapsies?" Alex asked, still grimacing from a combination of the potion and his lingering headache.

"No, thanks. The Sight does not appeal to me."

Mention of the Sight reminded Avery of something the Nephilim had said. "Alex, the spirit said the Children of Llyr have arrived. They must know Mermaids are here, on land."

He nodded. "I don't know how they know, though."

"It must be like Briar said—the earth trembles because they're here. Maybe they sense that."

"Maybe," Nate said, "the earth trembles because the Nephilim are here."

"True," Avery admitted. "Eve, if needed, is your magic strong enough to drive the Mermaids back to sea? Especially combined with Reuben's ability to manipulate water?"

Eve gazed into her cup and swirled her tea around, releasing steam and scents of cardamom and ginger, before she finally looked up. "I doubt it. While the weather can influence tides and obviously waves during storms, I'm not

173

sure how effective it would be against Mermaids. The water is their strength, their habitat, not ours. It would probably be best to fight them on land. An earth witch would have greater power there."

"Maybe. We just know so little about them. It's infuriating!" Avery exclaimed, feeling hopeless all over again.

Nate frowned. "Are you sure they're on land? How do you know?"

"Well, Oswald said Ulysses could tell in Mevagissey. And then this morning, we found out that three fishermen disappeared overnight, and their empty boat was found drifting this morning. Reuben traced Mermaids to the Devil's Canyon, a small cove outside White Haven. We're pretty sure they're now in the town. We need to find a way to identify them, before any more men disappear."

"You should speak to Ulysses about that," Eve said.

"Really? Why's that? Is he a Mermaid detector?" Reuben asked.

Nate looked at Eve as if weighing whether to tell them something, and then said, "Rumours are that Ulysses has Mermaid blood inside him."

Avery almost dropped her mug in shock. "What? How does that happen?"

"Oswald doesn't talk about it, and neither does Ulysses. But those are the rumours. And if you'd ever met him, you'd know why."

"Has he got scales or something?" Reuben asked, only half joking.

Nate shook his head. "I'm saying nothing. It will be a surprise."

"Okay," Avery said, wearily. "One more thing to add to my list. I presume you aren't worried about Mermaids in St Ives?"

Nate shook his head. "No. But we're not the ones with a big cloud of magic over us. Maybe it's just the south coast of Cornwall that will be affected." He looked at Alex. "Apart from the warning, what else did the Nephilim say? What was the general tone?"

Alex thought for a second. "I can only guess that the blood on the capstone must have triggered it. As soon as I touched it, I felt an intense flood of emotions. I immediately connected to the spirit I linked with last time. I recognised him straightaway, and he knew me." He hesitated and then said, "I think that he had no control over our linking, either. It seemed to me there was a few seconds when he didn't register that I was there at all and his feelings were unguarded. I could see through his eyes, too. He was somewhere dark and damp, and there was a smell around him that I couldn't quite place. I sensed his joy at being released, but also anger and fear. I guess the fear is from us, and the fact that they know we are looking for them, but also there was anger about the Mermaids. Anyway, the connection was short but intense. As soon as it recognised me, I could feel him mentally trying to shake me, and he warned me to stay away. The more I think about it, actually," he mused, "the more I realise how much he was thinking about Mermaids. His thoughts were full of them."

El frowned. "That's pretty scary, Alex, that you could connect so strongly."

"I know. Anyway, the shock was huge for both of us, but after a few seconds he was able to cut it. *After* warning me to back off."

"I think that you should be able to connect again," Nate said. "If you want to."

"I'm not sure I do," Alex said, finally draining his cup. "What do the Nephilim have against the Children of Llyr?"

175

Avery's grin broadened as a realisation hit her. "The Flood, of course, when the seas rose across the land, wiping the Nephilim from existence. God wanted to eradicate them and used Llyr to do it. I guess that's a pretty big score to settle."

18

When they arrived back in White Haven, Avery left Alex at his flat where he was heading for an early night. Nate's potion seemed to be working, but the psychic link with the Nephilim had left him drained.

As soon as she entered her own flat, she smelled smoke and violets. *Helena.* She looked around, wondering if she'd manifest, but other than her smell, there was no evidence of her. Avery wasn't sure if that was a good thing or not. She'd warded her bedroom against her presence, but otherwise, Helena was free to drift in and out as she pleased. She knew it was odd, especially as Helena had tried to kill her, but she couldn't bring herself to banish her completely. She was connected to her. She was family, after all.

Avery flung open the door and windows, letting the cool evening breeze drift through the rooms in an attempt to get rid of Helena's scent. Circe and Medea were pleased to see her, and rubbed against her ankles affectionately. She rubbed their silky heads and headed to the kitchen to feed them, before curling up on the sofa in the attic with a collection of books on history and myths and legends. She intended to gather every bit of information she could on the Nephilim and the Children of Llyr.

She'd only been reading for an hour or so when her lamps flickered, the music she'd been listening to stopped, and the scent of violets returned, and Helena manifested abruptly in front of her. She was wrapped in her dark cloak, a peek of her long dress beneath, and her dark hair flowed down her back and over her shoulders. She was not as *solid* as she had appeared beneath All Souls, and Avery could see through her to the room behind. Nevertheless, Helena's intense stare was unnerving; the narrowed glare of furious dark eyes that had seen who knows what in the spirit world.

Avery met her gaze, refusing to flinch. "Helena. Nice of you to stop by. Can I help you?"

It was ridiculous to speak to her; Avery knew she couldn't answer, but what else should she do? She couldn't just ignore her.

Helena's gaze was imperious and slightly resentful. It seemed she hadn't forgiven Avery for regaining control of her body, and Avery had no intention of letting her in again. Her eyes fell to Avery's neck and the amulet that El had made her recently, to protect against spirits. She drew her lips back in a snarl.

"Calm down, Helena. This isn't meant for you. What do you want?"

Helena pointed to the table where the grimoires lay. Immediately her grimoire, the original, flipped open and the pages turned rapidly, fluttering like wings before they finally stopped. Helena turned to Avery, hands on her hips.

Intriguing.

"All right. I'll bite," Avery said, unfolding from beneath the papers and heading to the grimoire. Helena hovered behind her left shoulder as Avery conjured a witch light.

The spell in front of her was old, located towards the beginning of the book. This meant it was probably written in the 14th century. The writing was cramped, the language difficult and archaic, and the illustrations obscure. And there, revealed by the witch light, was an image of a Mermaid perched on a rock. She had a beautiful face surrounded by long, flowing hair, and her long fishtail was coiled around her, detailed with tiny scales, but her smile was filled with razor-sharp teeth.

Avery gasped. *A spell about Mermaids.* She turned around to see Helena's predatory smile spread across her face. "Thank you, Helena." But Helena was already vanishing, leaving just a trace of violets behind.

Avery tried to decipher the spell's writing. The title said *Geyppan Merewif.* She turned to the shelf behind her, fingers grazing the reference books until she found the one she wanted, an Old English Dictionary. A few minutes of searching found the meaning. It meant essentially, "To Expose the Water Witch."

Avery grinned. A spell to reveal a Mermaid. If they couldn't banish them, at least they could see them, and that was a start. She pulled the grimoire towards her, grabbed a pen and started to translate the spell.

***

The next morning, despite only a couple of hours' sleep, Avery bounced into Happenstance Books. It had taken hours, but she had finally deciphered the arcane spell, and now she had a way to reveal the Mermaids. She needed to speak to Briar for help with some of the herbs.

She brewed a strong coffee and then walked around her shop, renewing protection spells, and the spell to help visitors find that special book, lit incense, and generally stoked the magic, so that by the time Dan arrived, the place hummed with energy.

Dan loped in through the front door, wearing his university t-shirt and jeans, and a messenger bag slung over his shoulder. He looked around the shop and then at her with narrowed eyes. "You must have had a good Sunday."

"I had an excellent Sunday, thank you. Did you?"

"Pretty good—pub lunch, a walk along the beach, played some football. But enough about me," he said, setting his bag down on the counter by the till. "What have you been up to?"

"I've been researching Mermaids, and have had a little success. I might actually have a way to identify them now." She looked at him speculatively. "I don't suppose you've seen any new women around town, have you?"

He groaned. "Are you kidding? There are loads! It's summer. There are positively gaggles of them, all giggling and surfing and drinking. I got chatted up tons last night. It was great." He grinned, and then his face fell. "Hold on. Are you saying I was being chatted up by *Mermaids*?"

Avery shrugged. "I don't know. But after yesterday, we know they're here, in town somewhere. Didn't you hear about the missing fishermen?"

Dan nodded sadly. "Yeah, I did. It's pretty crap. I didn't know them, but I know friends of them. You think it was Mermaids?"

"It was a calm night, they were in an area not known for the best fishing, and far away from the other boats. We think they were lured there, and then…" She didn't need to finish the sentence.

Dan sat heavily on the stool behind the counter. Fortunately, they had the shop to themselves. "Are they *that* powerful?"

Avery nodded. "We think we found where they've come ashore—the cave in Devil's Canyon Cove. Within seconds they had bewitched Alex, Reuben, and Newton. Not enough to make them jump overboard, but they were distracted, vague—dreamy," she said, searching for a better word. "For some reason Nils was spared, probably because he was at the front of the boat. But," a sudden flash of worry flashed through her mind. "Maybe we should check, just in case."

"And all they want is men? Mates?"

"Yes, we think so. We also think that the magic we released has attracted them here. I suppose like anything that's supernatural, they have their own magic, but are drawn to the magic of others, too. But they're not of the Earth. They are *Other*."

Dan's bright and breezy attitude had disappeared. "For the last few days, there have been about half a dozen long-haired, long-legged young beauties flirting the night away at The Kraken, just off the harbour. They've been attracting men like flies around shit. Including myself. Now that I think about it, it does seem weird. I mean, people flirt in pubs all the time, but these girls exude glamour, confidence. I wonder?" He looked into the middle distance, lost in his thoughts for a second. "I must admit, when you're close by them, it's hard to look away. But, well, they're attractive and funny. It's not that unusual."

Avery fell silent, thinking and watching Dan. "It's a big pub, isn't it? Pretty loud, bands on sometimes?"

"Oh, yeah. It's not the pub I usually go in, actually, it's a bit full-on for me, but my mate, Pete, wanted to go in Saturday night. It has a big party vibe on a weekend, lots of young people out to have fun. One of *those* pubs."

Avery nodded. She knew exactly what he meant. It was the type of pub she usually avoided, too. But maybe she should make an exception. She ran through all the pubs in White Haven. There were quite a few, a mixture of family pubs, upscale bars, chain pubs, those who catered for all sorts, like The Wayward Son, and then there were the party pubs that only wanted singles or couples. Kids were actively discouraged. There were only a few that would fit that description. The Kraken, The Flying Fish, and The Badger's Hat. If she were a predatory female, looking for the biggest selection of young men who'd be drinking, up for fun, flirting, and sex with no strings attached, those would be the pubs that would offer the biggest pool of men to choose from. And she presumed they *were* choosing them. If Avery could perfect the spell, then she could try it out, maybe tomorrow.

Avery looked up at Dan. "Can you spare me for a few hours?"

"I guess so." He looked momentarily confused. "I thought you were worried about Nephilim?"

"Oh, I'm worried about both now."

"Great, just great," he murmured. "Bring me coffee and cake when you come back."

***

As usual, Briar's shop smelled divine. This time it was the scent of basil, rosemary, and...*what?* And then it struck Avery. Tomatoes—fresh, sun-warmed tomatoes. *Delicious.*

Briar looked up and smiled, and then went back to serving her customer, putting the finishing touches on her wrapping.

There were already quite a few customers drifting around the displays, trying out lotions, and sniffing soaps. Another customer, a young woman, carried some creams to the counter, so Avery strolled around the shop, trying out hand creams while she waited.

When Briar was finally free, she joined her at the counter. "What are you doing with tomatoes, Briar?"

"You can smell them? Oh, good. Gardeners' soaps. It's a new range. Delicious, isn't it? And a little something to soothe the joints, too," she said conspiratorially.

"Nice! Well, I know you're busy, but I wondered if you had a couple of dried plants I can have. They're not that common. Well, I haven't got them, anyway."

Briar frowned. "Such as?"

"Agrimony root and Blessed Thistle leaves."

"Follow me." She headed through a door into a room at the back of the shop, and the pungent smell of plants hit Avery like a hammer. The room was filled from floor to ceiling with shelves, and on them were jars and baskets stocked with dried herbs, tinctures, fatty creams, roots, cuttings, and real plants in pots. Everything was meticulously labelled. Above their head were rows of wooden beams, and hanging from them were bunches of drying plants. A long bench ran beneath a window, a little bit like in El's shop, and empty jars sat there, waiting to be filled, as well as ribbons and bags for decoration.

"Wow," Avery said, looking around. "Very impressive."

"I need a lot of stock," Briar explained. She pulled a short step-ladder towards her and used it to reach a small brown jar, and then headed to another shelf and pulled down a bundle of roots. She carefully carried them to the counter, pulled a strand free of the roots, and placed it in a paper bag. Then she measured out a small thimbleful of the dried plant from the brown bottle. "This is strong, so I trust you're using it sparingly. What are you doing with it?"

Avery lowered her voice. "Trying to identify Mermaids."

Briar's eyes widened. "Do you need help?"

Avery thought for a second. "Yes, please. I don't want to take Alex, or any of the men, actually."

Briar nodded. "So what's the plan?"

"I have a spell to unveil Mermaids, but I need to be close by them to use it. I have a few places to try. Which reminds me. Have you got something to aerosolise my potion?"

"Like an old fashioned perfume dispenser?" Briar asked, reaching to the shelf above her and grabbing a beautiful, cut-glass dispenser with gold edging, a fancy purple pump at the top.

"Perfect! You fancy meeting me for a pub crawl after work tomorrow? We'll start at The Flying Fish."

"I'm intrigued. Consider it done. And El?"

"I'll ask her, too. So, another two bottles, please."

***

Before Avery headed back to the shop, she decided to visit James. He had no idea that the spirit had vacated All Souls, and she knew he'd want to use the church again. She hoped he wasn't going to ask her awkward questions.

He opened the door to the vicarage and frowned. "Avery, has something happened?"

"Good news only, you'll be pleased to know."

Relief washed over his face. "Excellent, come in, the kettle's on." He turned and led the way to a large kitchen at the back of the house, overlooking a small square garden filled with children's toys. "Tea?"

"I'm sorry, I can't stay," she said. *Hopefully the less time she spent there, the less awkward questions he might ask.* "I've got to get back to my shop."

"Of course," he nodded, pouring hot water into the teapot. "So, what happened with the spirit?"

"It's gone."

He paused mid-pour. "Gone? How? Where? When?"

Should she lie and say Alex had banished it? That might have repercussions later.

"I don't know where." *That was true.* "Sometimes spirits just disappear back to where they came from, or it may have gone somewhere else. But we checked the church yesterday, and it's safe," she said vaguely.

"But, I thought spirits usually remained in one place, somewhere familiar to them."

"Usually, but not always. However, I don't think you need to worry. I'm sure it wasn't responsible for Harry's death after all, and that it was just a horrible coincidence. The police are still investigating."

"Well, how do you know it isn't just hiding again? And how did you get in?" His voice was rising with annoyance.

Oh shit. "Look James. I can't explain everything to you, but trust me, it's gone. Me and Alex have ways of investigating these things."

James fell silent for a second, studying her. "Why do I get the feeling you're not being honest with me?"

"I'm being as honest as I can. But I can confidently say that you can safely use All Souls again." She smiled tentatively. "Hopefully this will be the last time you'll have a restless spirit in All Souls. We'll keep monitoring the local area, just in case it's gone somewhere else."

He narrowed his eyes. "You know there was a death in Harecombe too?"

"Yes, but no reports of spirits," she said, hoping the vicar there hadn't felt a presence. Surely not, or they'd have heard about it. "Anyway, I better go. I just wanted you to know the church is safe again."

"You know what some of the town believes about you, Avery?"

She felt her heart start to pound, and she took a deep breath. "Yes, I know. Because of the things in my shop and my ancestor, people think I'm a witch. This town runs on rumours of magic. That's how we make our money, you know that."

"Where there's smoke, there's fire," he said, watching her intently.

"Not always," she said evenly. "And you came to me, remember."

"I accept there are many things in this world I don't understand, Avery. I needed help. Maybe desperation was my weakness."

"Not a weakness. You needed help and I gave it, and will do again. You can trust me. If anything else happens let me know."

And before he could ask anything else, she left.

***

When Avery dutifully arrived back at Happenstance Books, she carried fresh pastries, Dan's weakness, and lattes. She spent the rest of the day serving customers and reviewing the instructions to the spell in her head, and as soon as the day was done, she headed up to the attic to start. She lit the fire in the small brick fireplace, stoking it until it burned hot and bright. Then she pulled out the cauldron she kept for such work, and set it on her wooden table. Finally, she started to assemble her ingredients.

It was hours later when Avery finally finished, and the potion was now simmering down. Her stomach grumbled, and it was already becoming dark out. The dormer windows were open, and the scent of summer and dust drifted in. Beyond, just visible in the grey twilight, bats swooped for insects. She sighed with pleasure, and once again thought on how much she loved White Haven, and would do anything to keep it safe.

She headed down to the kitchen to feed the cats, now watching her with resentment, and to make some toast, bringing it back up with her to watch the potion like a hawk. One wrong move now and she'd have to start again.

She sat on the rug, eating absently, when her phone rang and she saw Ben's number.

"Hey, Ben. How are you three doing after Saturday night?"

His voice sounded excited, which was a relief. "We're great, thanks, just psyched about the whole night and really pleased with some of our footage. If you're free tomorrow, you should come round to the office we've got set up."

"Sounds intriguing. I think I could do that. Where's your office?"

"We've bagged a room at the university. It's small and poky, but better than nothing."

"Sure—can anyone else come?"

"Whoever's interested," Ben said.

"Cool. Mid-morning okay?" she asked, thinking she could get back and relieve her staff for lunchbreaks afterward.

"Perfect. See you then."

Avery knew most of the others would be working, but Alex might be free in the morning. She called him, looking forward to hearing his voice. It rang half a dozen times before he picked up, and she could hear music from the pub. "Hello, gorgeous," he answered.

"Hello gorgeous, yourself. You busy?"

"Hold on," he shouted, and then the sounds disappeared and she realised he must have moved into the kitchen area behind the bar. "Sorry, had to move. Yes, very. It's a sign tourist season has hit. How about you?"

"The usual. Look, I won't keep you, but do you want to come with me to see our friendly neighbourhood ghost busters tomorrow morning? At the Uni in Penryn?"

"Yeah, why not. Any chance I could come to yours tonight? I can finish in another couple of hours."

She felt the warm pleasure at seeing him flood through her. "That sounds great. Do you need anything? Food, drink?"

"Just you."

She felt her heart skip a beat and she smiled. "Well, I'm all yours."

"Later, then," he said, and rang off, leaving her grinning at the cats like a lovesick fool.

19

Penryn University was a well-designed mixture of old buildings and new, set in green fields close to Falmouth, a town on the south coast of Cornwall.

Alex and Avery arrived close to 10:00 AM, pulling onto the visitors' car park in Alex's Alfa Romeo Spider Boat Tail. The day was overcast but muggy, and they had driven with the roof down and music blaring, both of them singing loudly and laughing all the way.

As Alex parked, Avery called Ben to let him know that they'd arrived, then they checked the map on the visitors' board and strolled across the campus to the entrance of the Pendennis Building where Ben had agreed to meet them. There were very few students around. It was the summer holidays, and the university had opened up for summer school and short courses only.

They approached a dark red stone building, the large windows glinting with reflected sunlight. Ben was leaning on the wall, scrolling through his phone as he waited. He looked rumpled, occasionally running his hand through his short dark hair. His Penryn University t-shirt was creased, his jeans had dropped from his waist and were perched on his hips, and his feet were barely in some old green Adidas trainers. He looked up and grinned when he heard them approach, put his phone away, and shook Alex's hand. "Hi, guys. Glad you could come. You're going to love our stuff," he said, leading them inside.

The interior of the building was modern. The entrance was huge, and bright artwork decorated the expanse of white walls. Granite tiles covered the floors, and a sleek staircase was in the centre, next to the lifts.

"I didn't know you had office space," Avery said, looking around with interest.

Ben headed to the lifts, and pressed the button. "We didn't until about a month ago, when my website really started to take off, and we got lots of referrals. I approached my tutor and stressed that what I was doing was fundamental research, and after all, that is what this building—and this university—is all about. Obviously there's a central research area we all use, but I wanted my own space." He dropped his voice. "He wasn't very happy or very eager to help, but one of the other research projects had just been canned, and the semester had ended, so I argued I should have the spare room. And since it's the holidays, no one's here."

The lift *pinged* as it arrived, and they stepped in, Ben pressing the button for the fourth floor.

"Well, I guess congratulations are in order," Alex said, looking vaguely impressed.

"We've only got it for six months," Ben shrugged, "but it's better than nothing. We'll set up in my flat afterwards if we have to."

When they arrived at the fourth floor, Ben led them through a maze of halls and doors, passing room after room, until they came to the end of the corridor at the back of the building. He flung open the door. "Ta da!"

The room beyond was small, with a tall, narrow window on the far wall looking out over a mixture of buildings and fields. In the distance was a glimpse of the sea and the sprawling town of Falmouth. The room was packed with workbenches, a desk, computers and electronic equipment, huge white boards filled with pictures and scribbled writing, and the hum of electricity buzzed in the air. In the middle of all this were Dylan and Cassie, staring at monitors.

"Welcome," Ben declared. "*Mi casa es su casa!*"

"So, this is where you investigate all the things that go bump in the night?" Alex said, looking around with amusement.

Avery prodded him in the ribs. "This is pretty cool! And exciting."

Dylan slid the earphones he'd been wearing around his neck. "Make us feel legit. I'm going to have business cards printed next."

Cassie laughed. "Your faces are a picture, but he's not kidding. Over the last few days, we've decided we're going to make a go of this."

"Come in," Ben said, shutting the door behind them and ushering them to some spare seats.

"But I thought you were doing post-grad studies, and had—" Avery floundered for the right word, "*other* careers planned."

"When you study parapsychology this *is* the perfect career," Cassie said, leaning back in her swivel chair. "I mean, of course we'll finish our post-grad studies, obviously, but I only had vague plans of what to do with it. Research, of some sort. This is the perfect fit."

"Seriously?" Alex said, looking at her, baffled. "You looked massively spooked at the castle the first time we met."

"It was a shock, I admit that. None of us had ever seen anything on that scale before."

"And potentially won't again," Avery tempered, feeling she needed to add some reason to the conversation. "Ghosts don't normally manifest like that."

"True," Cassie agreed. "But I came back, didn't I?"

Dylan was perched on the end of his chair, his right foot on his knee. The screen next to him appeared to be showing an audio file that he'd paused halfway through. "We know that not every event will be as big as the stuff we've seen recently. Don't worry, we're not getting the wrong idea. But there's way more out there than I realised. And knowing you, and what you are—it's opened our minds to all sorts of things. We're going to be a bit more than just ghost-hunters."

"You are?" Alex asked.

"And we'd like your help," Cassie added.

"You would?" Avery asked, glancing at Alex.

"Nothing that would unveil your identify," Ben tried to reassure them.

"I'm not Batman," Alex said, looking amused.

"No, just a paranoid witch," Dylan said. He held his hands up in mock surrender as Alex glared at him. "I get it, just saying!"

Ben stepped in. "Hold on. We're getting ahead of ourselves. Can we show you some stuff first?"

"Of course you can," Avery said, trying to ignore Alex bristling next to her. "We're all ears."

"First things first. Don't go summoning any of your witchy magic in this room—unless we ask you to. Our stuff's pretty sensitive, and we don't want you shorting it out."

"No problem," Avery said, nodding.

"Great. So, Dylan—want to roll the video?"

Dylan turned to one of the computers behind him. "This video is from the other night at St Luke's. I've edited it a bit…the first part didn't show much. It's in infrared, so the

192

dark blue and green colours indicate cold, and yellows, reds and oranges are heat."

It was odd to see themselves as thermal images. The church was in shades of blue, while their bodies were rendered in a strange, orangey hue, particularly their heads, where they were warmest.

"It's interesting," Cassie said, looking at them, "that all you witches look a brighter range than we do—redder, actually. I think it must be your magic."

"You're right," Alex agreed, nodding. "That is interesting."

"When you use magic, the flare of heat is even greater," Dylan explained. "I think it's the energy you summon, the way you manipulate the elements—or whatever it is you do. I'm going to have to ask you more about that one day."

Great. Now they wanted to study them. Avery had no idea how she felt about that. Surely the magic of magic was its unknowability. She wasn't sure she wanted it reduced to science and graphs. But, on the other hand, the footage *was* fascinating.

For a while, nothing much happened onscreen as they moved around the church, and Alex prepared the circle. They could see the flare of the candle flames and the bright buzz of energy around Avery when she lit the candles using magic, and the glow from the light bulbs.

And then the Nephilim arrived.

"Here," Ben pointed. "You can see a shape behind the altar, a slightly paler blue than the surroundings. Turn the audio up, Dylan."

Again the thermal imaging showed the wide sweep of wings, and they could hear a whining buzz of static as the electric lights started to flash and then overload and blow out, showing as very bright, orangey-red pulses on film. The sound of shouts filled the air, and the zap of magic buzzed again and again. The Nephilim started to get brighter in colour, too, swelling with power, and they saw Caspian sail across the room, caught by the Nephilim's wings. When Estelle started to throw balls of energy at it, it was immediately obvious that it absorbed every single one, becoming brighter and brighter as it grew. When Caspian joined in, they could see its limbs forming out of what was an almost shapeless blob with wings before.

"Wow," Avery said. "That's amazing. I mean, I know, I was there. I saw it happening, but to see it again like this! You can actually see it absorb Estelle and Caspian's magic."

Ben grinned. "I know. This is way better than we expected. Watch this," he said, pointing back to the screen.

Everyone was now back in the circle, except for Alex and Avery, who had left it to get Caspian and Estelle. *They had only just made it*, Avery thought, feeling a chill run through her as the Nephilim advanced on them. They saw the punch that Alex threw at Caspian, the bright burst of blood from Caspian's nose, and then a huge red flare as Avery activated the circle, creating a wall of protective magic around them.

"And that's your magic, Avery," Cassie said admiringly. "That thing can't get close."

The Nephilim stalked around the outside, and then flared brighter again as it headed for the window and smashed through. A wave of yellow flashed across the walls, and then faded.

"That's the spell breaking that sealed the church," Alex noted. He leaned back in his chair, exhaling heavily. "That's actually amazing, to see magic and elemental energy as infrared. And the Nephilim absorbing it."

All three of the paranormal investigators grinned. Dylan said, "I've isolated some of the audio. Listen."

He turned to another computer and played the audio he had displayed on the screen. Over the whine of static they heard a strange, guttural language.

"That's the language Alex was speaking the other night!" Avery said.

"Yep. I recognise that," he agreed.

"I can't believe you've captured that."

"That's all we've got," Ben said, "seconds only. Any idea what it says?"

"Not a clue," Alex said, shaking his head.

"Have you noticed how much brighter your energy is, compared to Caspian's and Estelle's?" Cassie pointed out.

"I suppose it is," Avery said, watching the screen closely. "Must be our new influx of magic."

"Anyway," Ben said, "we have some more footage to show you of some other places we've been. Nothing as good as this, but stuff that happened in different houses around Cornwall. We thought you might like to see some of the spirit activity we've captured."

"Sounds good," Alex said. "But first, you said you wanted to ask us something. What did you want?"

Ben glanced at Cassie and Dylan. "We wondered if we set up a paranormal business, could you help us, if we needed a bit of support with any cases? We'd pay you, of course. We're going to charge for this. Or could you recommend someone who could help?" He looked slightly perplexed. "You know, most of the time, it should just be us recording and observing, but we could offer a service, too—to banish unwanted spirits, ghouls, dark magic…" He trailed off, looking hopeful.

Alex glanced at Avery. "I don't mind helping, but I'm pretty busy at the pub, and I'm guessing Avery's pretty busy at the shop, but we could have a think to see if there's someone who could help more often than us."

"Awesome, thanks guys," Ben said, relieved.

"After what we've seen, it would be good to have some support," Cassie added.

"We could probably teach you some simple protection and banishing spells, nothing that needed too much magic," Avery said, already thinking of some basic spells that would work.

"Great! Thank you."

And then Avery had another idea. "You know, I was talking to Briar the other day. She's pretty busy at her shop. She doesn't have help like we do, but I get the feeling she was thinking about looking. Obviously she wants someone trustworthy."

"Me!" Cassie said immediately. "I'd love to help, and it's a great opportunity to learn."

Avery smiled. "Cool. I can't promise anything, but I will talk to her for you."

"Right," Ben said. "Let's show you what else we've been up to."

20

At 7:30 PM that night, Avery was dressed in her heels, skinny jeans, and a slinky top, ready to meet Briar and El for a night out, identifying Mermaids.

After she and Alex had left Penryn in the afternoon, they both headed to work. She had decided to lie to Alex about her plans for the night. She knew he would disapprove and worry.

"I'm just having a quiet night in, catching up with some reading and spell casting."

"Well, I'm working, so have fun."

"If a gaggle of young, nubile women come to your pub, looking improbably glamorous, be on your guard."

"Spoilsport," he said, winking. He dropped her outside of her flat and pulled her close for a lingering kiss. "I'll see you soon."

She spent the remainder of the workday in the shop, and once she was back in her flat, filled the three perfume bottles with the finished potion. She held one up to the light, admiring the pale amber colour. It was always satisfying to successfully complete a spell. *Let's hope it works.* She then fed the cats, grabbed her leather bag, and headed out the door.

Avery strolled through the streets and down to the harbour, enjoying the evening's warmth. Down by the harbour, the smell of brine and seaweed was strong, and she inhaled deeply, feeling invigorated by it. The tide was low, and the boats were half beached. The fish and chip shops were doing a brisk business, and people were perched on the sea wall, eating chips from paper. The scent of the food, and the underlying sharp smell of vinegar, mixed with the salty air of the sea made her smile; she was comforted by the reassuring scents. This was the White Haven she loved.

She was meeting El and Briar at The Flying Fish, the pub perched on the rise of the hill overlooking the harbour, on the road that ran next to the beach. She paused outside it and looked up. It was a large pub, set back slightly from the pavement, allowing a few tables to be set up outside. But it was the large, first floor deck that was the busiest, and the sound of music and the chatter of people filled the air from above. The deck provided shelter for the ground floor seating, and it was edged with pots of greenery and strings of lights. Avery weaved through the already crowded tables, looking for groups of women, but most people on the ground floor were couples or small groups of three or four, both men and women.

Avery headed upstairs, and the noise of music, laughter, and chatter hit her like a wall. This place was *busy*. She leaned on the bar and bought a glass of wine, and then made her way to where El was perched on a bar stool at the far end, sipping on a pint of beer. Her long, blonde hair was loose, cascading down her back, and the light caught her piercings; she was drawing lots of admiring glances.

"Hey El, how are you?"

El nodded and jerked her head back over her shoulder. "This place is nuts."

"I know. I haven't been here in years. I forgot it got so busy."

"I came here once, and that was enough. But, you're right. This is a great place to start looking."

Avery glanced around the room, and caught a glimpse of Briar emerging at the top of the stairs. She waved to attract her attention, and Briar waved back, weaving through the crowd to meet them. "I hate this place already," she said as she joined them. She caught the bartender's eye and ordered a drink.

Avery laughed. "Come on, ladies, it's just a bit of fun. Well, until the Mermaids turn mean."

"So, what's the plan?" El asked.

"I think we just need to keep an eye on the groups, maybe wander around a bit, do some eavesdropping, and spray a little potion," Avery said, reaching into her bag for a perfume bottle for each of them.

"This is your potion?" Briar asked, examining it. "It has a slight amber tinge."

"Yep. It's supposed to. Let's hope I've made it properly, and that it works."

"Do I need to say anything?" El asked.

Avery nodded. "Let's find a quiet spot."

El led the way through the jostling bodies to a corner of the balcony, where the music was quieter, and Avery shared the short incantation. "We just use it like perfume, spray it, but just casually miss yourself, and spray whoever's next to you, say the words, and it should unveil the glamour of their appearance, revealing them properly to us."

"Will they know?" El asked.

Avery frowned. "Not sure. But hopefully not."

"Great," El said, sarcastically. "So reassuring, Avery."

"Sorry," she answered, feeling slightly annoyed. "But it's better than doing nothing."

"Fair point," El agreed. "Why don't we get this party started?" She looked around at the small group of girls behind her, all giggling and chatting together, then spritzed herself and murmured the words to activate the spell. Avery gave the potion a little push with the breeze, allowing the fine spray to reach the group. They didn't even notice. And nothing happened.

"Well, that's one group eliminated," El said, grinning. "Shall we keep going?"

Over the course of the next hour they worked their way through the room, checking out every available group. Every now and again one of them would visit the toilets and try in there, but with no success. Eventually, they stood at the corner of the bar surveying the room, the thumping bass of the music making conversation difficult.

"Should we move on?" Briar asked. "I think we've covered everyone."

"I think so," Avery agreed. "Let's try The Kraken. The Badger's Hat has the club in the basement, so we should leave that to last."

"Do you think a Tuesday is probably a dud night?" Briar asked, looking around doubtfully.

"It's jammed in here," El said incredulously. "And I don't think Mermaids keep work timetables, either."

The Kraken was closer to the harbour and had a large beer garden out the back. Like The Flying Fish, the music was loud, and the atmosphere was raucous. They separated and started to sweep the room, the same as they had done before. It wasn't long before Avery felt a tap on the shoulder, and looked around to see Dan, standing with a tall, blond man.

"Hey, Avery!" Dan nodded towards his companion. "This is my mate, Pete."

"Hi, guys," Avery leaned up and kissed Dan's cheek. "Couldn't keep away, then?"

"He couldn't," Dan said, looking at Pete.

Pete laughed. He was attractive, his blond hair slightly long and falling over his face. His eyes were blue, with laughter lines in the corner, and his attention was on a group of young, pretty girls by the bar. He extended his hand. "Hi, Avery. I've heard all about you. Dan tells me this bar could be bad for my health."

Avery's eyes opened wide at Dan, but he gave a vaguely imperceptible shake of the head that made her think that whatever he'd said, Pete had no idea she was a witch. He laughed and said, "Avery doesn't want you to be fodder for these voracious females."

Avery agreed. "I care about the wellbeing of my friends, that's all." She looked at the girls who were undoubtedly all glowing with youth, vitality, and an undeniable sexiness. Every single one was taller than the average woman, slim, with long hair and fair skin. The more she looked at them, the more she thought they might be Mermaids. "Which one's caught your eye?"

Pete shrugged. "They're all gorgeous and they've been here all week, teasing us mercilessly."

I bet they have. Time to try the potion.

"Let's hope they don't break your heart, Pete."

"I'd recover," he said, smirking. "Come on, Dan. You're my wingman."

Pete turned and headed back to the group, who were already surrounded by men, and Dan hesitated a second. "Do you think…?"

"Maybe. I'll head over soon and test my theory. Are you feeling okay?" she asked, examining his expression carefully for signs of vague dreaminess. "No odd compulsions, or the feeling of being bewitched?"

He looked at her, amused. "No different than usual."

"Well, be careful," she said. "I'll find you later."

Avery saw Briar and El by the entrance to the toilets, and threaded her way through the crowd to join them. It was getting darker now, and the low lights of the pub created shady spaces where couples could gravitate.

El broke her conversation with Briar. "Any luck?"

"Maybe, over by the bar. There are half a dozen women who all look possible." She pointed at them discretely. "They are very good looking, flirting massively, and have a harem of men to choose from."

Briar rose up on her tiptoes to see over the crowd. "Maybe. You tested the potion yet?"

"Just about to. You had any luck?"

They both shook their heads, but El answered. "No. Why don't you go and check those, and then let's move to the last place. I feel my soul being sucked out of me here."

Avery knew what she meant. There was almost a smell of desperation about this place. It should have felt fun, but instead it seemed predatory and sad. She headed to the bar on the pretence of putting down her glass. When she got close enough, she pulled the spray and angled it behind her. She prepared herself to see something unpleasant, and maybe to be recognised.

But absolutely nothing happened.

No one changed or unveiled their appearance; they continued to flirt unashamedly, and didn't seem to notice Avery in the slightest.

Avery worked her way around them all, squirting her potion discretely. And still nothing. She caught Dan's eye and gave him the thumbs up, and he smiled with relief.

She headed back to Briar and El, who had been watching from a distance. "Nothing. Damn it. I felt sure they were them."

El sighed. "So, we have to go to The Badger's Hat?"

"'Fraid so, unless my potion sucks," Avery agreed, as they headed to the final pub for the night.

***

The Badger's Hat was situated in the centre of White Haven, in the middle of a run of shops. Like many buildings, it had stood there for several years and had a certain old world charm. The ground floor of the pub catered to all groups, and it had an extensive menu, but the owners had extended down into the basement, turning it into a club, with a dance floor at the far end.

It was almost 10:00 PM as Avery led the way inside. The restaurant area was on the left, and most of the tables were still occupied, but the kitchen had stopped taking orders and customers were eating desserts and cradling coffees. She didn't linger there; instead, she turned right and heading for the door in the corner with a sign overhead, reading, The Badger's Set. Avery laughed at the name. That was new—but then again, it had been years since she'd been here.

The door opened onto a small landing in a dim stairwell lined with exposed brick walls, lit with shaded sidelights. They went downstairs to the bar and as soon as they stepped inside, Briar said, "Wow. This is cool!"

And it was. The ceilings were low and lined with beams, the walls were of exposed brick, with the occasional smoothly plastered section painted in dark greys or purples. The lights were low, the bar was long and covered in gleaming polished steel, and the seating was funky. It was a great mix of old and new. And it was hot and crowded inside, the murmur of voices a steady undercurrent to the music, which wasn't too loud—yet. Avery could just make out the dance floor on the far side of the room, empty at present.

El headed to the bar, striding confidently through the crowd, and taller than most. "Come on, girls. This round is on me. I think this is the place."

Avery knew exactly what El meant. It did have a feeling of promise in the air. But maybe that was just the mix of alcohol, sweat, perfume, and hormones.

El handed her a glass of red wine, which she sipped with pleasure. None of them had drunk anything except lime and soda water in the second pub, wanting to remain mentally alert and ready for anything.

Briar slipped her shoes off, and pretended to rub aching feet. "Oh yes. I can feel them. I may not be on bare earth, but I can sense a change."

"I guess we are *in* the Earth, in this basement," Avery said. She felt goose bumps run across her skin. *They were here.*

"So, do we split up again?" Briar asked, scanning the crowd.

El shook her head. "No. I think we stick together. There are no easy exits out of here, and I don't want anyone, especially us, feeling cornered, if they work out they've been spotted."

Avery agreed. "Let's start by the entrance and work our way in."

After a half an hour of targeting the bigger groups, and ignoring several terrible chat-up lines, they had still drawn a blank, and they were all feeling frustrated.

"Maybe my potion sucks," Avery said, flopping against the wall and closing her eyes.

"No. They have to be here," El said, remaining determined. "Look at all these side-booths that we haven't tried yet."

She was right. All of the seating was along two sides of the room, and the seats were long, padded benches situated around a table, all partially sectioned off from its neighbouring table to allow for discrete conversations, which left the central area free for standing.

"It's not going to be so easy to spray them though, is it?" Briar observed.

El grinned and pointed to the air conditioner on the wall. "Let's get creative."

She reached up and quickly sprayed the potion several times in front of the vents, and said the spell as the potion was carried across the room. Nobody noticed. They were all too intent on their conversations. "And another couple just to make sure," she said, spraying again. "Now, every couple of minutes I'll keep spraying, and you two will have to go and look."

Avery nodded. "I'll use a little breeze to help."

Halfway down, Avery saw something that made her catch her breath, and she felt Briar stiffen besides her. They both glanced away to avoid staring.

"Do you see them, too?" Avery asked quietly, her heart hammering in her chest.

"Yes. Oh, wow," Briar swallowed, desperately trying to hide her shocked expression. "That's probably what I should have expected them to look like, but still…"

There were four Mermaids seated together in a booth, each next to a man who was gazing deeply into their eyes. With their glamour, they looked like average, attractive women in their late twenties, two with long hair, two with shoulder-length, all with slim builds and nice clothes, but nothing too flashy. With the aid of the potion, they were revealed to be sharp-faced, and their skin was green with a slightly metallic sheen to it. Their hair was long, curling down their backs and coiling on the seats around them, and coloured all shades of blue, green, and purple. But it was their eyes that made them look *Other*—they had a flat, shiny surface, like metal, that reflected the light in an odd way, gleaming with a feral intelligence, and they were completely round—fish eyes. They were flirting with their companions, and every now and again, the Mermaids laughed, revealing tiny sharp teeth, and on the side of their necks were gills, lying flat and unused for now.

Briar and Avery stepped back, trying to watch them discretely through the crowd, and then as Avery turned to look for El, she nearly dropped her drink. At least half of the booths were filled with Mermaids, and she saw another couple at the bar.

She turned her back immediately, trying the hide the panic on her face. "Shit. Briar. We're surrounded."

Briar glanced around and went pale. "What now?"

"Beat a hasty retreat? This was about finding them. And we have."

El joined them, keeping her expression admirably blank. "First, well done. Your potion worked. Now what?"

Avery glanced nervously between them. "I think we need to get out of here, before they realise they've been identified. There are way more of them than I thought there'd be. And then we decide on a plan."

El led the way to the door. They were a long way from the entrance, and trying to get through the press of bodies was slow going. They were doing well, until a Mermaid turned from the bar to get back to her booth, coming face to face with them. Avery couldn't help it. She blinked and averted her gaze, and she knew immediately she'd made a mistake. The Mermaid frowned and turned to look after her, and Avery *knew* she knew.

Within seconds, like ripples in water, head after head turned to watch them, the humans remaining oblivious. Avery felt the atmosphere change, becoming predatory, and the smell of brine bloomed around them. *What was happening?*

They arrived at the door leading to the stairs and freedom, and stepped into the dark entryway, ready to run, when they came to a sudden stop.

A Mermaid stood on the stairs, waiting for them, and one stepped into the narrow stairwell behind them.

The Mermaid on the stairs smiled maliciously, the dim light shimmering on her iridescent scales and glinting off her sharp, white teeth. Her eyes observed them dispassionately. "What are *you* that you can see us?" she asked in a silky smooth voice.

El didn't even bother bluffing. Her hands balled with fire as she said, "We're witches, powerful witches, and we're investigating *you*. What are you doing in White Haven?"

The Mermaid didn't answer El's question. Instead, she narrowed her strange round eyes, stepped forward, and sniffed deeply. "Ah, yes. I see it now. You carry your magic well. It drapes around you like a cloak." Her eyes fell to their bags where they carried the potion bottles, and she smirked. "A clever spell. With all the magic in this pretty place, it was well disguised. And I was a little distracted with all of your lovely men."

"I asked you a question," El said.

"You know what we seek, human," she continued in her lilting voice that carried the soft *shush* of waves. "Searching for mates. And this place is rich with them."

"They are not yours to take!" Avery said, rage flashing through her. "They have families and loved ones here. They do not belong beneath the waves."

The Mermaid smiled seductively and played with her hair, and then turned to catch the light, and Avery realised that she was trying to seduce *her*. "Oh, but they do. Their life will be long and pleasurable with us. They shall want for *nothing*. It is surprising how quickly they forget their human life."

Despite Avery's immunity from the Mermaid's charms, her manner was unnerving, and she had to resist the urge to step back.

"But why White Haven?" Briar asked. Avery noticed her shoes were in her hands, her bare feet planted solidly on the floor.

The Mermaid laughed again. "The magic—*your* magic— falls through the sky." She held out her hands as if to catch something. "It falls even now, like rain, into my hands and into the sea. The currents brought it to us, out in the deep, deep ocean. It called us. It *feeds* us. It falls on your men, even though they don't know it. And now we want them. It is rare to find magic in such rich supply." She looked at them speculatively. "And I think there is nothing you can do about that."

"You need to leave," Avery said, adrenalin making her bold. "You will not take anyone."

"You dare to threaten us?" The Mermaid laughed, and the one behind them joined in. "We are the Daughters of Llyr. We will leave only when we are ready."

The magical energy in the small stairway was strong now, emanating in waves from all of them, and Avery realised with a horrible clarity that the Mermaids had a powerful magic of their own.

El was well aware of it too and she said, "You have your own magic. I can feel it. Why do you need ours?"

"All magic is useful, witch, surely you know that."

The Mermaid stepped closer to El, and then in a lightning strike, pushed El against the wall, her hand against her throat, and Avery noticed her webbed fingers and long nails like talons. Water started to trickle from El's mouth as she struggled to breathe and started to turn blue in front of them, the ball of fire in her hands disappearing.

Avery reacted instinctively, the wind already teasing her hair, and she slammed the Mermaid behind her against the wall as well, lifting her several feet off the ground. "Stop. We can both play that game."

The first Mermaid ignored her, focussing only on El, her face inches away as she watched El struggle. Briar stamped her foot, causing a strong root to snake out of the wooden stairs. It caught the Mermaid around the ankle and pulled her away from El, breaking her concentration. El fell forward onto her knees, spewing up water, and dragging in ragged breaths, but Avery kept the second Mermaid firmly pinned against the wall. She could feel her prodding at her magic, trying to release herself, and hissing with annoyance.

The first Mermaid bent forward and reached for the root, grasping it firmly. Within seconds the wood turned soft and rotten and fell away, and she looked up at them triumphantly.

Avery couldn't believe Briar's spell had been disarmed so easily, but she tried not to show her surprise or any sign of weakness. She stared the first Mermaid down. "This is not a debate. You need to leave White Haven *now*."

Fortunately the stairwell had remained empty, but any minute now, someone could arrive, and Avery wanted to end this quickly. This was not the place for a fight. And she had the feeling they were horribly outgunned.

The Mermaid appraised her with cold eyes. "We are many, little witch, and you are few. We leave when we're ready, and if you continue to threaten us, we will take *all* of your men with us. Now, release my friend."

For a few seconds they locked eyes, and then the door slammed above and voices carried towards them.

Avery dropped the Mermaid to the floor and in seconds, the Mermaids returned to the bar, leaving Avery, El, and Briar to make their way out.

They ran out to the street and down the road, their hearts pounding, and leaned against the wall of the closest chip shop, taking refuge in the handful of people milling around.

"That didn't go so well," El said, her breathing still ragged and uneven as she gingerly felt her neck. Her skin had a horrible pallor to it. "Ugh, I can still feel her webbed hands on me."

"Did she hurt you?" Briar asked, moving El's fingers to examine the area.

"No, I'm fine, honestly. My chest aches a little, and I'll just be a bit bruised." She looked annoyed and shocked. "As is my ego. She was faster and stronger than I expected."

Avery nodded, reflecting on their encounter. "She *was* quick—and she tried to drown you, on dry land! I mean, I knew they had magic, but I guess I really didn't appreciate how much."

Briar rested her hands for a few more moments on El's neck, and Avery felt a pulse of healing magic. "That should help," she said, finally moving away. "Let me know if you need a poultice."

El smiled ruefully. "Thanks, Briar."

Avery glanced at her watch. "If we hurry we can get to The Wayward Son before last call—I'd like to tell Alex what happened."

"I have a feeling Reuben is there, too," El said. "The football's on."

They almost ran to the pub, and got to the bar just as the bell for final orders was ringing. The bar staff were busy serving customers getting their last rounds in, and the hum of noise and familiar surroundings were comforting. Alex was pulling pints with the rest of his staff and he glanced up, noticing Avery's arrival. He shouted, "Be with you in a minute!"

Reuben and Newton were sitting on stools at the end of the bar, watching a repeat of the weekend's Manchester United versus Chelsea match on the television mounted on the wall in the corner, both with a fresh pint in front of them. As the girls joined them, El placed a kiss on Reuben's cheek.

"Ladies," Newton acknowledged, turning around. He looked them up and down and frowned. "What have you three been up to?"

"Investigating," Avery answered nervously. She knew he would not be happy.

"Investigating what?" Newton asked suspiciously.

They were surrounded by people in the pub, and although there was a steady buzz of conversation, it wasn't private. "We've been looking into our latest problem."

"Which one?" Reuben asked. "The sea-related one," Briar answered enigmatically.

"Oh, so that's why you were so vague earlier," Reuben said to El. "That was very sneaky of you."

El bristled slightly. "For a very good reason!"

"Why is your neck red?" Reuben asked accusingly.

"Er, things got a little ugly."

"What!" he said, eyes wide with worry.

"Please calm down," she said, reaching forward to reassure him. "I'm okay. *We're* okay."

"I think," Briar said decisively, "that we should check out in here—just in case. Glass of wine, please, Avery. El—care to help?"

"My pleasure. Get me a pint of Doom, please," El said, following Briar deeper into the pub.

"No problem," Avery replied, fishing inside her bag for her purse.

Alex finished serving his customer and moved closer until all four of them were leaning together around the bar.

"What have you done?" Newton asked, looking increasingly annoyed. "And what are they doing?" He gestured toward El and Briar, now lost in the crowd.

"I identified a way of finding our *visitors*. And it worked." Avery looked at their astonished faces, trying not to look too pleased with herself. "We have located a healthy number of *visitors* in The Badger's Set. In fact, unhealthy would be a better word. They are already choosing their prey. El and Briar are just making sure there are none here."

"Are you kidding?" Alex said, visibly annoyed. "That was incredibly dangerous. You should have involved us."

Avery looked incredulous. "Really? After you were so quickly seduced the other day? I don't think so."

"It was minor and you know it," he argued.

Reuben looked slightly sheepish. "It wasn't that minor really, Alex. We were enthralled."

Alex grimaced at him. "You're supposed to be on my side!"

"Yeah, shut up, Reuben," Newton added. He adopted his interrogation face and looked at Avery again. "Was the bar in thrall to them? And how many are we talking?"

"I'd estimate at least a dozen, maybe more. And no, the bar wasn't 'in thrall.' Well, not the *entire* bar. They were getting cosy in the booths." They were all glaring at her, and she turned to Alex. "Look, can you at least get me some wine before this interrogation continues?"

He sighed and rubbed his face. "Bloody Hell, Avery. You're exasperating. All right. And then I want to hear every detail!"

By the time El and Briar returned, the bar had quieted down and Avery had informed them about their encounter on the stairs.

Alex asked, "Anything I need to worry about here?"

"Clean bill of health," El said, visibly relieved. "But I think we should do regular checks every night."

"I agree," Briar said, pulling up a stool and sitting down before taking a sip of wine. "There's some potion left."

"And I can make some more," Avery added. "But identifying them is now the least of our worries. They are strong. Or at least the main one we spoke to was. I'm worried our magic is no match for theirs."

"It will be," Alex assured her. "We just need to find their weakness."

"I'll let Genevieve know," Avery said. "I feel we need to keep the Council informed about everything. And perhaps they can help. Someone must know some way to fight them."

Reuben grinned. "I bet Ulysses does."

21

Halfway through the morning the next day, on a break between customers, Avery phoned Oswald. His voice was warm. "Avery, how can I help you?"

"It seems we have a Mermaid infestation, and I was hoping to speak to Ulysses."

Oswald was silent for a moment. "May I ask why?"

Avery faltered for a second, and then thought she should just be honest. "I was told that Ulysses had Mermaid lineage, and thought he might have valuable insight, but if I'm wrong, or we shouldn't know…" she trailed off apologetically.

There were a few more seconds of silence and Avery wondered if she'd just made a horrible mistake, when Oswald finally said, "Let me speak to him and I'll call you back."

Avery then spent an uncomfortable few hours trying to distract herself. She reorganised bookshelves, changed stock, decided to increase the defences on her shop and flat, and drove Dan mad.

After she finally slowed down, Dan said, "Do you want to tell me what's going on? In fact, let me rephrase this. Avery, sit down and tell me what's going on." He gently placed his hands around her upper arms and directed her to the sofa under the window.

Avery felt flustered. She'd been trying to avoid this conversation all day, because she didn't know what to say.

But this was Dan, and he'd helped her, and she felt she had to tell him. She just didn't want to terrify him. *But maybe he should be afraid.* "After we left you last night, we moved on to another couple of pubs, and, well, we found *them*. It was all a bit weird."

"By 'them,' you mean…"

"Yes. *Them*."

"Wow. So they're really here. Should we be worried?" he asked, sitting down next to her as if for a long story.

"I don't know. Yes, probably? There are a lot of them." She rubbed her face, as if hoping to rub all of her worries away.

He exhaled forcefully. "Okay. I admit to not taking this as seriously as I should. Now, I'm a little bit freaked."

"I don't wish to alarm you, but join the club. We're a bit freaked, too."

He stared at her. "Not exactly reassuring. Is this in any way linked to the weird deaths in churches?"

"No. Completely unrelated."

"Great. Nephilim and Mermaids, operating independently, both deadly." He raised his eyebrow. "Anything else you want to share?"

"Avoid The Badger's Hat for now. Well, The Badger's Set, to be precise."

"Good tip. Thanks. You didn't mention this earlier, because?"

"I was trying to think of a solution before I freaked you out. Too late!"

"Ha!" he laughed dryly. "You know what? I'm going back to work now, and then I'm going to give up on socialising until all this is over. But I will update my pastry quota. Sugar always helps."

"Pastries on me," Avery said, grateful for a distraction. "I'll go now. Give me five minutes."

She was on her way back from the shop, laden with twice as many pastries as normal, and two mochas for that extra sugary blast, when her phone rang. It was Oswald. She juggled her bags and phone, and tried to keep her tone even as she answered. "Hi, Oswald."

Oswald kept it brief. "Tonight at eight, at mine."

"Can I bring the other witches?"

"I suppose so. But not that Newton man."

And then he rang off.

***

"When I grow up, I want to live in a castle," Alex said, looking up at Crag's End admiringly.

"Idiot. It's not a castle," Avery said, looking at him with affection. He always looked so hot, and tonight was no exception. He'd dragged his hair back into a half man-bun, and all she wanted to do was nuzzle his neck.

"It's pretty bloody close," he answered, unaware of her lustful thoughts.

"It's all right," Reuben said, trying to look underwhelmed. "I prefer my manor house."

"Bragger," El said, narrowing her eyes.

Reuben grinned. "I know. You can stay anytime."

"Only if I get my own wing," she shot back.

"Depends how well you behave."

Briar laughed at all of them, and led the way to Oswald's huge wooden front door. Newton knew about their appointment and was annoyed he couldn't come. Avery still had no idea if Briar and Newton had any type of relationship beyond friendship, and if they had, Briar wasn't telling.

It was a few moments before Oswald answered the door, and when he did, he slipped outside to join them on the covered porch, as if within the house Ulysses would have heard every word. *Talk about paranoid.* His sharp eyes appraised them, and Avery introduced him to Alex, Briar, and El, who he hadn't met before.

He licked his lips nervously. "I would like to point out before I introduce you to Ulysses that he doesn't generally like to talk about his parentage. But, he does acknowledge that many witches are aware of it. It is up to him to introduce the subject, and he often never will. You are lucky this evening. Now, follow me."

He turned and led the way inside, leaving the others to turn and look at each other with stunned expressions, before they hurried after Oswald.

Oswald led the way through a maze of ground floor corridors, panelled with oak, and herringbone wood floors, before finally leading them into a room on the side of the house overlooking an abundant rose garden. It was a sitting room, with elegant, velvet-covered armchairs in rich blues and greens, and a large peacock-blue chesterfield sofa that Avery immediately coveted. The walls were covered in pale blue Chinoiserie wallpaper and decorative lamps were dotted on side tables. It was utterly charming, and very Oswald.

Charmed as she was by the space, Avery's attention was quickly drawn to the man standing in the window with his back to them. It was dusk out, and the room was full of shadows, so that even when he turned at their arrival, it was hard to see his features immediately. One thing was apparent—he was huge. His shoulders were broad, and his arms and thighs were powerful.

"Ulysses," Oswald said. "Thank you again, good friend, for coming. Here are the White Haven witches."

As Oswald introduced them one by one, they all met in the middle of the room, and Avery felt her hand squashed by Ulysses's enormous one. The lamplight threw his face into relief, and she saw the most startling pair of emerald eyes, deep set into a long face, and overcast by a heavy brow and magnificently wild eyebrows. His hair was similarly wild, falling down his back in straggling waves, and his expression was fierce.

Avery smiled nervously, her confidence faltering. *By the Goddess. He looks like Aquaman, but in his fifties. And he's terrifying.*

If Alex or the others had any such fears, they hid them well, but other than muted greetings no one said anything.

Oswald ushered them into seats before bringing over a tray of drinks and glasses. There were cut glass decanters of sherry, whiskey, and port, and Oswald politely filled everyone a glass before pouring himself a sherry and sitting down next to Ulysses, looking like a dwarf in comparison.

Ulysses cradled his whiskey while staring at them suspiciously. As yet, he hadn't said a word.

"Welcome, all," Oswald said. "Before Ulysses tells us about himself, perhaps you could all explain a little about yourselves and your particular problem?"

Oh my God. This is like some hellish chat show or work icebreaker.

"I'll start," Avery said, seeing everyone's slightly baffled expressions, and she told Ulysses about her shop and her family, and about the hidden grimoires, and then Alex carried on, until eventually they had all introduced themselves, downed their drinks, and were still looking at Ulysses's sullen expression. Avery started to wonder if he was mute.

Oswald smiled encouragingly, topped off their drinks, and then said, "Ulysses and I have known each other for many years. He is the only other witch in Mevagissey. His magic is a mix of earth and water—and by that I don't mean the water element itself, of which you young Reuben are a novice, but the magic of the deep oceans, the underwater abyss, and Llyr himself."

Ulysses nodded and finally spoke, all the while looking down into his glass. "Thank you, Oswald. You are very kind, as usual."

Ulysses's voice was not what Avery was expecting. She'd presumed it would be cracked and broken, a barely used rasping thing, but instead it was deep and rich, like hot chocolate, and utterly beguiling. *And actually*, she reflected briefly, *if he were the child of a Mermaid, it would be. Their voices carried the powers of seduction.*

He looked up at them finally, and she tried not to blink and shy away from his bright green eyes. "I don't like to talk about my past, my mother, because it's very painful for me. Even now." His lips cracked a thin smile. "You may feel it's ridiculous, given my age."

"Not at all," Briar said kindly. "The scars of our past can linger a long time."

Ulysses's shoulders dropped a fraction and his smile softened. "What Oswald is not telling you is that he found me, as a child, on the beaches beyond Mevagissey, when he was very young himself. He knew immediately what I was, because of my eyes, and these."

He spread his hands wide, and whatever glamour he was using disappeared, revealing the webbed fingers of the Mermaid, and the slightly green tinge to the skin. Within seconds his glamour returned, and he looked human again.

He continued, "A storm had raged for days, and my father had taken advantage of it. He brought me ashore, desperate that I should avoid the life that he had." He looked around. "You are confused, I can tell. I still haven't got any better at telling this story."

"Perhaps," Oswald said gently, "you should start with your father."

Ulysses nodded. "My father was a witch, and had lived here in Mevagissey with his family, as had generations before him. This was a long time ago. Back in the 1700s. As they do, from time to time, a Mermaid came here searching for a mate, and my father went willingly. He told me he was curious, and of course, my mother was enchanting. But life was not as he expected. The Mermaids' magic will change a man, allowing him to breathe beneath the sea. He grows webbed hands, his legs become a tail, and he develops gills. But even so, the seas are dark and cold. They had many children, and I was their youngest." He paused a second, the memories clearly painful for him. "For some reason, my mother rejected me. I was too *human*. I don't know why—" he spread his hands wide, "some quirk of genetics. My mother tolerated me for a few years, but as I grew older, I became more humanlike and she decided to kill me. My father interceded, bringing me to shore in the storm. My own natural magic allowed my body to change once I reached the shore—my tail disappeared and I could walk the land. But I was otherwise lost."

Oswald jumped in, continuing with his part of the tale. "The day after the storm, I was on the beach—storms always throw up the best things that are useful for magic. When I found him, he was naked, hungry, and covered in seaweed. I knew immediately what he was. There was no sign of his father or mother, and even though I waited with him all day—terrified, I may add—as you well know, Mermaids are not to be trifled with, no one appeared. In the end, I brought him here. My family has lived here for many years, and it is very private. I have essentially been his father since then."

"It was here that I learned to master my magic," Ulysses explained, his expression haunted and vulnerable. "My father's and my mother's, and learned to live with humans. My father refused to stay, bringing me only to the shore, promising me it was for my own safety, and then he returned to the deep. He was to tell my mother I had died in the storm. As far as I know, he lives there still. Life is long in the depths. I still dream of it."

He fell silent, and Oswald watched him for a second. "So, as you can see, Ulysses is one of a kind. I named him after the great adventurer who battled the seas to finally return home. It seemed fitting."

"And you have never seen another Mermaid since?" Briar asked.

"Never. Until I sensed them the other day in Mevagissey. I confess, I have avoided them. I would see through their magic immediately, and they through mine, even though I cloak myself well. I do not wish to invite conflict." Ulysses's expression was grim. "Because make no mistake, if they knew of me, they would wish me dead, and I would have to fight for my life."

"I have figured out a way to monitor them," Oswald said, "but we are convinced there are only a couple here, and at the moment, they watch and wait."

"Unfortunately, there are far more in White Haven," Avery said. "At least a dozen."

"How do you know?" Ulysses asked.

"I found a very old spell in my grimoire. It has allowed us to unveil their glamour, and we had an *encounter* in a club.

They know that we know they're here, but we have no idea what to do next. And they know it." Avery appealed to Oswald and Ulysses. "They're strong, and we're in trouble. It would be awesome if there's anything you can tell us to try to fight them. Of course, we don't expect you to get involved."

Alex placed his glass on the table. "I am curious as to why they want our magic if their own is so powerful. The Mermaid told Avery that all magic was desirable, but I don't buy it."

Ulysses laughed, and it transformed his face. "Of course they desire our magic. Llyr is greedy, and despite his own power, he has always resented the magic of earth and his brother, Don, the Brother of Light. Llyr made his Daughters specifically so that they should need a man of earth to mate with and breed—something to perpetually taunt his brother with. So, when magic is so freely available as it is over White Haven right now—" he shrugged. "It's like Mardi Gras."

El nodded. "She said magic was falling like rain, covering everything and everyone."

"How do we get rid of them?" Reuben asked.

"They are born of water, so that element is like air to them. The air itself does not really trouble them too much, and fire they quench easily. But dry earth—that is a different matter. It is heavy, it suffocates, it saturates water, and could bury them. Of course, powerful blasts of energy will always be effective."

"Well, short of an earthquake, what are we supposed to do?" Briar asked, wide-eyed. "I can rupture the earth, but not on such a scale, and besides, it would be catastrophic for everyone around, not just the Mermaids. We can't just wait for them to take what they want and hope they don't come back. Five fishermen have already gone missing."

"And will never return," Ulysses said seriously, his eyes filled with regret.

"You have a mix of both magic," Alex said. "Does that give you any special abilities?"

Ulysses met his eyes briefly and looked away. "I can swim longer and deeper than any of you could." He dropped his glamour again, lifted his hair, and showed them the gills on either side of his neck. "And I have power over the oceans, but not as much as they have."

Avery looked at the others, and their faces reflected her own disappointment and frustration. She turned back to Ulysses. "Thanks for your time, and for sharing your past. I know it wasn't easy. Based on what we now know, we'll just have to try and figure something out."

"I'm sorry," he said. "I know you wanted more. But one final thing. They have one moon cycle only to live on land, and then they must return to the sea, so they will choose their mates soon—your time is running out."

22

"Genevieve," Avery said, feeling very frustrated. "Surely there's something the Council can do to help us? Men are at risk!"

Genevieve's voice rang out clear and direct over the phone, and Avery held it slightly away from her ear as she paced the room. "No, Avery. I have consulted the covens on this, and although they were happy to admit White Haven to the Council, they feel that this is your problem and that you must deal with it."

"Are you kidding me? Thirteen covens—the magic we could wield together would be huge. I thought that's what witches did? Band together in times of need."

"While some are sympathetic to your plight, many are fearful that becoming involved would invite disaster to their own communities. It seems that only White Haven is subject to this invasion."

"And Mevagissey," she injected.

"Small only, and probably because it is so close to you. No other communities are at risk from Mermaids. And now that the threat of the Nephilim has also gone, many witches wish to keep a low profile."

"The Nephilim are quiet for now. It does not mean they have gone for good."

"May I remind you, Avery, that your magic has caused this. *You* caused this. You insisted on releasing the binding, and now you are paying the consequences."

"But we had no idea what the consequences would be!" Avery shouted. "None! And that is *your* fault for excluding us for so long!"

There was a brief silence, but if Avery expected a change of heart, she was sadly mistaken, because Genevieve ploughed on, regardless. "I'm sorry, Avery, but that is our final decision. If individuals choose to assist you that is different, but there will be no official convening of the covens."

Avery was tempted to scream abuse down the phone, but she resisted. "In that case, we shall manage without you and I won't bother you again."

"Wait," she said, quickly. "We still wish to include you. The celebration of Lughnasadh is approaching, and we are planning to observe that together. It is something we should like you to participate in."

Lughnasadh was one of the big fire festival celebrations, and fell on the first full moon closest to the first of August. It celebrated the start of the harvest, and was a time for giving thanks for plenty, and celebrating the turn of the seasons.

I cannot believe she has the nerve to invite us to this.

This time, Avery decided to celebrate her temper. "Genevieve, go screw yourself." She threw the phone onto the chair in the corner and looked at Alex, who raised an expressive eyebrow.

"Trouble?"

They had returned from Oswald's only an hour or so ago, and Alex was lying in her bed, his hair loose and his chest bare, reading a thriller novel. Medea had curled up on the end of the bed, and Circe was purring contentedly in the crook of Alex's arm.

"That bitch has refused to help us in any way."

"I gathered that," he smirked. "Is this our penance?"

"It seems so. That, that … *Utter cow!*" She continued to pace, desperate to blast something, anything, and when Helena manifested in the doorway, she yelled, "Not now!" and slammed the door in her face with a powerful gust of wind.

"Come and sit down," Alex said calmly, patting the bed beside him.

As fantastic as he looked, the last thing Avery wanted to do was sit down. He had shaved before bed, and now had a very swashbuckling, piratical goatee that added to the wicked glint in his eye.

"I'm too annoyed! Do you know that after refusing to help us, she had the nerve to invite us to Lughnasadh celebrations?"

"Ah! That's what incensed you. And fair enough, too. Clearly, we won't be joining them?"

She had a sudden attack of guilt. "That was terrible of me. What if the others want to go? Do you?"

"No. I'd rather us do our own thing. And I'm sure the others would, too."

"Even Reuben?"

"Even Reuben." He smiled, and she started to calm down.

"You're adorable."

"I know. So are you. Even when you're mad as hell. Now, come and sit down."

She sidled over to the bed, slid beneath the sheets, and slipped under his arm, nestling close to his warm body. "What have we done? What have *I* done?"

"If I tell you I have a plan, will that help?"

She turned abruptly, looking him right in the eye. "Have you? What is it?"

"We have two powerful new arrivals as a consequence of our magic, who fortunately happen to hate each other. Well, the Nephilim hate the Mermaids, the Daughters of Llyr. I have no idea if the Mermaids even know of the existence of the Nephilim. Anyway, it seems the Nephilim merely wish to be left alone, and they seem to pose no risk to us—at least right now. I was thinking, that maybe they wish to avenge themselves. And help us in the process." He smiled enigmatically.

"And just how would they know to do that?"

"I'll contact them again. I have a psychic link."

Avery sat up, sliding from under his arm. "No. it's too dangerous."

"No, it's not."

"Yes, it is. They threatened you last time. You might not survive another link."

"I will. Trust me."

"I trust *you*. I don't trust them."

He smiled, and reached over to brush a lock of hair from her face, sending shivers all over her. "It's nice that you care."

"Of course I care. I don't want anything to happen to you."

"And I don't want anything to happen to you, and yet you rushed off the other night to tackle Mermaids, and didn't say a thing."

"I was protecting you!"

"And who's going to protect *you*? That's my job."

Her heart almost faltered, and she felt locked within his gaze. She didn't think she'd ever felt so—dare she say it— *loved*.

227

He didn't wait for her to answer, instead pulling her close and kissing her deeply, his tongue exploring her mouth as he pressed his lean, muscled body against hers, pushing her down onto the mattress. She heard the grumpy meow of the dislodged cat, but pulled him closer, one hand exploring his back, the other cradling his head. He smelled and tasted so good.

Alex pulled back, staring at her with his warm brown eyes. "Feeling calmer now?"

Avery teased him. "Not really, but for all different reasons."

"Good," he said, his gaze still serious. "Because we can solve anything together, Avery. Never forget that."

***

The next day at work was busy, especially because Sally was still on leave. A coach of American tourists had arrived at White Haven, part of a tour of Cornwall, and they added to the general busyness of the town.

Avery could tell those that were part of the touring group. She watched them through the window as they clustered together, following the tour guide as he strolled down the street waving a long, red folded umbrella to summon them to see various sights. Avery wondered what they'd think if they knew they'd be seeing witches and Mermaids as part of their tour. Quite a few of them came into her shop, clustering around the books on the locality, and also taking pictures of the occult displays. All she kept hearing was how 'cute' and 'tiny' everything was, and she caught Dan suppressing smirks as he was serving them.

She took a thirty-minute lunch break and headed into the garden to soak up the silence and sunshine, wishing she had all afternoon to potter among the plants. With reluctance, she dragged herself back inside, and then had a horrible shock.

Dan was outside the shop, tending to a young woman who looked as if she had fallen over. He was helping her to her feet, and picking up some of her fallen bags, and he was grinning from ear to ear. Avery could only see the woman's back, but something about her was very familiar. A cold chill started to run down her spine, and she tried to hurry, noting how Dan was focussing only on the woman, oblivious to everything else.

Unfortunately, a customer stepped in front of her and started to ask her about local books she could recommend. Avery tried to deal with her as quickly as possible without being rude, but she was still held up for several minutes. By the time she got to Dan's side, he looked dazed and devoted.

Avery could now see the woman's face, and she felt her own expression stiffen with horror. It was the Mermaid from the other night, glowing with health and beauty. Her long, dark hair had red low-lights running through it, and her skin glowed. She smiled at Avery with triumphant malice, and Avery had to bite down the urge to respond.

"Hey, Avery," Dan said. "This is Nixie. She's visiting White Haven for a while."

So, that's her name.

Nixie held her hand out, waiting for Avery to shake it, and reluctantly Avery reciprocated, feeling Nixie's strong grip. "So nice to meet you," she murmured in her soft, sibilant tones. "I was so silly, I just fell over, and your delightful shop assistant came to help."

"Yes, he's very helpful," Avery said, forcing the words through her clenched jaw. "Dan, can I have a quick word?

It's about our earlier conversation. You know, our *visitors*." She sent out a tendril of magic, hoping to break whatever spell it was that Nixie had so quickly and skilfully woven, but she was met with a wall of desire wrapped tight around him.

Dan was oblivious. "I'll catch you later, if that's okay? I'm having lunch with Nixie, down at the Beachside Café."

Avery felt fear rush through her. *What if Dan didn't come back?* But a small queue had started to form inside the shop, and a woman was gesticulating at her, an annoyed expression on her face, as Dan turned away to walk down the street. *She wouldn't take him now. The time wasn't right. This was a threat, surely. A show of power.*

Avery looked at Nixie and her snaky grin. "Sure, Dan, have fun. Look forward to hearing how lunch went."

Nixie answered for him. "Oh, we'll have a great time. See you again, Avery." And then she turned, tucked her arm into Dan's, and led him away.

Avery served the next couple of customers in record time and then called El, relieved when she answered. "El. Thank the Gods. I need your help."

"Hey Avery, what's happened?"

In hushed tones she related Dan's encounter. "Any chance you can have lunch at the same café? I'm completely tied up here, and I know you're close. I'm really worried about him." As she was talking, she noticed Dan's hex bag lying on the shelf under the counter and her blood ran cold. "And he's taken off the bloody protection I made him."

El's voice hardened. "That bitch. Yes, no problem. I'll make sure he's okay."

For the next hour Avery tried to stay focussed, but with every minute Dan was away, she felt her fear rising. Only the regular texts from El kept her from locking the shop and running down the road. El, having found a table in the corner of the café, was watching their every move. She'd said hello to Dan and Nixie, so Nixie knew she was being watched.

When Dan finally arrived back in the shop over two hours later, Avery rushed over and hugged him. "You're back. Great. Are you okay?"

"'Course I'm okay. It was just lunch." He noticed the clock on the wall and the grin on his face slid off. "Sorry. I had no idea I'd been so long."

"Don't worry about the time." She ushered him behind the counter, and turned her back to the shop. "Do you know who that was?"

"Yes, Nixie. Unusual name, isn't it? Pretty, like her." His eyes started to glaze again, and a dreamy smile spread across his face.

"She's a *Mermaid*!" Avery hissed. "Are you mad? Don't you listen to me? And why have taken off your hex bag?"

Dan looked at her with patient amusement. "Oh, Avery. You have such a vivid imagination. She's just a woman. Well, an incredible woman. We talked about everything, from books, to art, to football. I'm meeting her tonight, too. For dinner." He pushed his dark hair back, raking it up into unruly tufts. "And she's invited me to the Lughnasadh celebrations on the beach next weekend. Quite a few of her friends are leaving the area for good—it will be a final farewell, or something of the sort."

Avery blinked, and things started to slide into place. "I'd forgotten about that."

White Haven liked to embrace its witchy roots, and the town Council always put on events to honour the pagan celebrations. The mayor particularly liked to officiate, and Stan Rogers, one of the local Councillors, became their local druid, dressing in robes and chanting around the fire, making libations, and generally kicking off the celebrations. During the summer, the celebrations always took place on Spriggan Beach, on the edge of the town. The beach was edged with sand dunes, and the bonfire was sited close by, on dry sand, above the tide line. The fire was already being built of driftwood and old pallets. During the winter, the celebrations moved to the castle grounds, where it was protected from the strong winds.

These events were always well attended by both locals and visitors, and they attracted people from neighbouring villages. *If the Mermaids had already identified specific men, could they be planning to take them on that night?* Part of her thought that would be crazy. There would be so many people around. But that was also the advantage. Loads of people would be there, drinking and dancing, and although it was a family-friendly event, once the families had gone, the celebrations became wilder, lasting far into the night. If the Mermaids led the men into the sea, one by one, quietly disappearing, no one would notice a thing until it was too late.

"Dan, I think that would be a really bad idea."

Dan frowned. "Honestly, Avery, she's lovely. I have no idea what you're talking about. In fact, she told me to invite you along. Anyway, I'm going to go and tidy some shelves while you stop being so weird."

She looked after him, flabbergasted. Yesterday, he had been rational and worried, and today, he didn't care. The Mermaids' powers of seduction were impressive. But, what were they waiting for? Why didn't they just take the men they wanted now?

And then suddenly she remembered that Nixie had just invited her, as well. She *wanted* the witches to know when they were leaving. It was a challenge to find out whose magic would be stronger, and clearly Nixie thought it would be theirs.

23

"It's a good thing we weren't planning on celebrating Lughnasadh with the covens," Briar said, looking horrified at the news. "We'll have to be at the beach with the rest of the town."

All five witches and Newton were at Alex's flat after work, sharing pizzas and information, and all of them were worried about Avery's latest announcement.

"We're talking about mass kidnapping," Newton said, looking at them in disbelief.

"Yes, we know." Reuben said, waving his slice of pizza about. "And we're going to do everything possible to stop it."

"But what?" Newton asked, annoyed. "It seems your magic is no match for theirs."

"Wrong," Alex said. "We just have to think creatively. Earth magic is their biggest fear. Well, that's what Ulysses was suggesting, anyway. And I have another idea."

"One that I don't like," Avery added, looking at him with concern.

"Why?" Newton looked between them. "What's wrong with it?"

"It means Alex making another psychic link with the Nephilim."

Newton looked baffled. "And what will that achieve?"

"I'm going to ask for their help."

El almost choked. "You're going to *what*?"

Alex grinned. "You heard me the other day, after I linked with them. They hate the Mermaids—or more generally, the Children of Llyr. They want revenge. If I share the information about Lughnasadh, they may want to help."

"And they may not," El said, ever sceptical.

"So, we'll need a back-up plan," Alex said calmly.

Reuben laughed, a dry un-amused sound. "We haven't even got a main plan!"

"We need to separate them somehow from the men they've chosen. Get them on their own."

"But their Siren call is captivating. They could just use it on the whole beach, then all of you would be affected, too," El pointed out. "The consequences would be catastrophic."

"They are choosing their men with care," Avery said thoughtfully. "They don't just want anyone."

"But if the ones they don't want just drown, they won't care about that."

"Maybe," Avery said, thinking through the possible permutations. "But that would be messy."

"Maybe they want to drown the whole town. Maybe that's why they're waiting for the celebrations," El suggested. "After all, they've done it before."

"The village of Seaton," Briar said quietly. Seaton was once a thriving fishing town, but myths said that after a local man insulted a Mermaid, she cursed the town and it was swallowed by the sands.

"And the Doom Bar," Reuben added, referring to the huge sandbank that was responsible for the floundering of many ships just off the coast of Padstow, again rumoured to have been raised by a Mermaid. "Maybe not the town, just those on the beach. One massive wave would do it."

"Could you counteract that, with our help?" Avery asked.

He shrugged, looking doubtful. "Water is their element, far more than it is mine. I don't know."

"But we know a half-Mermaid, and a weather witch," Avery pointed out, starting to get excited. "Eve can control storms. She could bring a storm in on the night of the celebrations, driving people off the beach. And the great thing about a storm is that it uses all elemental magic. That would be overwhelming to the Mermaids, surely."

"And Ulysses would be able to help counteract their magic with our help." Briar nodded, looking impressed.

El disagreed. "But he wanted to avoid them. He said Mermaids would kill him if discovered."

"But at that point we'd be driving them out of White Haven, back into the sea, and their defeat would be strong enough to put them off ever coming back," Avery said, her voice rising with excitement. *This could work.*

Alex mused, "And if we get the Nephilim on board, the odds are well stacked in our favour."

Newton was not so sure, and he snorted with derision. "And just how are you going to do all this magic stuff with a huge amount of people on the beach?"

"We'll think of something," El said confidently. "The dunes are huge. We can hide ourselves in there easily. And if people start to scatter with the storm, there won't be many around anyway."

Newton looked doubtful. "Why don't you just make a storm and have the event cancelled entirely?"

"Because," Alex pointed out, "they'll just go elsewhere. At least we know—or think we know—where it will happen now. But, I think Avery's right. This *feels* right. They are waiting for the celebrations. There are huge levels of energy that come off crowds of people. They will surely feed off that, especially combined with their own magic and ours already drifting across the town."

Newton still looked doubtful. "I agree with some of that, but I still don't want the Nephilim involved. They killed people. Five people! Don't forget that. They are not our allies."

Avery had to admit that was a sobering thought. She had been so relieved that they hadn't killed again, she was almost feeling positive about them. "No, you're right, of course, Newton."

"What has happened with the police investigation into that?" El asked.

"It's come to a big bloody full-stop," he answered grumpily. "I know what's happened, but I can't say, of course. Everyone would think I'm mad. And there are absolutely no clues at all. No DNA, no fingerprints, no motives. The police chief is going nuts, and there are rumblings about black magic or some religious lunatic, particularly because the deaths were all in churches." He looked at them, and Avery could see the exhaustion etched across his face. "Do you know how bloody complicated my life is right now?"

Briar reached across and touched his arm gently. "We're sorry, Newton. We'll try and resolve this as quickly as possible."

He met her eyes, a flash of longing passing across his face for a brief second before it was quickly veiled again. "But we'll still have five unsolved murders, and the families are still grieving. And of course, there are five missing fishermen, presumed drowned. We know they'll never be seen again. I don't want any more deaths."

"None of us do," Alex said, all humour now gone. "Sorry. We sound flippant right now, but we're not."

"I'm horrified by this," Avery said. "It's eating me up every day. I'm losing sleep over it! And I'm infuriated that the Council won't help. It's not us they're punishing, it's everyone else."

"Right," Alex said, standing up and brushing crumbs onto his rug. "Let's try to reach the Nephilim now. While I prepare, Avery, can you call Eve?"

"Sure." She pulled her phone out, glad to be doing something. "I'll call Oswald tomorrow. I'd rather arrange to see Ulysses in person."

"What should we do?" Reuben asked, as he started to clear pizza boxes and beer.

"Prepare the space. You're all going to help me," Alex said.

***

The only light in Alex's living room was from a few candles, and a low fire burning in the grate. The coffee table had been moved, the rug rolled back, and a huge circle made from salt was in its place. The witches sat holding hands within the circle, and Alex was in the centre, bent over a new crystal ball. Newton had retreated to the kitchen, where he sat watching the events on a stool.

El, Avery, Briar, and Reuben represented the four elements, and they chanted a spell together, summoning their powers to enhance Alex's skills. As the spell intensified, everything outside the circle fell away into darkness, until there was only the five of them and the blackness of the glass orb held within Alex's hands. The room was quiet and hot, and Avery felt sweat trickle down her spine.

For what seemed like several minutes nothing happened, and Alex murmured in frustration. "They are resisting me. I can feel him, the one I spoke to, at the edge of my consciousness, but he's pushing me away." He looked up at them. "Do you trust me?"

"What?" Reuben asked, confused. "Yes, why?"

Avery frowned. "What are you thinking?"

"I have an idea." He shuffled back so he was part of the circle, not removed from it, and linked hands with Avery and Briar, who sat either side of him.

"I'm going to try again, so don't get freaked out. I need your power directly, so you'll feel me draw on you."

They started the spell again and summoned the elements one by one into the circle, magnifying their power, while Alex stared into the crystal ball. Sparks started to dance across its surface, and once again, the outside world fell away until only the crystal ball and its swirling darkness remained. And then, with a sudden snap, Avery felt as if she had plunged headlong into its darkness, falling at a giddy speed she couldn't control.

For a few seconds she was terrified, but then she felt Alex's strong, calming presence, and then Briar, Reuben, and El as their spirits all linked and their thoughts swirled around hers. The darkness cleared slightly, and Avery could make out the indistinct shape of a room. With a shock she heard raised voices, and saw the huge shapes of the Nephilim, still cloaked in shadows.

A deep, resonant voice boomed out, and Avery found she could understand every word. "You intrude again, witch. Have you learnt nothing?"

Alex spoke. "We need your help. I only want to talk."

"You have no right to ask for anything. Leave this place, and leave us in peace."

"I have *every* right. It is thanks to us and the doorway that we opened that you are here. Without *us* you would still be trapped in the spirit world."

A silence fell briefly before their voices rose again, arguing with each other. Eventually, their spokesman asked, "What would you have us do?"

"The Daughters of Llyr are threatening us. We need your help."

Avery felt the anger ripple around the room. "We will not interfere in the affairs of men."

"You have already interfered," Alex insisted. "You are here, killers of innocent humans. You need to make amends."

"We slaughtered cattle."

"And before them, five humans. My memory is not that short. We demand penance."

The figures shifted, moving closer and murmuring together, until another spoke. "You seek to draw us into the light to destroy us."

"No. That is not our plan." Alex's voice was calm and reasonable. "The Daughters of Llyr will kill many. We need help. We are not strong enough to defeat them alone."

"And what will we get in return?"

"What do you want?"

"To live once more among men."

"But you are Nephilim, the sons of angels and human women. Your reputation is one of violence."

"Your stories lie. We were feared for our strength, but we threatened only those who threatened us."

Alex persisted. "But how will you live? Do you even look human? We have seen only your spirit form. The world is not as you left it. Many creatures that are not human have to hide their true nature or risk persecution. Even us."

Again there was silence, and the tension around them was palpable, the shadows deep and impenetrable. Despite her best efforts, Avery could not see the Nephilim. She could feel the other witches, their fear and curiosity, but she could also feel the Nephilim and some of their desperate need to find a way into existence. And then, as if they had come to some unspoken agreement, the shadows lifted and they emerged out of the gloom.

The light revealed seven tall men, all naked, their hair long, faces bearded, and their eyes intense. Swirling tattoos covered their arms and their chests. And they were perfect male specimens. Avery wasn't sure if her spirit form could be seen, but she knew she was staring. She couldn't help it. Their limbs had sculpted muscles, and their abs were well defined, but some were blond, others dark-haired, and their skin colour ranged from brown to white. They looked like warriors.

"Where are your wings?" Alex asked.

One of the Nephilim spoke, his familiar voice indicating he was the one Alex had the psychic link with. His hair and skin were dark, his eyes a bright blue, and his teeth gleamed white in the light. He looked amused as he stared at them, making Avery think he could see them in some way. "Invisible to you now. We can hide them, but they are a part of us and always will be. Are we human enough for you?"

"Very. But you should find some clothes," Alex said, amusement in his voice. "You can speak English now?"

"We are the sons of angels, our language will adapt to anything."

"But how will you *live*?"

All seven Nephilim laughed. "We will find a way. This place," the dark-haired one gestured around him, and Avery realised they were in an old mine shaft, one of dozens spread across Cornwall, "is temporary. A place for us to find our strength. There will be no more killing of humans or cattle."

"Good. In that case, once you have helped us banish the Daughters of Llyr, we will not pursue you, and you will be free to live in peace—as long as you do not kill humans again," Alex warned. "Otherwise, there will be consequences."

The spokesman looked at his companions, and they all nodded. "It is agreed. We will destroy the Children of Llyr. Name the place, witch."

"White Haven. The place you first found when you left the spirit world."

He nodded. "The place that sits beneath the magic."

Avery felt her heart sink. *What the hell were they going to do about that?*

"Yes, that place. On the night of Lughnasadh, under the full moon. Nine nights from now."

"Agreed."

Doubt crept into Alex's voice. "How will we find you?"

The Nephilim smiled, but it didn't quite reach his eyes. "I will contact you again. Our word is law. We *will* be there."

And then they were plunged back into darkness, and Avery felt Alex pull them back into the circle.

***

"Holy crap!" Reuben exclaimed, "That was insane."

Even though the light was low, all of them blinked as they adjusted to returning to their own bodies. *Except they hadn't really left their bodies*, Avery reflected, *not like spirit walking.*

Her heart was pounding and her mouth was dry, and she felt Alex give her hand a squeeze, and she looked at him and smiled. "Well done."

El nodded, stretching like a cat. "Yes. Well done, Alex. That was so odd. I've never done that before."

"Or met a Nephilim, for that matter," Briar said. "Well, seven of them."

Newton stepped in front of them and crouched in front of the fire, just outside of the circle. "Success?"

"You couldn't hear anything?" Alex asked, a frown creasing his face.

"Not a thing. You all fell very silent and still. Like you'd turned to statues."

Reuben grinned. "Like I said. Insane! And yes, success. They will help us, in exchange for letting them live."

Newton looked incredulous. "They have killed five people!"

"And will help save many more," Alex said. He released the power in the circle and broke the ring of salt. "We need them, Newton."

"We shouldn't make deals with murderers."

"The police make deals all the time with lesser offenders in order to catch the big guys," Reuben pointed out.

Briar spoke softly. "So, what's your solution to the Mermaids, then?"

Newton glared at her, and then stood, pacing off his anger. "I haven't got one. Can't you use your magic?"

"We *are* using our magic, but we need them. You know we do," she said, appealing to him.

"Bollocks! I don't like this," he exclaimed.

Avery started to clear the circle, thinking on their options and the days they had left. "Newton, in a few days' time, we could lose many men to these Mermaids. We're running out of time. Our plan is a good one. Sometimes, you have to choose your enemies. I trust the word of the Nephilim. It doesn't mean I like what they've done, but they're trying to survive."

Newton strode to Alex's fridge, grabbed a beer, and took a long drink.

Briar leaned on the counter and watched him. "What will you do about the five deaths?"

"We'll have to blame some nut job who's now disappeared. They will remain unsolved. What else can I do?"

"I'm sorry," Briar said. "But at least you know it won't happen again."

Newton shook his head. "My morals feel very ambiguous right now. I don't like it. It's like I'm living a double life." He stared into the distance for a few seconds, and then downed his beer. "I have to go. I'll be in touch."

Without a backward glance, he strode across the room and out the door, leaving the others staring after him.

24

The next day was Friday, and Avery was relieved it was the end of the week. She was looking forward to Sunday and a day off. She contacted Oswald and arranged to meet Ulysses at lunchtime in a pub in Mevagissey. For some reason, Oswald had insisted on coming too, as if Ulysses needed a minder. Avery didn't care, as long as she could talk to Ulysses again. She had a minder of sorts, too. Alex was joining her.

"I feel two of us will be more persuasive," he argued along the way.

"Alex, you can come with me anywhere," she teased.

Mevagissey was undoubtedly one of the prettiest places Avery had ever visited. It was a small town, little more than a village, nestled on a sloping hill overlooking the sea, and its winding streets ran down to the harbour, the buildings jostling together.

They took Avery's Bedford van, following the main road down to the harbour, where the streets became increasingly narrow. Before they went too far, she found a parking spot on one of the side streets, and then set off on foot to the pub.

Alex pulled her into his side, wrapping his arm around her as they continued to walk. "I hope Ulysses thinks logically. He didn't look too keen to get involved the other day."

"No. But we have a plan now," Avery reasoned.

They rounded a corner and found the harbour spread before them, glittering in the sunlight. Avery could smell fish and chips mixed with the cool scent of briny water. She smiled. *Seaside towns all smelt the same.* It was reassuring.

The Salty Dog Tavern overlooked the harbour, and the sound of voices spilled out of the open door onto the street. They edged through the crowded entrance, where a few smokers hung around, coughing into their cigarettes, and then made their way to the bar. As Alex bought drinks, Avery checked the room out.

It was a small pub with a long bar and a mismatched collection of tables and chairs, and it was filled with sea and sailing paraphernalia—old nets, buoys, shells, and lobster pots. The smell of food filled the air, and most of the tables were occupied.

They found Oswald and Ulysses in a large back room, sitting at a table in the corner beside an empty fireplace. They both looked at them warily.

"Hi guys," Avery said breezily, sitting down next to them and taking a sip of the pint of Guinness that Alex had bought her.

"You don't have to look so worried," Alex told them.

"I think we do," Oswald answered. "You want Ulysses's help. He's said no."

"I get that you're worried, Ulysses, but we have a plan," Avery explained. There was no point in making small talk; Oswald had made that pretty clear.

Ulysses's bulk was still impressive, particularly in a small, crowded pub. He leaned back, staring at them impassively, his green eyes giving away nothing.

She lowered her voice. "We think they will make their move during the Lughnasadh celebrations on the beach in White Haven. I know because Nixie, their leader of sorts, told me herself. She's challenging us to some kind of show of power." Avery could hear her voice rising with frustration. "The Nephilim have agreed to help us. So has Eve. She will bring a storm in on that night, big enough to mask us and what we must do. The storm will dispel the crowds, too, and hopefully allow us to fight the Mermaids unseen."

"The Nephilim?" Ulysses asked, his voice smooth as butter. "And what made them agree to help?"

"The promise of freedom," Alex said.

Oswald's eyebrows shot up. "Freedom? Is that wise?"

"Yes, I think so," Alex said, confidently. "They are now fully physical in appearance, and they want to live among men again. They promise they will not kill again."

Oswald snorted. "So you've made a deal with devils."

Alex leaned forward, his eyes hard and his expression grim. "Your precious Council will not help because everyone's scared, but Genevieve didn't really want to call it that. And of course, it's a punishment of sorts for our transgressions in breaking the binding spell. Except we're not the ones being dragged into the murky depths. We're not the ones who will lose partners, fathers, husbands and sons if the Mermaids succeed! I'm not prepared to just let that happen, Oswald. Are you?"

Oswald swallowed and looked nervously at Ulysses. But Ulysses still watched them, impassive and silent.

Avery spoke, her hand on Alex's arm. "If we do this, the Mermaids will be gone for good. I'm presuming the ones in Mevagissey will join the celebrations in White Haven. They won't be here to threaten you any longer, and they will know that we are too strong for them. They won't come back."

"I knew you would return," Ulysses said, watching them with sadness. "It was inevitable, and it is my fate." He closed his eyes briefly. "I was a fool to fight it."

"I promise we will help you," Avery said.

"You will draw on your reserve of magic above the town?" Ulysses asked.

Avery frowned and blinked. *Of course they could, why hadn't she thought of that? It was theirs to use as they chose.* "Yes. And so will Eve."

Ulysses shifted his massive bulk as he made himself more comfortable. "Let me use it too, and I will help you."

Alex and Avery glanced at each other, surprised. "You'll help?" Avery asked.

"Yes. But I'll need to draw on your magic. The Mermaids will mix with the revellers, they will charm and bewilder, until everyone, man and woman alike, is almost drugged with pleasure. And then they will take their chosen men to the water's edge, and walk them to their doom. The sea will rise to swallow them, and drown those that are left. They have challenged you to a duel. I will need to stop the giant waves, and I must draw on your magic to do so."

"Yes, of course," Avery agreed. "We will lend our strength to yours, and the Nephilim will take on the Mermaids, too. We will attack on several fronts—it's the only way."

"In that case," Oswald said, making a sudden decision that caught them all off guard, "I will be there, too. We will see you on Lughnasadh." And with that declaration he stood, closely followed by Ulysses, and left Avery and Alex gaping at their backs.

***

When she returned to the shop, Dan was there, dreamy and pale, and clearly focussed on other things. Fortunately, Sally had returned to work that morning.

"What's going on with Dan?" she asked, drawing Avery into a quiet corner of the bookshop. "I've never seen him look so distracted."

"Girl trouble," Avery said, watching him surreptitiously.

"Oh, that's nice, isn't it?" Sally asked, falteringly.

"No, not at all. He's in thrall to a Mermaid."

"He's *what*?" Sally exclaimed. "Can't you do something?"

Avery looked at her, annoyed. "I am doing everything I can. Mermaids are very powerful, and their magic is different from ours, rooted in the oceans and the power of Llyr. It's making life difficult."

"But what will happen to him?"

"He'll become a Merman—unless we can break their spell and terrify them with our magic so much that they will not return. We're currently making deals with everyone who can help."

Sally looked horrified. "A Merman! Is that a joke? No, of course it's not, you wouldn't joke about that. Is the Witches Council going to help?"

"No. They're bloody useless. I could strangle that Genevieve woman."

"Oh. So no more Council meetings?"

Avery frowned. "No, I'll keep going to those. We still need to know what's going on. Besides, I'll prove there's more to us, and that we don't *need* them to fight."

"Is there anything I can do? Or," Sally hesitated, "anything I shouldn't do?"

"Do *not* go to the beaches, or The Badger's Hat. And do not go to the Lughnasadh celebrations."

Sally's face fell. "But I love them, and the kids are looking forward to it."

"Not this year, Sally. Trust me. A storm's coming, and you don't want to be caught in it."

***

Over the next week Avery kept herself busy with the shop, and at night she practised spells she thought might come in useful for Lughnasadh. She didn't dare risk returning to The Badger's Hat, but Dan was at work most days, and other than looking utterly lovesick, he remained well.

"So, how's it going with Nixie?" Avery asked him as innocently as she could the following Friday, the day before the celebrations.

He grinned. "Fantastic. She's amazing. We'll be going tomorrow with quite a few of her friends, and my mate, Pete, will be there, too. He's hooked up with one of her mates. We might even have a midnight swim. You should come, too."

Avery's heart sank. She had been trying to convince herself that the Lughnasadh celebrations would be just one big party on the beach, and that perhaps she'd got their plans wrong. She agonised over the fact that she'd persuaded Eve, the Nephilim, and Ulysses to turn up and attack the Mermaids, but that it would all be an elaborate ruse, and they would instead be luring the innocent men to their deaths in some other spot. But Dan's latest update convinced her she was right, and they were looking for confrontation, as if to prove their superiority and unassailability.

"We'll be there," she promised. "We wouldn't miss it. Tell Nixie, thanks."

"Will do." A momentary flicker of confusion passed across his face. "You must have made quite an impression on Nixie. A couple of times she's asked how you are, and if you'll be coming tomorrow. She'll be pleased to know you are."

I'll bet she will be. "Obviously, I don't want to cramp your style, but we'll say hi," Avery said, lying furiously. "Don't you think you should put your hex bag back on?"

"I don't need it anymore," he explained, utterly failing to see its importance. *Too late now, anyway.*

Later that afternoon, Newton came into the shop, looking preoccupied and tired. Avery led him into the back room and put the kettle on for some tea. "You look like crap, Newton. What's going on?"

Newton sat at the table, staring into the distance for a few seconds, before he finally focussed on her. "I'm trying to tie up the investigation into the church murders without creating further complications, but I don't like it. At all."

"I know, and I'm sorry." Avery placed a cup of tea and a plate of biscuits on the table, and then sat down in a chair opposite him. "I wish we could help, but we can't, and you'd never be able to bring anyone to justice."

"I know, but I'd prefer magical justice of some sort at least, and they won't even get that!" He fell silent and sipped his tea.

"But they will make amends," she said, trying to be positive. "They will help save so many people at the beach tomorrow."

He met her eyes with a stony gaze. "Will they? Or will it turn into one big fight with a whole load of casualties caught in the crossfire?"

"You know that's not what we want, and that we'll do anything possible to prevent that."

"I know, but it doesn't mean it will be successful."

"There'll be a police presence there though, won't there?"

"Of course, in case of crowd unrest, but it will be small."

"Will you be there?"

He nodded. "It's not normal for me to be there, but I argued that it's a pagan festival, and that after the church murders anything might happen. So yes, I'll be there in an official capacity."

Avery smiled. "Good. As soon as Eve summons the storm, you must help get people off the beach. We'll isolate the Mermaids."

"And what about the men they've enthralled?"

"We'll separate them as best as we can. I think they'll be confused, anyway. Well, I'm hoping so."

Newton took a biscuit and crunched through it in two bites, and then quickly had another two, as if he hadn't eaten in hours. "We're leaving a lot to chance."

"We're as well prepared as possible," she insisted. "Look, Newton, it's as frustrating for us as it is for you. I'm sorry we can't do more." Avery couldn't help but wonder if Newton's mood was related to Briar, and although she hated to pry, he might want to talk. "Have you caught up with the others since the other night? Reuben? Briar?"

He shook his head. "No, I've been busy at the station, but I might drop into Briar's later."

"Great. Say 'hi' from me."

He lifted his gaze from the table top. "I know what you're thinking, Avery."

"No, you don't," she said, flushing and speaking far too quickly.

"Yes, I do. You're a romantic. I'm single, she's single, and she's attractive. Very attractive, and for a while…" His voice trailed off, and he looked anywhere but at her.

Avery waited, watching his anguished expression.

When he finally looked at her again, his expression was sad. "I know about magic, about your histories. I accept that. I'm your friend, a friend to all of you, and I always will be. And I thought that maybe me and Briar—" he shrugged. "You know. But I think the magic, the blurring of boundaries, is too much. For me, anyway."

"There *is* no blurring of boundaries, Newton. None. We wish no harm—you know that. Especially Briar. She's a healer, a green witch."

"But you're making deals with the Nephilim."

"Just like the police make deals with lesser criminals to get the big guys," she argued. "There's no difference here. You know the Mermaids will kill more."

He shook his head and stood up, brushing crumbs off his shirt absently. "I'd better go."

She stood, too and moved around the table. "No, wait. Don't go yet, I've got time to talk."

"It will solve nothing."

"Things seem complicated right now, but they won't always be. Our lives were peaceful before all of this. They will be again."

He smiled, but it didn't quite reach his eyes. "Will they? I'm not so sure. I'll see you tomorrow."

He left through the back door and Avery watched him, full of regret, without a clue how to make him feel better. And she hoped Briar would be okay, too.

25

Avery stood on the sand dunes overlooking Spriggan Bay, watching the sea and the crowds of people stretched across the sand.

It was the day of the Lughnasadh festival, and in a few hours' time, the bonfire would be lit and the celebrations would begin. For once, it was actually the full moon tonight. On previous years, the full moon had fallen either before or after the celebrations, but the town bonfire was always planned for the Saturday night, regardless. Not that they could see the moon. It was already overcast, grey clouds scudding across the sky, showing only brief glimpses of blue. It wasn't cold, though; instead, it was muggy, a clamminess that kissed your skin. Even the breeze was warm.

A few hundred meters to Avery's right was the harbour wall, and the bonfire was to her left, placed in the fullest curve of the bay, allowing lots of people to be able to spread around it. Even from her height on the dunes, it looked huge, a massive stack of driftwood and pallets, built during the preceding week. Families, couples, and friends of all ages were spread across the sand already. Many had been there all day, but some had arrived recently, laden with chilly bins, rugs, picnic blankets, and baskets of food.

The tide was steadily working its way out, the slow ebb and flow of the waves mesmerising. By nightfall it would be fully out and the Mermaids would have a way to walk to reach the sea.

Avery looked behind her. Below, in the dip of the dunes, the other witches, including Eve and Nate, had set up a base camp. They had picked this spot because it was fairly isolated, sitting a few minutes away from the wooden walkways over the dunes, and out of sight of those on the main beach. They had already placed a spell of protection over the area, causing anyone who did walk that way to turn around and leave.

Behind them were about a hundred metres of dune, all the way back to the road, and above them, on the low hills of the coast, were some houses with commanding views of the sea. The dunes would protect them from their view, too.

Avery took some deep breaths and tried to calm herself down. Her heart was fluttering with anxiety and her mind was racing through all sorts of possibilities. *What if the Nephilim didn't come? What if Eve couldn't summon the storm? What if, after everything they were planning, the Mermaids were too strong and succeeded in taking the men?*

Avery felt movement behind her, and then Alex appeared. He snaked an arm around her waist and pulled her in close, kissing her temple. "Stop worrying," he murmured in her ear.

"I can't help it. This could be a disaster." She turned to look at him, and ran her hand across his cheek. "And I'm worried about you. They could ensnare you, too!"

He smiled, took her hand, and kissed her palm. "That won't happen. You're the only one who can steal my heart, Avery."

"Stop teasing me," she said reproachfully.

"I'm not teasing. I just wanted you to know how I feel, in case anything happens."

What was he saying? I think my heart might explode. I have no idea what to say.

"Avery," he said. "Speak to me. You've gone mute."

"You say the sweetest things. It sort of takes my breath away," she mumbled.

He kissed her hand again. "I'm just being honest. Please be careful tonight. And don't worry about me. I've warded the amulets El gave Reuben and me with extra protection. We'll be immune."

"I'm not convinced. Dan took his protection off, and I still don't know why because he gives me evasive answers when I ask. On the positive side, my protection has held up on the shop. Nixie couldn't get in."

"There you go. They aren't invincible. Anyway, come down to the fire. We're strategising," he said, pulling her by the hand down into the dunes.

The campfire was glowing brightly, the salt in the driftwood burning all shades of blue. The witches sat in a ring, and Eve had a small wooden box next to her, the top open, revealing small glass vials of herbs and potions, all jostling tightly together. A small leather book was open on her lap.

"It's busy, and getting busier," Avery told them as she sat down on the soft, cushiony sand. "There's no wind, it's warm, and the cloud will keep it that way. It's the perfect night for a beach party."

"Not for long," Eve said, rummaging in her box for something. "I'm going to start the spell now. It takes a while to build a good storm. I have to harness energy from all directions, and of course, we want it to look as natural as possible, so slow is better. It's fortunate you have a large pool of energy over White Haven. I'll draw on that."

"Have you ever had to summon a storm quickly?" Briar asked.

"No, never. I summoned rain when we had a massive drought, years ago. The harvest and the cattle were suffering. I also headed off a huge storm a while back, but nothing like I'm planning to do tonight." She smiled. "But don't worry, the principals are the same."

"Do you need us?" Reuben asked.

"No. Nate will help, so that will free you up to get to the beach. What time do they usually light the fire?"

"Not until about eight," Alex explained. He was lying on the sand, chewing a piece of dune grass. "It will be twilight then, sunset is around nine. The cloud cover will of course make it darker."

"Good. I presume the Mermaids won't take the men until it's dark anyway, so I'll aim for the full force of the storm to hit around the same time as nightfall. People should be heading away with their kids then, and the storm will drive off the rest. Then, under cover of the dark, wind, and rain, you can engage with the Mermaids." Eve spread her hands wide. "Of course, weather magic is not always predictable, but it should work out well."

"And what about the Nephilim?" Nate asked. "When do they arrive?"

"In another couple of hours," Alex answered. "I hope."

Nate raised an eyebrow. "I'm curious as to what they're going to look like. And what they're going to do."

"Me, too. I just hope they're dressed," Alex said. "Or things will get really interesting."

Briar smirked. "Part of me hopes they're not. They sure looked good naked."

Eve laughed. "Remind me to ask you more about that later, Briar. In the meantime, while you're all here, lend me your energy to get the ball rolling, and then you can go."

Nate quickly checked that the spell keeping their privacy was still effective, then they linked hands around the fire and Eve began the spell. She tipped her head back and closed her eyes, her voice low as she began the incantation.

She started with an appeal to the four elements, marshalling them to her will. Her long, dark dreads were threaded with beads and framed her strong features, which appeared rigid with concentration. Avery could feel the pull on her magic as it flowed from her and around the circle, mingling with the others'.

Then Eve did something amazing. She opened up and appealed to the four points of the compass, stretching out across the skies above, and with a *snap*, Avery felt the forces start to gather—wind, fire, earth, and water. The magnitude of the distance over which her magic was spread was overwhelming. Eve sat within it all, holding everything together calmly.

She opened her eyes and looked at them. "It has begun."

***

Avery wandered aimlessly across the beach, Briar at her side, taking in everything. The crowds of people, the music that came from all directions, the buzz of conversation, and the hum of energy—no wonder Nixie wanted to return to the ocean here. It was the perfect place.

Historically, men had gone missing alone, or in groups from boats out at sea. This surely had to be a one-off, for so many to be taken at one time. Once again, Avery's thoughts drifted to the power they had released. This was their fault for breaking the binding. But perhaps Nixie and the others had overreached here, and greed would help their downfall.

"A penny for your thoughts," Briar said, and Avery turned to see Briar looking at her, a sad smile on her face.

"Just hoping we're strong enough to do this."

Briar nodded. "It does feel huge. But we have a good plan—well, as much as we can. We don't really know what could happen." She hesitated for a second, and then asked, "Have you seen Newton?"

Avery stopped and turned to face her. "Not since yesterday. He popped into my shop. Have you?"

"Not since then either. He came to see me, too." She sighed heavily. "Magic is freaking him out."

"For now."

"Forever, I think." The smile had disappeared completely from Briar's face, and she turned to face the horizon.

"But he's still our friend. He still cares what happens to us. To you."

"But magic always gets in the way." She shrugged. "I honestly thought that, you know, things might happen."

"You liked him, then? I wasn't sure."

"Yes, I did. He grew on me. Apart from his smoking," she added.

Avery sighed, disappointed for her friend. "Things might happen yet. You're gorgeous, Briar. Trust me, you won't be alone forever."

"How selfish do I sound? Considering what may happen tonight."

"We all want to be loved, and find someone who understands us," Avery said, touching her arm gently. "To find someone who'll put up with our foibles and petty crap.

258

And you will. Not that you have any petty crap I'm sure," she added hurriedly.

"Oh, I'm sure I have," Briar said. "At least you have Alex."

Avery's thoughts flew back to their earlier conversation. "Well, yes, I think so."

Briar laughed dryly. "Avery! Stop it. You doubt yourself, and him. He loves you. It's all over his face. He might not have said so, but it's obvious."

All of Avery's doubts rushed through her. "Seriously? Do you think so?"

"Has he said it?"

"Well, I don't know…he said something earlier."

She huffed with impatience. "I won't ask what. But whatever it was, accept it."

Suitably chastised, Avery nodded. And then she saw Nixie and lots of young and very attractive women on the edge of the crowd, clustered together around a campfire. With them were a number of laughing men, and among them were Dan and Pete.

"There they are," Avery said, turning towards them, but resisting the urge to point.

Briar frowned. "Great, let's go and let them know we're here."

"Is that wise?" Avery asked, catching her arm.

"Yes. It's a game, and we're in play. There are certain moves you have to make, Avery. This is one of them." And then Briar marched off, with Avery running after her.

Before anyone noticed her, Briar strode to the edge of the group. "Evening, ladies. Enjoying yourselves?"

Heads whipped around, and Nixie looked up, a lazy smile on her face. "Avery and a friend. How lovely that you have come to join us."

Dan looked around and smiled, but stayed sitting on the sand next to Nixie. *Like a dog at his master's heel.* He greeted them weakly. "Guys, you came!"

"We're not staying," Avery said, standing firmly beyond their circle. "Just a quick hello."

Most of the group had now fallen silent, and the Mermaids watched them with narrowed eyes and pursed lips, while the men looked contented and oblivious.

"That's a shame," Nixie said, her voice like a caress on the skin. "We're planning on a swim later."

"I'm sure you are," Briar said. "We'll be around, so I'm sure we'll see you later."

"Maybe," Nixie said, her sharp eyes flashing in challenge. "But probably not."

Avery was watching Dan, and she caught a frown pass across his face, but it was quickly gone once Nixie turned her beaming smile on him.

They turned and walked away, aware of being watched. "There are well over a dozen women there," Briar said, worried. "And they looked mean. I'm not sure we're going to manage this."

"We bloody well have to," Avery said, her resolve strengthening. "None of those men had any will left, and I do not mean to lose them. Not one."

On their way back to the others they saw Newton talking to one of the PCs, patrolling as part of the community policing. He waved and strolled over, looking uncharacteristically nervous. "Are we on track?" he asked without preamble.

"Yes," Avery said immediately, hoping to instil a sense of calm. "How about you?"

"Just waiting for the storm." He looked around, perplexed, and Avery noticed he seemed to be avoiding looking at Briar. She had a sudden urge to slap some sense into him. "If I'm honest, it looks unlikely. Are you sure this Eve woman knows what she's doing?"

"Of course she does," Briar said scathingly, and Avery looked at her, surprised. She had never heard Briar sound so abrupt, and neither had Newton by the look on his face. His head jerked back and he focussed on her fully.

He stuttered, "I didn't mean to doubt…"

"Yes, you did. Can't quite make up your mind about magic, can you? But it's fine when it suits you," Briar snapped and walked away, leaving Avery and Newton staring at her back.

A red flush started to creep up Newton's neck, and he couldn't take his eyes off Briar. He looked horrified.

"Sorry, but you did kind of ask for that," Avery said, as gently as possible.

He tore his gaze away from Briar and looked at her. "I didn't mean anything by that! Shit. She hates me."

Avery patted his arm. "No, she doesn't. I better go. Stay safe tonight, and keep well away from—" she pointed across the sand, "*them*. By the campfire, where the crowd is thinning."

She headed back to the dunes, and hadn't gone far when there was an excited yell, and Ben, Dylan, and Cassie materialised out of the crowds. "There you are! We've been looking for you," Ben said.

"I didn't know you were coming," Avery said, shocked. "Are you mad? Things may get rough tonight."

Cassie laughed. "But this is Lughnasadh, and if the Nephilim are coming, we want to see them. It will complete our investigation, sort of."

"I've brought my camera, too," Dylan added, gesturing to his bag. "We don't scare that easily."

Avery eyed them warily. "Well, please be careful. A storm's coming, and we need to stop the Mermaids. We won't necessarily be able to watch out for you, too."

"It's fine," Ben reassured her. "We can look after ourselves." And with that, they headed into the crowds.

***

By the time the festivities were about to begin, the skies had darkened, and the clouds were thick with the promise of rain. Not that this development curtailed anyone's excitement.

The councillor, Stan, was dressed in white wizard robes, and he was holding a long, wooden staff. His hair was short and grey, but he had a beard that he had dyed, for some unknown reason, purple. He stood behind the mayor on a small wooden platform in front of the fire that faced the crowds.

The mayor, a woman called Judy Taylor who had bold red hair and short curls, gave a short speech about the importance of honouring pagan traditions and remembering the heritage of White Haven and the witches who once had lived there. Avery and others were standing on top of the dunes, watching the scene below, and they smothered smirks at that. Then, Judy passed the ceremony over to Stan.

With much pomp, Stan raised his staff and offered thanks to the Gods for the beautiful summer, and the promise of a bountiful harvest to come. He gestured to the flowers and fruits that had been placed on the small platform as gifts, making clear they were offerings. He then reminded the onlookers about the church service at the Church of All Souls, which would celebrate Lammas in a more traditional way. The Council were always inclusive. He then turned dramatically and pointed his staff at the bonfire. Two young men stood ready with a flaming torch on either side of the pile of firewood, ready to ignite the fire, but before they could move, a small *bang* emitted from the centre of the pile of wood, and it sparked into life of its own accord. The young men looked momentarily startled, and then lowered the torches to the wood hurriedly, as if it was meant to happen all along, and the crowd clapped and cheered. Stan looked shocked, but he smothered his surprise quickly as he turned and bowed to the crowd, and then proceeded to throw a large glass of beer into the fire as a libation to the Gods.

El was watching with a very large smile on her face.

"Naughty," Reuben said, equally delighted.

"I thought it would be a nice touch," she said with a wink.

Some people stuck around, watching the fire intently, while others drifted back to their groups, their blankets, and their booze.

Now that the fire was lit, the skies seemed even darker. The flames spread quickly and smoke eddied in the air, coinciding with the first stirrings of wind.

Avery stood next to Alex, and she nudged him gently. "How are you? I haven't seen you for hours."

He looked pleased with himself. "I've been contacting the Nephilim."

She frowned, worried. "Are you okay? You managed it alone."

He nodded. "I'm fine. Now that I have a connection, it's easier. And it helps that they're willing to be involved. You'll be pleased to know they're here."

Relief flooded through her. "Thank the Goddess! Where?"

"Beyond the dunes. I'm going to go and fetch them." He kissed the top of her head. "See you soon."

She watched him for a few seconds until he disappeared from view, and then looked at Briar, standing silent, her gaze on the horizon. "Briar, are you all right?"

For a second she didn't answer, and then with visible effort she said, "I'm sorry about earlier."

"You don't need to apologise for anything. I was feeling pretty annoyed with him, too."

Briar finally turned to face Avery. "I'm aiming to work out some of my aggression on those bloody Mermaids."

"Good. Me, too."

Avery looked behind her, down into the dunes, and for a second saw nothing. The veil of magic that protected the space had fallen like a blanket. She whispered the word of unveiling, and it shimmered and disappeared like smoke. Then she saw Eve crouched over their own small fire, and next to her were Nate, Ulysses, and Oswald.

"Come on, Oswald and Ulysses are here."

The small hollow in the dunes was protected from the rising sea breeze, and the fire warmed it beautifully. Even though it wasn't cold, there was something special about sitting around a fire and warming your hands.

Eve's eyes were glazed in concentration; her arms were raised and reaching towards the sky, and she chanted quietly to herself for a few moments. Avery felt the surge of magic around them and its connection to the storm building above, and she shivered with anticipation. When Eve finished, she reached into the small wooden box next to her, chose some herbs, and threw them into the flames. The fire changed colour, sparking with purples and greens, and with it came a huge rumble of thunder in the distance. She smiled at Avery across the fire. "It's shaping up nicely."

"When will it hit?" Ulysses asked.

"In about an hour, as promised. I'll bring the wind before rain. That should start to drive people off the beach."

Reuben laughed. "There's a few down there that will need more than wind to drive them away."

"And that's what the torrential rain will be for," Eve said, grinning. "I have a spell that I'll use to keep me dry here. This, essentially, will be the eye of the storm. I'm afraid the rest of you will get very wet."

Reuben stirred. "Well, I'm going to keep an eye on the Mermaids, in case they decide to bring their plans forward. And I need a hot dog."

"I'll come with you," El said, rising to her feet. She turned to Avery. "We'll stay well hidden in the dunes, and let you know if anything happens."

Ulysses and Oswald had fallen into silence. Oswald, as usual, was wearing his slightly odd, old-fashioned clothing, even on the beach, but he'd replaced his shoes with hiking boots, adding to the incongruity of his appearance. Ulysses was dressed in a t-shirt and jeans, and was barefoot, his hulking build making everyone else look like dwarves.

Avery was restless. "Is there anything I should be doing?"

Nate shook his head. "The action won't start until the crowds have reduced."

"But I feel I should do *something*!"

"This was your plan," Briar pointed out. She was barefoot too, and she dug her toes in the sand, wriggling them playfully.

"I know, but now it feels lame."

"That's how they want you to feel. Overwhelmed and underprepared. You've been *manoeuvred*, actually," Oswald said, suddenly sparking to life.

"What do you mean?" Avery asked.

"As you already know, tonight is a challenge of power. If I'm honest, they have the upper hand. After all, they picked the time and the place. You had no choice but to turn up."

"I know," Avery answered, annoyed. "But what else were we to do? Say, 'no thanks, have a nice night, and help yourself to our innocent men?' That's why we asked for help!"

Ulysses stared into the fire. "Mermaids are wilful, strong, and vindictive. It gives them great pleasure to thwart the Daughters of Don."

"I prefer to think of myself as a daughter of the great Goddess," Briar said archly.

Ulysses carried on regardless, his green eyes reflecting the firelight, which had now returned to a bright orange flame. "To take the men from beneath your very eyes will give them great pleasure."

"We've talked about the possibility of them raising a huge wave to drown the town, or us. Do you still think that's likely?" Avery asked, curious for Ulysses's opinion.

"It's possible," he said nodding. "I thought perhaps they would bring a great wave to wipe the beach, but now I'm not so sure. I think they will want you to survive—to remember their victory."

Nate watched Ulysses thoughtfully. "That makes sense. Our failure will be painful, and horrible."

Ulysses frowned. "It is possible that they will raise a wave over White Haven only."

"But the town is only a few hundred metres away. Could they make a wave so targeted?"

"Absolutely. The tide is coming in, isn't it?"

"It will be soon," Avery answered, wondering where he was going with this.

"And you are bringing in a large storm. This will make it easier to create a monster wave," he mused. "It may not happen, but I think it's a very good guess."

"And what can we do about that?" Briar asked. "We'll have enough trouble saving the men!"

"That's why you have me," Ulysses said, looking up finally. He rose to his feet. "My power over the sea is greater than all of yours. Come, Oswald. We must head to the harbour."

"But we need your help with the Mermaids," Avery said, standing, too.

"You'll have to manage those alone, I'm afraid." And with those ominous words, Ulysses disappeared into the night with Oswald at his side.

Only seconds later, Alex entered their secluded hollow, and behind him stood seven very tall men. The Nephilim had arrived.

26

The Nephilim were dressed in a mixture of army combat trousers, jeans, t-shirts, and boots. They had all shaved, and several had cut their hair, revealing their hard, angular faces, with high cheekbones and square jaws. They looked ex-military and their muscular builds were still apparent, but who knew where their wings were. Every single one of them had an intense stare; the look of those who had seen too much.

There was a second of silence, and then Alex spoke. "Are we interrupting something?"

Avery felt a wave of panic wash through her, and then she took a deep breath and exhaled heavily. *This will be okay.* "Ulysses thinks that the Mermaids may seek to drown White Haven in a massive wave. He and Oswald have gone to the harbour."

Before Alex could respond, Nate leapt to his feet. "So, Alex, are you going to introduce us?"

"Avery, Nate, Eve, and Briar," he said, pointing them out in turn. "We're all witches, and we're here tonight to stop the Mermaids from taking men. There are another two with us who aren't here at the moment."

"Reuben and El are watching the Mermaids," Avery explained.

Alex gestured to the Nephilim. "I'll let you introduce yourselves."

A dark-skinned man detached himself from the group, and Avery recognised him from the cave as the one who had done most of the talking, the one she presumed Alex had the psychic link with. "I'm Gabreel, and this is Eliphaz, Barak, Nahum, Othniel, Amaziah, and Asher."

Each one nodded in turn as he was introduced, but none of them spoke, and Avery knew she'd never remember their names. She wondered if they had any magical abilities, or if brute strength alone was all they needed. If your father was an angel, it must give you some special abilities. *Time will tell.*

There was another ominous rumble of thunder, a gust of wind ran through the dunes, and then there was a flash of lightning far off in the distance.

Eve spoke from where she still sat beside the fire. "I need to concentrate now. I'm going to draw the storm closer—it's going to be big. You better get going."

"I'll stay with you, just in case," Nate said, settling beside her again. "Good luck with the Mermaids."

"Good luck to you, too, and thanks again," Avery said, leaving the warmth of the fire as she led everyone else back to the top of the dunes.

The wind hit them, scouring their skin like sandpaper. Below them the fire still burned bright and hot, and there were a good number of people still on the beach. But it was almost dark now, and Avery could see a stream of people leaving, burdened with blankets and chilly bins.

The wind carried the sound of music from various smaller campfires, the shrieks of children, and the laughter of adults. Silhouettes danced around fires, and there were a few people at the water's edge, barefoot and shouting.

"Good," Alex said. "At least some of them are going. Where are the Mermaids?"

"That way," Briar said, pointing to the left toward an almost deserted area.

They walked down onto the main beach and hadn't gone far when El arrived, out of breath. Her eyes flickered across the Nephilim. "There's some movement in the camp. It looks like they're making a start."

"Right," Avery said, glad to be doing something after hours of waiting. "Alex, how do you want to play this?"

"We've decided that we'll hang back, until the storm fully hits, and then when they're getting close to the sea, the Nephilim will block them."

Gabreel smiled like a shark. "It will be a nice surprise for them."

"What about their Siren call? Will it affect you?"

He shook his head. "No, but they can try."

"Okay," Avery said decisively. "El, take everyone to Reuben, and when they make a move, we'll intervene. Me and Briar will test the waters—sorry, terrible analogy," she said, grinning. "Ready, Briar?"

"I've been ready for hours."

Avery and Briar threaded their way through the remaining partygoers. A flash of lightning illuminated the Mermaids ahead, clustering around the flames of their own small fire.

As they approached, Avery felt the power of their magic, and her skin rose in goose bumps. The wind carried their wild music that emanated from some mysterious unseen place, making her want to run across the sand and fall at the feet of the beautiful women with their pale skin, long hair, and beguiling eyes. She resisted its pull, but quickened her pace, Briar right next to her.

They were only a short distance away when a figure left the fire and walked to meet them. It was Nixie. "Stay away, witches. You won't win."

Avery peered behind her. "Where's Dan?"

She grinned, and her glamour briefly fell away, revealing a row of sharp teeth. "Out of your reach. Do you want to say your goodbyes?"

"You're very confident, aren't you," Avery said. "To invite us here and think we can't stop you? It's not a game. These men will die."

Nixie considered them both for a long moment, her eyes full of hate. "Life beneath the sea is not death. They will have long lives and father many children."

"But," Briar said scathingly, "you're not really giving them a choice, are you? Maybe if they were going willingly we would have less of a problem with this."

"Yes," Avery agreed. "Drop your magic and ask them now. We won't stop those who choose to go freely." Nixie didn't answer, and Avery laughed. "Exactly. No one would go. Blame Llyr for your predicament. The Gods love foolish games, but we won't tolerate it."

Nixie was clearly furious, and she did something so quick that Avery barely registered it before the sand turned into liquid beneath her feet, sucking her in until she was knee deep, and she saw Briar floundering next to her.

At the same time, there was an enormous crack of thunder, and lightning sprang across the sky, slicing it into pieces, and with an unexpected suddenness, rain started to fall in huge, freezing drops, stinging her skin. Within seconds it was pouring down, and then the storm really raged. Crack after crack of thunder and lightning followed.

Excellent. Nobody would notice what she was about to do.

"You'll have to do better than that, Nixie." Avery summoned air, using it to pull her and Briar from the sand, until they were both floating just off the ground. Then she pushed back, hitting Nixie full force in the chest.

Nixie shrieked as she flew over the sand, landing with a *thump* several metres away. She rose to her knees, her face furious, lifted her head, and keened like a banshee.

It seemed this was the signal.

As one, the Mermaids pulled the men close and started to walk towards the sea. They didn't run. Instead, they performed a laughing, teasing dance across the sands. Even from a distance, Avery could see the men's glazed expressions.

Avery saw the Nephilim break free of the dunes, the other three witches next to them, charging towards the mesmerised group.

Briar ran to join them in a pincer movement, but thick strands of seaweed caught around Avery's ankle, dragging her back. Avery whirled around, but Nixie was upon her, tackling her to the ground, her glamour completely gone now. Her nails scratched and pulled and she snapped her sharp teeth at Avery's face. In seconds, Avery felt her lungs start to fill with water and the sand suck her down. Terrified she was either going to drown or suffocate, Avery blasted Nixie away, and spewed water, coughing furiously. She was keenly aware that Nixie would attack her again, so summoning all her energy, she leapt to her feet and then hit back with ball after ball of fire, doing the same to the seaweed still rising out of the sand like tentacles.

Avery harnessed the wild wind that now shrieked around them, muffling all other sound, whisked it into a small tornado, and sent it after Nixie. It pulled her into its whirling circle, and carried her away into the darkness.

Avery didn't bother watching her. Instead she turned and ran after the others. The sand was sodden with water and it splashed around her, slowing her speed, and the torrential rain almost blinded her. They were all now halfway to the sea, the Mermaids still so sure of themselves that they didn't rush, but lazily danced onwards, as oblivious to the weather as the men who followed them, laughing with dazed excitement.

Avery glanced behind her, back to the main fire, and saw it had virtually gone out. The beach, what she could see of it in the darkness and through the sheets of rain, was deserted.

She stood for a second, letting her eyes adjust as she swept her hair back off her face. The witches were darting around the men, desperately trying to break the enchantment, fend off the Mermaids, and blast them out of the way. The men were so beguiled that they were fighting the witches off, too. It was a disaster, and it was clear they were struggling.

And then she saw the Nephilim, black silhouettes beneath the lightning, forming a barrier between the sea and the Mermaids.

Avery ran, finally coming to halt at the edge of the group, which had come to dead stop. The Mermaids faced the Nephilim in a line, the men behind them. Their glamour had disappeared, revealing their silvery, scaly skin and their webbed hands and feet. Their singing rose, but the Nephilim were indifferent to its charms.

Avery ran into the middle of the men, joining the others in trying to break the enchantment. One by one, she jolted the men with a blast of fire, letting it curl up their arms, enough that she hoped to break the spell, as it had done for the witches in the pub. Unfortunately, whatever enchantment they were in now was far more powerful. They shrugged, blinked, and then returned to their dazed state. She found Dan and shook him, but his eyes were vacant.

Frustrated, she caught Briar's eye. She looked frantic, and as impotent as Avery was. There was no sign of Nixie, and Avery wasn't sure if that was good or bad.

Gabreel called out, his voice booming out over the storm. "Return to your ocean, Daughters of Llyr, or you will regret it. These men do not belong with you."

One of them stepped forward, her face contorted with fury. "What men are you that resist our song?"

Gabreel shouted, "We are no men! We are the Nephilim."

The Mermaid's confident manner faltered. "No. It cannot be. You are dead. Fallen in the great flood that destroyed the world."

"And now we are back for vengeance. Flee now, or you shall all die."

Another Mermaid spoke, her voice carrying on the wind like the call of a seagull. "It's a bluff, they're powerless against us."

Gabreel laughed. He flexed his shoulders and two enormous wings spread from his back. He rose into the air and headed straight to the Mermaid. With his strong grip he lifted her high into the storm. Her shrieks made Avery's skin crawl.

The rest of the Mermaids ran at the Nephilim, leaving the men unguarded behind them.

Avery shouted, "We have to act now! We can't break their enchantment, but we can shield them."

"I agree!" Reuben shouted back.

They quickly gathered together, linked hands, and threw out a powerful shield of magic, encircling the men—but they were still transfixed and immovable.

"What now?" Alex yelled.

"Air!" Avery yelled back. "We'll float them back."

Much as she had pulled herself and Briar from the quicksand, she sent a cushion of air beneath the men's feet so they floated inches above the ground, and then with the shield around them, they shepherded them slowly back to the dunes.

Avery looked over at the battle, because that was the only word for it. The Nephilim had taken to the air, plucking the Mermaids up in ones or twos, and they dragged them high over the sea into the heart of the storm. In the searing flashes of light, she saw their broken bodies plummet, and she winced. The ones left on the ground must have decided to salvage what they could, because they turned back to where the men had been, and as soon as they realised they were no longer behind them, they fled into the sea.

The lightning flashed, again and again, illuminating the rising waves as they crashed on the shore. As Avery glanced to her right, back towards White Haven, her breath caught in her throat. An enormous wave was building beyond the harbour. It must be Nixie. She had to trust that Ulysses and Oswald could deal with it alone.

The group arrived at the edge of the dunes, wind-swept and soaked, and she released the spell, floating them back to the ground. Avery sighed with relief as the decked path that led from the beach back to the car park appeared out of the gloom.

A groan grabbed her attention, and she looked around to see Dan rubbing his face. "Where the hell am I? What's going on?"

Beyond him, the other men were stirring, too. Avery shouted, "Not now, Dan. Come on, we need to get off the beach."

With El leading the way, the men followed, all of them awake, but utterly confused.

Before the beach was lost to view, Avery turned and looked back to the edge of the sea, but the darkness and rain obscured everything. Another flash of lightning showed a soaring black shape in the sky, and then it was gone. She hoped the Nephilim would be okay. She turned and trudged after the others, and with every step, Avery felt her worry ebbing away, and exhaustion starting to take hold.

She caught up to Briar, who was drenched and shivering. "Are you all right?"

She grimaced. "Nothing a strong drink and a bath won't cure." And then she allowed herself a smile. "We did good! With help."

"Yes, we did," Avery answered. "But it's not over yet."

A shout up ahead distracted them. For a second, Avery couldn't work out what was happening, and then Newton appeared, running through the men, encouraging them onwards. As soon as he saw them, he grinned.

"You're okay!"

"Of course we are. There was never anything to worry about," Avery said as confidently as she could. But he wasn't really looking at her. Not that Briar seemed to care. She nodded and pushed past him, and Newton turned and followed, leaving Avery to walk alone.

A flash of red and blue lights were visible in the darkness, and as they reached the car park, Avery saw a couple of police cars and an ambulance, and a few people who looked as if they'd come from the houses opposite the beach. The rain was easing to heavy rather than torrential, and a few uniformed officers ran up to the men, ushering them to the shelter in the nearest house. Alex and the others were talking to one of the officers. Newton had stopped following Briar and was standing alone, soaked and smoking a cigarette as he leaned on his car. She headed to his side. "Thanks for organising this."

He nodded to some of the houses behind them. "Someone called it in—which was good, because otherwise I would have had to. I didn't want to risk one of the PCs seeing what was happening and getting involved. They said the lightning showed a group of men on the beach, who looked to be struggling." He gave her a long look, his face clouded and uncertain. "Let's hope there's no video footage. Or it's too unclear to see." He paused for second. "I saw the Nephilim out there battling with the Mermaids."

"We couldn't have done this without them, Newton. Their magic had these men utterly captivated. We might have saved a couple on our own, but that's all."

He nodded as he looked into the distance, and then his gaze drifted to Briar for a brief second, where she stood at the back of the ambulance, wrapped in a towel. A myriad of emotions crossed his face. "All right. Thanks, Avery. I better head to the station and see what comes out of all this." Another couple of police cars turned up and he walked away, as Avery looked for Alex.

She saw him deep in conversation with Dan and she ran over, putting her arm around Alex's waist. "How are you two?"

Alex kissed the top of her head. "We're fine."

"Speak for yourself," Dan said. He looked white and his jaw was clenched, whether from fright or the cold Avery couldn't tell. "I might never go on another date again."

"Can you remember what happened?" Avery asked.

"I remember the beach party, and then things get a bit blurred." He looked behind him to the police. "I better go. I want a lift home. I'll fudge stuff as much as I can with the police. And thanks, guys. I owe you. And you," he said to

Avery, "can explain to me exactly what really happened tonight with coffee and a pastry at work."

"Done!" Avery said, smiling.

While the police were distracted with the other men, the witches headed back into the dunes. Briar was visibly shivering, and it made Avery realise how cold she was now that the adrenalin was wearing off.

"There's a big wave heading to White Haven," Avery told the others. "We need to get Eve and Nate to safety, and then head to town."

"Avery," Reuben said, shaking his head. "We don't need to worry about town. Ulysses will deal with it. Come on." And with that he headed across the dunes towards their original campfire.

***

Eve and Nate were still crouched around the fire, in a perfectly warm, dry circle, protected from the raging storm by Eve's magic.

"So glad you two are so cosy here," Reuben declared as they warmed themselves.

"The advantages of being a weather witch. Lesson number one is how to keep dry. Did you save them?" Eve asked.

"Yes, thanks to you," Avery answered. "The men are safe, and the Nephilim were pretty brutal. We left them to it."

"Should we go back and try to help?" El asked. "Although, I would imagine they've finished by now."

Alex shook his head. "Gabreel was pretty clear that we shouldn't interfere. I'll try and contact him later. And they didn't look like they were in trouble."

The three women laughed, and Briar put in, "No. They weren't bothered by the Mermaids at all. I don't think I'll ever forget the sight of them and their huge wings. That was impressive."

El nodded. "Revenge is a dish best served in the heart of a huge storm."

Eve smiled. "Good. Sit with me a few minutes while I ease this bad boy down."

"Much as I hate to leave your toasty fire, I want to see White Haven," Avery said, unable to forget the image of the rising wave. "Anyone want to join me?"

"I'll come," Alex said, rising to his feet.

"Me, too," Reuben volunteered. "It's not every day you see a giant wave."

They reached the top of the dunes and looked towards the town. A rogue wave was rolling in. It was enormous, towering over everything and visible only as an intense blackness against the charcoal grey of the night sky. Avery felt her breath catch, and she heard Alex swear. Viewed through the rain it seemed like a mirage.

"Are we sure Ulysses can handle this?" she asked, alarmed.

But even before she'd finished her question, they saw the wave start to break, well outside of the harbour walls, falling in on itself, and then a wild, keening cry of grief was carried to them on the wind. *Nixie*.

It was over.

"I think we need a nightcap," Reuben said. "Let's head to mine."

27

Reuben's enormous living room was crowded, the fire was roaring, and everyone sat around cradling beer, wine, or whiskey.

Ulysses and Oswald had arrived last with Avery after she went to find them at the harbour, and they both looked very pleased with themselves.

"So, don't keep us in the dark," Eve said, grinning. "What happened?"

Ulysses laughed, his voice as rich as chocolate ganache. "Well, she sure didn't expect to see me."

"Nixie?" Avery asked. She sat on the floor between Alex's legs, who was seated on the sofa behind her. She had managed to dry herself off, and warmth was flooding through her.

Ulysses nodded. "We found her on the harbour wall, calling up the sea. It was her song that led us to her."

Oswald agreed. "She was oblivious and thoroughly enjoying herself. Her face," he mused. "It was vicious. And then she saw Ulysses."

Ulysses laughed again. "It was a good thing you made such a brilliant storm, Eve. No one was around, or I'd have been arrested, because I tackled her straight into the water. She might have been half my size, but she's full Mermaid and it's her element. But I was able to drag her out into the deep. There was more out there than just the wave."

They all looked at him, drinks halfway to lips. "What do you mean by that?" Alex asked.

"There was a pretty big deep ocean creature heading in; a Kraken. Don't worry—it's gone now. And it took Nixie with it. I don't think it was too pleased at being dragged out here."

"A Kraken?" Nate asked, almost choking on his whiskey.

Ulysses nodded. "They're vicious things, but fortunately it took out its annoyance on Nixie, and then I dispelled the wave."

Avery smiled. "Thank you. We owe you."

He shook his head. "No, you don't. And besides, we may need *your* help one day. And it was good for me, cathartic."

Oswald agreed. "I'm sorry the Council didn't help more, but you have proven yourselves tonight."

Nate laughed. "The Council can be a bit precious, especially Genevieve. She definitely wanted you back on the Council, but she always wants things her way. I think she was trying to prove who was boss. I'm not sure it worked."

"She's the lead witch, I have no problem with that," Avery said, "but it was more than us at risk tonight. I'm not sure I understand her stance. Many people could've died tonight—or as good as, to be condemned to a life beneath the ocean."

"You have to remember," Eve said regretfully, "that for many witches, our needs come before the needs of other communities. She didn't want to risk anyone knowing about us, or things becoming more complicated. That's the way it's always been."

With the lights low and the fire crackling, it was hard to believe that just a few hours earlier they had been battling on Spriggan Beach beneath thunder and lightning.

"Well," Briar began, "I'll be glad if life could return to some normality for a while. I have a business to run."

"Agreed," Alex said. He looked across to Eve and Nate. "Our magic that falls over the town. Can you still feel it?"

Eve nodded. "It's certainly fading, and I channelled some of it tonight, which is why my storm was so good. Yes, I still feel it. But you know, you shouldn't worry about that. While some creatures will sense it, not all will want to use it. Some are curious and are attracted to others like them. It can be a scary world out there for those with paranormal abilities. That's why it's best to keep them hidden."

Before anyone could answer, a heavy knock on the door disturbed them, and Reuben went to answer it. When he returned, Gabreel was with him, and his steely gaze swept the room.

Alex leapt to his feet and walked over to shake his hand. "Gabreel, thank you so much for tonight."

"Our pleasure. It felt good to defeat the Daughters of Llyr. They will not come here again. At least not for many years."

"Come and sit," Alex urged him.

He shook his head. "No, I must join my brothers. I wanted you to know we will be on the moors beyond the town. We have found somewhere to stay for now, but we may need your help to become more," he paused thoughtfully, "legitimate."

"We'll do what we can," Alex said, and Avery wondered what Newton would make of that.

He turned and left, saying muted goodbyes, and then Nate rose to his feet, too. "Come on, Eve, we should go. I'm knackered."

Eve drained her glass. "You're right. I'm going to sleep for a week I think. I'll keep in touch, Avery."

Avery stood to hug her. "Yes, please. Safe travels." She turned to hug Nate, too. "And to you. Thank you."

"Time for us to go, too," Oswald said, sounding weary.

After a round of hugs, handshakes, and promises to catch up soon, only the five White Haven witches remained.

"More alcohol, anyone?" Reuben asked. "I've got plenty of beds."

"Yes please, and can we order food?" El asked, stretching like a cat. "I'm starving!"

"It's nearly midnight. No one delivers at this time," Reuben said, reaching for the whisky bottle. "But there's food in the kitchen—if someone wants to cook."

As they were talking, Avery heard the crunch of gravel and a car engine idling up the drive. "Who's that?"

"It's probably Newton," Alex answered. "I thought I'd let him know where we were. I'll go let him in."

Avery glanced at Briar, but she was huddled in front of the fire, staring into the flames.

Newton hesitated at the threshold of the lounge. "Am I welcome?"

"Of course you are, you moron," Reuben said affectionately. "There's a glass here with your name on it."

"I've brought curry to bribe you with, if that helps," he added, and Alex followed him with another couple of bags packed with cartons.

El went to help him. "Brilliant, you must have read my mind." She kissed Newton's cheek as she wrestled a bag from his hands.

Avery smiled. "You don't need to bribe us. You're always welcome."

"Even if you're an ass," Briar added, glancing up at him.

Newton met her eyes and then looked at the rest of them, a rueful smile on his face. "You were all brilliant tonight, and so were the Nephilim. Well done, and sorry if I doubted you."

"You're allowed to," Alex said. "It was risky, but it paid off."

"I'm getting plates," El said, heading out the door. "Newton, sit down, relax, and get drunk with the rest of us."

***

The next day, Alex and Avery left relatively early and headed back to Spriggan Beach, strolling hand in hand across the dunes and onto the flat sands.

The sky was a pale, watery blue, as if the storm had scrubbed the colour from it. The beach was strewn with driftwood and seaweed, and the remains of the blackened wood from the bonfire sat in a soggy pile. The tide was out, and birds settled in the shallows and pulled worms from the wet sand.

"Hard to believe, isn't it, that there was such a massive storm and almost a mass kidnapping last night?" Alex observed, pulling her close as he turned to face her.

"It's surreal! It feels like a dream."

He smoothed her hair from her face. "We've gained some good friends out of this."

"Do you think the Nephilim are friends?"

"I think so. Different, yes, but still friends. And of course, there's Ulysses and Oswald. Oswald's a funny little man, but I like him."

"One of life's eccentrics," Avery agreed. "And I like Eve and Nate, too. Do you think things will be okay with Newton? I'm worried about him. I mean, I know he came round last night, but long term?"

"He'll always wrestle a bit with what we do," he mused. "But he knows we act with White Haven's best interest at heart, and ultimately, he's on our side."

Avery nodded absently. "I hope you're right." She hesitated a second and then said, "I was really worried for a moment last night, in case their magic worked on you."

He winked. "Our spell worked, really well. I could hear their song, but I could control my emotional pull towards it. You won't get rid of me that easily." He wrapped her in his arms, pulled her close, and kissed her until she was breathless. "In the meantime, let's go for breakfast and have an epically lazy day. We deserve it."

***

Over the next day or so, the papers and local news were filled with stories of Lughnasadh and the storm.

Unclear footage from camera phones showed strange shapes on the beach, and there was a report about a group of men who became confused and tried to go swimming at the height of the storm. They described how a few locals helped bring them to safety, and that was about all that was said. Quite a few speculated about angels of darkness and aliens on the beach, but most of the speculation died down quickly to muted rumblings.

Sally and Dan were full of questions for Avery on Monday morning, and the tourists who came in the shop couldn't keep the excitement out of the voices about the quaint little town and the beach activities. Every now and again someone mentioned the film *The Wicker Man*, and Avery tried hard not to giggle. And then she thought of what might have happened, and that sobered her up pretty quickly.

Ben appeared in the store halfway through the afternoon, bringing cakes.

Dan smiled in approval. "You know how to make yourself popular around here."

"I always aim to please," he said, helping himself to a cake. "So … Saturday was fairly epic."

"Did you film it?" Avery asked, worried over whether to be worried or not.

"The weather was too bad," he said, shaking his head. "Impressive storm."

"A friend helped," Avery said impassively.

"And the weird, winged creatures over the sea?"

"Our new friends, the Nephilim," she said, quietly.

"Okay," Ben said, nodding in understanding. "Well. The calls keep coming. There are still more spirits in White Haven and other towns. Any suggestions as to who could help us, if needed?"

"I haven't had a chance to ask yet, but I will. I promise. It's just been a bit busy around here." *Underestimation of the year.*

"All good. By the way, Briar called Cassie. She's starting with her next week."

Avery smiled with genuine pleasure. "That's great! I look forward to seeing her there."

"And as for me," Ben said, heading to the door, "I'll be in touch. I have a feeling things aren't going to stay quiet here for long."

"Is that wishful thinking?" Avery called.

"It's good for business," he said, and then waved goodbye.

Dan rummaged in the bag, pulled out a cake, and took a huge bite.

"Glad to see your appetite hasn't suffered after the weekend, Dan," Sally said, smothering a smirk.

"My appetite for cake is fine, not so much for women. But he's right, you know, your friend, Ben."

"Is he?" Avery said, wondering where this was leading.

"Oh yeah. I don't think White Haven will ever be normal again."

Avery groaned. She had the horrible feeling he was right. And then she allowed herself a smile.

What's so great about normal? Absolutely nothing.

End of Book 3 of the White Haven Witches.
White Haven Witches Book 4 will be out later this year.

Thank you for reading *Magic Unleashed*. All authors love reviews. They're important because they help drive sales and promotions, so I'd love it if you would leave a review. Scroll down the page to where it says, 'Write a customer review' and click. Thank you—your review is much appreciated.

Author's Note

Thank you for reading *Magic Unleashed,* the third book in the White Haven Witches series.

Thanks again to Fiona Jayde Media for my awesome cover, and thanks to Kyla Stein at Missed Period Editing for tidying up my draft.

Thanks to my beta readers, glad you enjoyed it; your feedback, as always, is very helpful!

Thanks also to my launch team, who give valuable feedback on typos and are happy to review on release. It's lovely to hear from them—you know who you are—and their feedback is always so encouraging. I'm lucky to have them on my team! I love hearing from all my readers, so I welcome you to get in touch.

If you'd like to read a bit more background to the stories, please head to my website, where I'll be blogging about the books I've read and the research I've done on the series—in fact, there's lots of stuff on there about my other series, Tom's Arthurian Legacy, too.

If you'd like to read more of my writing, please join my mailing list at www.tjgreen.nz. You can get a free short story called *Jack's Encounter,* describing how Jack met Fahey—a longer version of the prologue in *Tom's Inheritance*—by subscribing to my newsletter. You'll also get a FREE copy of *Excalibur Rises,* a short story prequel.

You will also receive free character sheets on all of my main characters in White Haven Witches—exclusive to my email list!

By staying on my mailing list you'll receive free excerpts of my new books, as well as short stories and news of giveaways. I'll also be sharing information about other books in this genre you might enjoy.

I look forward to you joining my readers' group.

About the Author

I grew up in England and now live in the Hutt Valley, near Wellington, New Zealand, with my partner Jason, and my cats Sacha and Leia. When I'm not writing, you'll find me with my head in a book, gardening, or doing yoga. And maybe getting some retail therapy!

In a previous life I've been a singer in a band, and have done some acting with a theatre company – both of which were lots of fun. On occasions I make short films with a few friends, which begs the question, where are the book trailers? Thinking on it ...

I'm currently working on more books in the White Haven Witches series, musing on a prequel, and planning for a fourth book in Tom's Arthurian Legacy series.

Please follow me on social media to keep up to date with my news, or join my mailing list - I promise I don't spam! Join my mailing list by visiting www.tjgreen.nz.

You can follow me on social media -

Website: http://www.tjgreen.nz
Facebook: https://www.facebook.com/tjgreenauthor/
Twitter: https://twitter.com/tjay_green
Pinterest:
https://nz.pinterest.com/mount0live/my-books-and-writing/

Goodreads:
https://www.goodreads.com/author/show/15099365.T_J_Green
Instagram:
https://www.instagram.com/mountolivepublishing/
BookBub: https://www.bookbub.com/authors/tj-green
Amazon:
https://www.amazon.com/TJ-Green/e/B01D7V8LJK/